A CHANCE SIGHTING

RAY HOBBS

Wingspan Press

Copyright © 2020 by Ray Hobbs

All rights reserved.

This book is a work of fiction. Names, characters, settings and incidents are either the product of the author's imagination or used fictitiously. Any resemblance to actual events, settings or persons, living or dead, is entirely coincidental.

No part of this book may be reproduced or transmitted in any form or by any means, electronic or mechanical, including photocopying, recording or by any information storage and retrieval system, without written permission from the author, except for the inclusion of brief quotations in reviews.

Published in the United States and the United Kingdom
by WingSpan Press, Livermore, CA

The WingSpan name, logo and colophon are the trademarks of WingSpan Publishing.

ISBN 978-1-59594-645-4 (pbk.)
ISBN 978-1-59594-958-5 (ebk.)

First edition 2019

Printed in the United States of America

www.wingspanpress.com

1 2 3 4 5 6 7 8 9 10

This book is dedicated to those engaged in rescue at sea, whose exploits often take place without media attention, and also to those who assist in the readjustment of returning service personnel and prisoners of conflict.

Sources & Acknowledgements

Winton, J., *Find, Fix and Strike* (London, B.T. Batsford Ltd, 1980)
Pitchfork, G., *Shot Down and in the Drink* (London, The National Archives, 2005)
Rowe, A.& Andrews, A., *Air-Sea Rescue in World War Two* (Stroud, Sutton, 1995)
Hillary, R., *The Last Enemy* (London, MacMillan & C0, 1942)
McKay, S., *The Secret Listeners* (London, Aurum Press Ltd, 2012)
Macksey, K., *The Searchers* (London, Cassell, 2003)
Gilbert, A., *P.O.W.* (London, John Murray, 2006)
Gillies, M., *The Barbed-Wire University* (London, Aurum Press Ltd, 2011)
Nudd, D., *Castaways of the Kriegsmarine* (Create Space, 2017)
BBC, WW2 People's War, recollections published on the internet (2003-6, archived)

I am indebted to my brother Chris for his technical advice regarding counselling, and for continuing to act both as soundboard and as a regular source of ideas, as well as helping to fuel my enthusiasm throughout the writing of this book.

RH

Glossary for Readers outside the UK

Note: ^{n} denotes naval terminology or slang.

Blackout:	the masking of light as an air raid precaution.
'Blackout(s)'^{n}:	female uniform drawers.
Wren:	member of the Women's Royal Naval Service.
Christian name:	forename or given name.
P O^n:	petty officer.
Wardroom^n:	naval equivalent of officers' mess.
'Shagbat'^{n}:	Supermarine Walrus amphibian (see back cover).
'Stringbag'^{n}:	Fairey Swordfish torpedo bomber.
Biscuit:	cookie.
Sainsbury's:	a chain of stores, now nationwide.
'Civvies':	civilian clothing.
Grammar school:	selective 11-18 school of the time.
Starboard^n:	right-hand side.
Fortnight:	two weeks.
'Lord Haw-Haw':	(William Joyce), a renegade propagandist.
NAAFI:	Navy, Army and Air Force Institute, retail facility.
RNVR:	Royal Naval Volunteer Reserve, civilian volunteers.
RNR:	Royal Naval Reserve (then) ex-Merchant Navy.
Writer^n:	naval clerk.
'Kriegie':	(*Kriegsgefangener*), prisoner-of-war.
'Goon':	Prison camp guard.
RAF:	Royal Air Force.

(Keep) 'mum':	keep a secret.
Solicitor:	attorney.
'Bun in the oven':	unborn child.
'Gen' (RAF slang):	general information/intelligence.
Flat:	apartment.
Barrister:	trial lawyer.
'Jenny'^{n}:	Wren.
Directly (dialect):	quite soon
'Oggin'^{n}:	sea.
'Subby'^{n}:	sub-lieutenant.
RAC:	Royal Automobile Club.
R A^n:	service ration allowance for living out.

Author's Note

It must seem incredible to many that rationing remained in force in Britain for nine years after the war, but that was nevertheless the case. Meat, the last foodstuff to be rationed, became freely available on the 4th July, 1954.

The reasons for the extended rationing were both economic and political. In those days, Britain was far from self-sufficient and relied heavily on imported goods. Such purchases had to be paid for and Britain's reserves of foreign currency were severely limited.

The First World War of 1914-1918 had left Britain almost bankrupt, so that when war returned in 1939 it was necessary to borrow heavily from the USA and Canada. Then, in 1945, the US Government terminated the Lend-Lease Agreement. To tide Britain over they granted a loan of $4.33 billion, one condition being that sterling was made convertible. Within a month, nations with sterling balances had withdrawn almost $1 billion, leaving British dollar reserves dangerously depleted. With what remained Britain had to make repayments to the US whilst feeding the home population and the British sector of West Germany as well.

Imports had to be financed by exports, and controls were placed on the domestic sale of manufactured goods, such as motor cars. New vehicles were impossible to acquire because they were reserved for the export trade.

In some cases food quality was also subject to government controls. In 1942, the government decreed that to preserve stocks of white flour the only bread to be baked would be The National Loaf, made from wholemeal flour with added salt, calcium and vitamins. It looked and tasted unappetising but was not abolished until after the end of rationing.

Another food to be standardised was cheese. Manufacture of regional cheeses was forbidden, and the milk previously used in their manufacture was now reserved for Government Cheddar, the only cheese available throughout rationing. When the control was finally lifted, manufacture of regional cheeses had to be planned and developed from scratch, and was therefore extremely slow to recover.

On the 31st December 2006, Chancellor of the Exchequer Gordon Brown wrote the final cheque in repayment of Britain's war debt. For such an important milestone, the news announcement seemed to pass almost without notice, coming as it did on New Year's Eve with its attendant distractions. By contrast, however, I am sure I am not alone in remembering the 4th July, 1954. For the first time, I was sent on an errand to the village shop without the ration book, because it was no longer necessary.

RH

Part One

1

WINCHESTER, HAMPSHIRE
JANUARY 1944

Cliff was now convinced he'd taken a wrong turning. It was an easy mistake in the blackout; the masked headlamps were pitifully inadequate and now the weather was an added problem. Squalling rain was obscuring the windscreen and the single wiper was struggling to clear it.

Taking a cloth from the passenger seat, he wiped the misted windscreen, still hoping to see some recognisable landmark. So far, each black shape had been much like its neighbour and street signs had long since been removed as a precaution against invasion.

The Austin ground along in second gear until Cliff became aware of a rectangular object emerging from the gloom and on his nearside. As he drew closer, he recognised it as a large bus shelter and realised that, by a fortunate accident, he'd found the bus station. Relieved, he pulled into the side of the road and parked beside the white-painted kerb to check his directions.

The car's windows were misting up again, so he lowered his side window an inch to reduce the condensation. As he did so, he heard raised female voices coming from the bus station. Lowering the window further, he made out a man and two women in what appeared to be a lively exchange. Whatever the cause of their disagreement, however, it was clearly their affair and he saw no reason to intervene.

He was about to continue on his way, when he realised that one of the women was particularly agitated. At that stage, he decided to investigate.

A Chance Sighting

When he approached them, he saw that the two women were Wrens. The man's uniform suggested that he was a bus company official.

'If there's a problem,' said Cliff, returning the Wrens' hurried salutes, 'maybe I can help.'

'These two girls have missed the last bus, sir,' the man told him.

'We were told it left at eleven forty-five, sir.' The girl who spoke made no effort to disguise her anger.

'Who told you that?'

'The woman in the bus office, sir.'

The man, who turned out to be an inspector, said, 'She must have been looking at the old timetable, sir. They put extra services on over Christmas, you see, and now they no longer apply.' He added awkwardly, 'The last bus for *HMS Flowerdown* leaves at ten-thirty.'

'She told us quite clearly that it left at ten-forty-five,' said the Wren who had spoken first, 'and now there isn't a bus until morning.'

'At six o'clock,' confirmed the inspector.

'It's a disgrace,' said Cliff. 'Have you any idea what punishment these girls can expect for being absent overnight?'

'No, sir, I haven't, and I'm sorry if they have to be punished. I've apologised but I can't do anything about it tonight.'

'No, I don't suppose you can.'

The girl who seemed to be acting as spokesperson for the two said, 'We'll just have to walk to *HMS Flowerdown*. It's not all that far – we'll be there by midnight but we'll be soaked to the skin as well as frozen silly.'

'Don't do that,' said Cliff. 'I'm going to the air station. I'll drop you both on the way.'

'Oh, will you, sir?' Resignation gave way to relief. 'That's very kind of you.'

'Thank you, sir.' The quieter of the girls made her belated contribution, and Cliff noticed for the first time that she was rather plain, a fact that might account in some way for her shyness.

The inspector also looked relieved. 'That's all right then,' he said.

'Small thanks to the bus company. If I were you, I'd speak a few stern words to that woman in the office.'

'I'll speak to the manager, sir. I'm only responsible for the drivers and conductors.'

'Well, if you show a bit of initiative, you never know where promotion might take you.'

'Yes, sir. Good night, sir. Good night... ladies.'

'Good night.'

The girls added their response and followed Cliff to the car.

'If you both get in the back,' he advised, 'there's a rug you can share.'

'Oh, lovely.' They squeezed into the back and draped the rug over themselves.

'There's just one tiny snag,' he said, taking his seat. 'I'm not at all sure how to get to the Andover Road from here.'

'That's all right, sir. We know the way.' The pretty girl leaned over the back of the passenger seat to reassure him. 'Just turn right at the end of this street, then left and then right into the High Street. After that, it's quite easy. I'll show you, sir.'

'It doesn't sound all that easy.'

'You'll see, sir.'

'I'm impressed. You should swap jobs with my observer.'

'What does an observer do, sir?'

'He navigates. At least, that's what he calls it. He spends most of his time getting us lost over the Channel.'

'I don't believe you.' She pointed ahead and said, 'Right here, sir, then left.'

'Thank you.' He followed her directions.

'Then right at the end, here, and you're in the High Street.'

'How do you know? There's no sign.'

'If you come here on foot, you have to ask your way around and you can't help learning the street names.'

Peering right and left, he made the turn into the High Street. As he did so, he became conscious that the other girl hadn't spoken since getting into the car. He really ought to include her in the conversation, however briefly, because they would soon be at *HMS Flowerdown*.

'What are your names? Just your Christian names will do.'

As usual, the pretty girl answered for them both. 'I'm Laura and this is Doris. We went to the pictures tonight to give Doris's spirits a bit of a lift. She's engaged to one of the boys at *Flowerdown* but they've changed his watch so she only gets to see him once in a while.'

'Oh, that really is a bugger....' He corrected himself hurriedly. 'I'm sorry, girls. That's a bad habit of mine. I mean it's bad luck, Doris, but congratulations on your engagement. I'm sure someone will see sense and put things right for you.'

'Thank you, sir.'

'What about you, Laura?'

'What do you mean, sir?'

'Have you got anyone in your sights?'

'No, sir. I'm not ready to settle down.'

That was good news. 'What was the film?'

'*The Adventures of Tartu*.'

'Good, was it?'

'Excellent. Anything with Robert Donat in it is worth seeing.'

'Did you enjoy it, Doris?' The diversion had been for her benefit, after all.

'Yes, sir, it was a good film.'

'Steady now, sir. We're coming to the end of the High Street.' Laura guided him through what felt like a maze before saying, 'This is the Andover road, sir.'

'Thank you. I'm even more impressed.' Returning to their previous conversation, he said, 'I read somewhere that Robert Donat suffers badly from asthma.'

'That's right, sir,' said Laura. 'It's one of the things that endear him to me.'

For a moment, he wondered if he'd misheard her. 'Asthma?'

'Yes, it appeals to my protective instinct.'

Cliff decided he would never understand women. It was probably safer to change the subject. 'You have excellent eyesight, Laura,' he said.

'Why do you say that, sir?'

'The way you've brought us through Winchester in the blackout.'

'Oh, that's because I know the area. I've seen it often enough in daylight and, besides, you get used to the blackout.'

'I'm not so sure about that, although I only fly in daylight, and most of the time I see nothing but miles of sea.' As he spoke, he glanced at her sideways, trying to imagine her with her hair down.

'What kind of aeroplane do you fly, sir? Or aren't you allowed to say?'

'Strictly speaking, I shouldn't, but I'll bend the rules in your case. "Agatha" – that's what I call her – is a Supermarine Walrus.'

'I don't think I've ever heard of that one.'

'She's not at all glamorous. I mean she's not like a Seafire or a Corsair, but I wouldn't swap her for anything. She's an amphibious biplane of a kind that's been around for almost ten years. Some people like to mock the dear old Walrus, but ditched airmen who've been picked up by one only ever sing its praises.'

'Is that what you do, sir? Air-sea rescue?'

'Yes.'

'It's necessary, and it must be very satisfying.'

'That's right. One day, my grandson, because it's not the kind of question a girl would ask, will say, "What did you do in the war, Grandpa? Did you kill Germans?" And I'll be able to say, "No, but I saved the lives of quite a few allied airmen and some enemy airmen as well." Mine is a decent war, you see. I leave the bloodthirsty behaviour to the heroic types.'

Laura leaned further over the seat to say almost confidentially, 'If I might offer the opinion of a humble PO Wren, sir, yours is a humanitarian calling, and I think that's just as important as heroism.'

Before he could respond, an anxious voice from behind them asked, 'Are we nearly there, Laura?'

'We'll be there in two or three minutes, Doris.'

'Good.'

'Are you crossing your legs?'

'Yes.'

'In that case,' said Cliff, 'don't stand on ceremony when we reach the gate. Just hop out and make a bee-line for the heads.'

'Yes, sir.' She corrected herself quickly. 'I mean, aye-aye, sir.'

'Good girl.' She observed the niceties, even in a personal crisis. He couldn't help smiling.

'Left here, sir,' said Laura.

A Chance Sighting

Cliff took the turning and drove along the track that led to the main gate of *HMS Flowerdown*.

'Off you go, Doris. Laura, may I have a quick word?'

'Of course, sir.'

He waited while Doris climbed out, saluted him and dashed to the gate.

'I wonder if you'd join me one evening,' he said. 'We could eat at a restaurant in Winchester and then you could guide me home again, rather as you did so expertly tonight.'

'It sounds like an expensive way to get through the blackout.'

'But it's highly necessary. I have absolutely no sense of direction.'

'Surely you don't mean that, sir.'

'I do. I only made it to the south coast because it was downhill all the way.'

'Where did you come from? Somewhere up north, I imagine.'

'Scarborough.'

She nodded. 'That is a long way.' She appeared to consider his request, and he wondered for a moment if she might turn him down, but then she said, 'We're not really supposed to go out with officers, sir, but I think I can bend the rules in your case.'

'Excellent. When are you free again?'

'My next free evening will be, let me think, Tuesday week.'

'Good. I'll pick you up here at eighteen-thirty if that's all right.'

'Perfectly, sir.'

'Just one thing. It's "Cliff", not "sir".'

'Okay. Goodnight, Cliff, and thanks again for the lift.'

'Thank you for the directions. I'll see you a week on Tuesday.'

2

It was the forenoon stand-easy, and the first opportunity Eileen Goodall had to speak to her friend.

'Come on, then,' she said, putting her mug of tea on the table and taking the seat opposite Laura. 'Tell me all about this new man of yours.'

Laura raised her eyes and said, 'I suppose Doris has been talking.'

'She only told us the bare facts. I'm waiting for you to fill in the details.' Eileen was fair-haired, with doll-like features and a permanently mischievous expression. She also took a detailed interest in the love lives of her friends.

'I don't know any details. I'm not seeing him until Tuesday week and, whatever Doris says, we met in the blackout and there's a limit to what you can learn about someone under those conditions.'

'But you agreed to meet him again.' Eileen was insistent. 'There must be something about him that appealed to you.'

'All right.' Laura rested her mug on the table, cradling it loosely between her hands. 'What can I tell you? He's modest and he's a listener, and that's very important.'

'It's rare in a man.' She smiled mischievously. 'Just imagine, Laura. He could turn out to be just the man you're looking for, and then you'll forget all that nonsense about requesting a draft.'

'You've been reading those magazines again, Eileen. You shouldn't take them so seriously.'

'But you never know.'

'No, I don't,' agreed Laura, 'but I do know that a draft is out of the question. They've taken the trouble to train me as a special telegraphist and they're not going to let me go now.'

'Where did you want to go, anyway?' Eileen's tone seemed to suggest that any draft would be a disappointment after *Flowerdown*.

'Anywhere where I can use my languages. I came into this circus as a German linguist and I spend most of my time reading coded groups. The only time I do any translation is when two idiots indulge in plain-language gossip.'

'It does seem a waste.' Eileen looked at her watch. 'It's time we were heading back,' she said, 'but before we go, what else can you remember about the mystery man?'

'He's only a mystery man as far as you're concerned because you're the one who's fascinated by him.' She thought for a moment and said, 'Mind you, there is something else that I think is important.'

'What's that?'

'He cares about people.'

Eileen shook her head in semi-disbelief. 'Do you mean to say you discovered all that on a ten-minute journey?'

'The journey took a good fifteen minutes, but yes.'

'Well I never.' Eileen digested the information and then asked, 'What's he like to look at?'

'It's difficult to say, really. I think he looks quite nice, but the only light was from the car's dashboard, and that was very dim. It's one of those little Austins.'

'A Ruby?'

'I've no idea – I don't know much about cars – but it was very cosy.' She thought again about Cliff. 'I think his hair is quite dark,' she said, 'but I couldn't swear to it. One thing I do remember, though, is that he smiles a lot.'

'Well,' said Eileen, getting up to leave, 'from that rather basic thumbnail sketch, the early indications are that you may have found the ideal man.' She wrinkled her nose. 'I wonder if he has a friend who's free and available.'

The conversation taking place in the wardroom of the Royal Naval Air Station at Worthy Down was on broadly similar lines, although Marcus Rhodes was less interested in detail and more inclined to regard Cliff's news as an occasion for good-humoured banter.

'All right, Cliff,' he said. 'Stand me a pre-prandial gin and I'll listen to your tale of lechery. The sun's well over the yardarm; at least, it would be if it bothered to put in an appearance.' He shivered at the cold, gusting, spectacle beyond the window. All flying was cancelled pending the next weather report but, even so, the two officers had the wardroom almost to themselves, at least for the time being.

Cliff attracted the steward's attention. 'Two pink gins, please, Edwards. I'll sign the chit. Lieutenant Rhodes seems to have mislaid his pen.'

'Two pink gins, sir.' The steward treated each glass to a dash of bitters and added a measure of gin.

'Thank you, Edwards,' said Marcus, taking one of the glasses. 'Lieutenant Stephens will have his little joke.' He added, 'And even by modest standards it was a very tiny one.' He watched Cliff sign for the drinks before taking his.

'Mud in your eye.'

Cliff raised his glass. 'Down the hatch.'

'All right, Bluebeard, tell me about this girl.'

'I know very little about her except that her name's Laura, she's a friendly soul and, although I only saw her by the light from the dashboard, I'd say she's pretty. She's a damned good navigator as well. I told her she should swap jobs with you.'

'She'd soon learn what you're like to fly with. That would do the relationship no good at all. Anyway, when are you seeing her again?'

'A week on Tuesday. It's her next evening off-watch.'

'What does she do?'

'Search me. No one at *Flowerdown* ever utters a word about what they get up to. It's obviously very hush-hush.'

'Yes, now I think of it, I got that impression at the last dance they had. Still, I suppose being a wireless station makes it hush-hush by definition. I imagine you told her all about the thrills and perils of air-sea rescue in a "Shagbat".'

'No, I didn't. I just relied, as always, on natural magnetism.'

'Then you've most likely scuppered your chances.'

'We shall see.' Cliff looked inquiringly into his glass. 'The tide's out, Marcus.'

'All right, I'll get them. There's no chance of any flying today or tomorrow.'

'Splendid fellow.'

Marcus ordered two pink gins. When the steward had set them down and returned to the bar, he asked, 'Have you any plans to take your new conquest up for a joyride?'

'None whatsoever.'

'Larry Olivier did, apparently.'

'Oh?'

'Didn't you know? It's in the station annals that he borrowed a "Stringbag" to take Vivien for a spin. Of course, he'd never admit it now, but that's the story everyone tells.'

'Only he could get away with it, Marcus. Actors and film stars live by different rules.'

'You're probably right, old chap. I'll tell you what, though.' Something else had evidently occurred to him. 'There's going to be a wardroom party soon.'

'Do you mean the week after next? I know we're entertaining the Americans from Bisterne.'

'No, not that. There's going to be another. They had to cancel the Christmas party because of the weather. It was pretty bad, as I recall.'

'I'd no idea. I was on leave at the time.'

'So you were, but you'll be able to show off the fair Laura to your comrades-in-arms now.'

'When's it going to be?'

'I don't know. I think it's only just reached the planning stage. We should hear something soon.'

'I hope so.' The idea appealed to Cliff. He was already looking forward to seeing Laura again.

3

The weather improved towards the end of the next week, so that flying was quickly resumed, and it was not long before Agatha was required to search for the crew of a Mosquito that had been damaged on a raid and had been obliged to ditch off the Normandy coast.

'We continue on this course for twenty-five minutes,' said Marcus in response to a question from Cliff.

Above and astern of them, the single radial engine roared, but they were still able to hold a conversation.

'When did they ditch?'

'About five hours ago.'

'Poor buggers. It's cold enough on dry land this morning. I hate to think what it's like down there in an open dinghy.'

Marcus shuddered. 'Let's hope we'll never find out.'

Cliff began to recite:

' "Freeze, freeze thou bitter sky,
That does not bite so nigh
As benefits forgot:
Though thou the waters warp,
Thy sting is not so sharp
As a friend remember'd not." '

'What brought that on, Cliff?'

'Just thinking about those poor sods in the dinghy.'

'But what is it from?'

'*As You Like It*. "Blow, blow, thou winter wind," and all that.'

A Chance Sighting

'I've heard of that.'

'I thought you might.'

'I know "All the world's a stage" as well. Isn't that from the same play?'

'It is indeed, and well done, Marcus.'

'I'm not the stranger to culture you think I am.'

'Possibly not. Where do you see us in the Seven Ages?'

Marcus considered the question briefly. 'I suppose we're the soldiers. The Navy hadn't been around very long in Shakespeare's time, so I imagine he overlooked us.'

'No.' Cliff shook his head confidently. 'Shakespeare never overlooked anyone. He was the most astute observer of the human race known to man. No, I think he probably realised that his audiences would be more familiar with soldiers than with sailors. I imagine most matelots spent very little time at home.'

'I wouldn't mind spending some time at home,' said Marcus wistfully. 'Anyway,' he said, returning to the original question, 'which age of man are you when you're not being an unlikely soldier?'

'On a cold morning like this,' said Cliff, 'I see myself as the schoolboy, "creeping like snail unwillingly to school."'

Marcus was unimpressed. 'I see you as something else entirely.'

'Go on, I'll buy it.'

'I see you as the lover, "sighing like furnace…" something.' Clearly recollection had deserted him.

' "Sighing like furnace, with a woeful ballad made to his mistress' eyebrow", ' prompted Cliff. 'Very funny, Marcus.'

'You're seeing her tonight, aren't you?'

'Yes, Marcus, I hadn't forgotten.'

Cliff was spared further intrusion into his private life when the third member of the crew appeared at his shoulder.

'How now, Woody?' Cliff greeted Cyril Woodbridge, his telegraphist/air gunner.

'I was wondering if you gentlemen were ready for coffee, sir.'

'Isn't this man a marvel, Marcus? He thinks of everything.'

'So he does, but it's a little early for me.'

'Yes,' agreed Cliff. 'Thanks for the thought, Woody, but not just now.'

'When you are ready, gentlemen, there are biscuits as well as sandwiches.'

'Really?' Cliff turned to look at him in surprise. 'But we never have biscuits. How did you work this miracle?'

Woody coughed modestly. 'Edwards, the wardroom steward, owed me a favour, sir, so I called at the wardroom pantry and made the plea on your joint behalf.'

'You know, Marcus,' said Cliff, 'in morning dress, he could be mistaken for Jeeves.'

'Quite easily,' agreed Marcus, 'and deservedly so.'

'We'll keep you posted, Woody, but carry on for now.'

'Aye-aye, sir.' Woody bowed out of the cockpit, the canopy being somewhat restrictive for his six feet.

They flew on without speaking and Cliff lit a cigarette. One of the aircraft's many endearing characteristics was that its engine and fuel tank were distant enough from the cockpit that smoking posed no fire hazard. After a while, Marcus left his seat and went aft to his chart table. He returned after a few minutes. 'We're approaching their last reported position,' he announced.

Cliff stared at the bare seascape. 'Not a sausage. I imagine the wind could have blown them further east.'

'Just what I was thinking, Cliff. The new course, if you're still of a mind, is zero-six-zero magnetic.'

'Oh-six-oh,' Cliff confirmed, setting the course on the verge ring of his compass. 'Let's try a box search on that.'

They began the search, making a series of 90 degree turns, with each leg longer than the last, in a gradually expanding pattern.

At the third turn, Marcus saw something. 'Fluorescein at ten o'clock, Cliff.'

Cliff saw the spreading yellow stain almost immediately. The occupants of the dinghy had thrown the dye into the sea as a marker, presumably when they saw the Walrus. As the dinghy, repeatedly obscured by the waves, bobbed into view, its occupants waved urgently to the aircraft.

'We're going down.' Cliff made the announcement as a warning to Marcus and Woody as he began a shallow, spiralling descent.

He brought the Walrus into a tail-down attitude, flying a few

A Chance Sighting

feet above the surface and parallel to it, and watched the pattern of the waves. When he had selected the best place to put down, he made a fully-stalled landing from about six feet. The Walrus made contact with the waves and threw a huge curtain of spray over the canopy and lower wings. The wipers finally cleared the windscreen and Cliff taxied towards the dinghy and its joyous occupants.

Woody made his way to the after hatch and hooked the ladder over the hatch coaming. When they were close enough, he threw a line to the airmen. One of them caught it and secured it to the dinghy.

A few minutes later, both men were on board, wrapped warmly in blankets and vocal in their relief and gratitude.

Airborne once more, Cliff summoned his air gunner.

'Woody,' he said, 'how are the survivors?'

'Much warmer now, sir, and quite cheerful. There's a message from base, sir. "Well done. Return to base." '

'Excellent. I think this calls for coffee and sandwiches all round. What are the sandwiches?'

'Corned beef, sir.'

'Yes, it was a silly question, wasn't it?'

'One can always dream, sir.'

'Quite.' Cliff was more inclined to be realistic. 'What's the biscuit situation?'

'We have about half a pound, sir.'

'I think we can be generous. Don't you?'

'Of course, sir.'

'Very well. Carry on, Woody. Oh, and well done back there.'

'Thank you, sir. Aye-aye, sir.'

Cliff swept the horizon and found it gratifyingly empty. He began to relax. It had been a successful morning. Now, coffee, sandwiches and biscuits beckoned and, best of all, he could look forward to his date with Laura.

4

Laura settled in the passenger seat and gathered the skirt of her coat so that Cliff could close the door. When he took his place behind the wheel, she said, 'You managed to find this place after all. Well done.'

'Thanks. It's not too difficult if you practise non-stop for two days. I even flew over it this morning, just to make sure.'

'You do talk nonsense.'

'You won't say that when we reach the restaurant.'

'Won't I?'

'No, because that's when I'll tell you how exquisite you look.' He released the handbrake and drove down the lane.

'Do I have to wait until then?'

'Of course you do. I can't see you properly in the blackout.'

'In that case, how do you know I look exquisite?'

'I'm playing a hunch. Trust me.'

'I hope you won't be too disappointed.'

'Don't worry, Laura. I can cope with most things.' He changed down and reduced speed as they approached the junction with the Andover road. Then, having negotiated the turn, he asked, 'Did your friend get her *fiancée*'s watch changed?'

'Doris? Not a hope. They say they're running a naval establishment and they don't want their people distracted by *fiancées*, sweethearts and the like. There's a war on, they say.'

'I was wondering what the blackout and sudden explosions were about. Poor girl.'

'Yes, I'm worried about her.'

'Really?'

A Chance Sighting

'Well, let's say I'm concerned about her. She's been under a lot of strain.' It was as if she realised she'd said too much, because she added by way of bland explanation, 'She's been working very hard.'

'I see.' He didn't, but it seemed an appropriate response.

'Cliff, I know I've asked you all about your aeroplane and that sort of thing, but I'm not allowed to say anything about what we do.'

'I know.'

'Do you?' She sounded surprised.

'Some of us came to a dance at *Flowerdown* last year. We were briefed about security.'

'Oh, good. Just as long as you know.'

'Take it as read, Laura.'

'Okay, but, Cliff....'

'What?'

'Before we go much further, where exactly are we going?'

'To the Cavendish.'

'How grand.'

'Ah, but war is a great leveller.'

'True. Menus are not what they were before all this nonsense began, but I'm still looking forward to it.' She peered through the gloom. 'Left at the next turning, Cliff.'

'Thank you.'

'Cliff?'

'Yes?'

'Is your name short for "Clifford"?'

'Yes. It's a bit serious for a chap like me, so I'm happy to be called "Cliff".' Then, feeling very much the centre of attention, he said, 'I'm quite taken with yours. It's unusual, isn't it?'

'My mother was keen on Christina Rossetti.' She sounded unimpressed. 'Actually, she still is.'

'Of course. *Goblin Market*.'

'You know it, obviously.' She broke off for a second. 'Next right, Cliff.'

'Thanks, Laura.'

'Carry straight on from here and the Cavendish is just a few hundred yards down this road.'

'It's fine. I know where I am now.' He drove on for a quarter of a mile, took the turning that led to the Cavendish Hotel's car park, and found a space without difficulty.

'You knew your way here after all.'

'You could say,' he said, leaving his seat, 'that I know it quite well.'

They walked into the opulent lobby and found the reception desk free.

'I booked a table for seven o'clock,' he told the receptionist. 'My name's Stephens.'

'Good evening, Mr Stephens. The receptionist crossed out his name.

A voice from behind them said, 'Lieutenant Stephens. Good evening, sir. Good evening, miss.'

'Good evening, Arthur.' Cliff greeted an immaculate, silver-haired waiter. 'How are you?'

'I'm well, thank you, sir, and your goodself?'

'In rude health, as ever, Arthur. Thank you for your concern.'

'Would you care to take a seat in the lounge, sir, to consult the menu? I should tell you that the fricassee of veal is no longer available, I'm afraid.'

'I shouldn't worry, Arthur. I wouldn't have ordered it anyway.'

'Quite, sir. Perhaps you would both care for a drink?'

Laura thought for a second. 'I'd like tomato juice, please.'

'Certainly, miss.'

'Gin, please, Arthur. I'll ask you later about the usual thing.'

'Of course, sir.'

Cliff led Laura to the lounge, where they found a sofa. A four-piece band was playing the Irving Berlin number 'Change Partners', which pleased Cliff. He was fond of Berlin's music.

'Now that we're out of the blackout,' he said, 'I can tell you that you look positively enchanting.' He meant it. With medium-brown hair, now touching her shoulders, she was certainly pretty; his recollection of her that night in the blackout had been accurate in that respect but, more importantly, she had what he saw as a sensitive face. There was instant response in her blue eyes, so his compliment was both genuine and insightful.

'Thank you.' She was smiling, and that made her even more attractive.

A Chance Sighting

'I like your frock, too.' It was the colour of claret and he found it modest and appealing at the same time. In accordance with King's Regulations, he was in uniform, which was neither modest nor appealing, but it meant that he didn't have to make a decision about what to wear.

'Thank you again.' Looking down, she said, 'Uniform stockings, I'm afraid. They're all I have.' As an afterthought, she added, 'I suppose they're all anyone has nowadays.'

'They're no detriment, believe me.' He waited until Arthur had set down their drinks and a jug of water. 'Thank you, Arthur.'

'Not at all, sir.'

Cliff took out his cigarette case and asked, 'Do you smoke?'

'No, I tried it but it somehow lost its appeal.'

'Do you mind if I do?'

'Not at all.'

'Thank you.' He lit a cigarette, resolving to stop sometime in the near future. Smoking suddenly lacked sophistication, he decided.

'You know,' said Laura, leaning backwards for a better view, 'you're much as I imagined in the blackout: dark-haired, with a cleft chin, soulful brown eyes and a calamitous sense of direction.'

'Quite ordinary,' he agreed. 'I could have told you that.'

'There's nothing ordinary about you, Cliff,' she assured him. 'There are men who would envy you your cleft chin, at least.'

'Thank you. I'll view it in a different light from now on. It's been a shaving hazard far too long.'

She picked up the menu. 'Should we have a look at this and make a decision?'

'No, it's never very exciting.'

'It's a familiar story, but we have to eat something.'

'Let's wait for Arthur.'

'Okay. While we're waiting, would you mind telling me something else? Why do you call your aeroplane "Agatha"? I'm dying to know.'

'Oh, I think it's all right for me to tell you that. It's the noise the engine makes when they start her up, a sort of *Agatha...Agatha... Agathagathagathaarrrrrr*, and then the old girl purrs along happily.'

'I'd never have known, but it makes perfect sense.' She looked up. 'Oh, here's the waiter.'

Arthur approached them smiling benevolently and said, 'When I knew you were going to be here tonight, sir, I took the liberty of reserving a little something for your consideration.'

'Spill the beans, Arthur. What is it?'

'Roast pheasant, sir, served with Brussels sprouts, carrots and roast potatoes.'

Laura stared at him. When she had recovered from the shock, she said, 'I haven't tasted pheasant since before the war.'

'I think that wins our vote, Arthur.'

'I am delighted, sir, and to start?'

'What do you recommend?'

'Without hesitation, sir, the chicken and leek soup.'

Laura was still in a trance, so Cliff said, 'In that case, we'll have the soup.'

'Very good, sir.'

'By the way, Arthur, how is your grandson's footballing career progressing now he's at the big school?'

'He's in the Under Thirteens First Eleven now, sir. We're very pleased with him.'

'You have every right to be pleased, Arthur. I'm delighted to hear about him too.'

'Thank you, sir. You're most kind.' For a moment, the waiter seemed to be searching his memory, and then he said, 'Now I think of it, sir, there's a red Bordeaux that would be an excellent accompaniment to the pheasant.'

'Then I'll be guided by you. Thank you, Arthur.'

Laura watched him go, and said, 'Pheasant, Bordeaux, and after five years of war. How do they do it?'

'It's better not to ask. It's classified information.' Then, suddenly remembering his manners, he asked, 'Is the red Bordeaux all right? I should have checked with you, only with Arthur doing it as a favour....'

'It's fine. I'm not a great drinker, which is odd, my father being a wine merchant, but I'm fond of Bordeaux.'

'A wine merchant? That's the kind of father to have. It must be Christmas every day at your house.'

'He's actually a grocer and wine merchant. He has a few shops, that's all.'

A Chance Sighting

'Really? Your name isn't Sainsbury, by any chance, is it?'

'No,' she laughed, 'it's Pembury.'

'At least I got some of it right.' The band was starting 'Love Walked In,' so he asked, 'Would you like to dance?'

'All right.'

He led her through the dining area to an almost deserted dance floor. It was the first physical contact he'd had with her and he felt a little awkward at first. Once into the dance, however, unease gave way to enjoyment and they moved naturally together.

They danced to the end of the number without speaking, and applauded the band before returning to the lounge.

'That was lovely,' said Laura. 'Thank you.'

He waited for her to be seated and then joined her on the sofa. 'I was about to say, "That was lovely. Thank you." But you stole my thunder.'

'I'm sorry. I'm too quick off the mark. It comes of being a Capricornian.'

'Isn't that where they make syrup of figs?'

'No, that's *California*, and you know what I mean.'

'If you're Capricorn... no, that's wrong.' He thought again.

'What's wrong?'

'Capricorn's January, isn't it?'

'December to January.'

'In that case, has your birthday been and gone, or is it yet to come?'

'Friday week, the fourteenth.'

'Ah.' Before he could say more, Arthur arrived to show them to their table. It was in a secluded corner and not too close to the band, just as Cliff had requested.

Over the soup, a question arose in Laura's mind.

'Cliff, when I told you my mother was keen on Christina Rossetti, you knew straight away which poem she was thinking of, didn't you?'

'Yes, I studied English for a year at university before I joined up. I think it's important to know what we don't like as well as the things that get us excited, and that's not a criticism of your mother. I just don't care much for Christina Rossetti.'

'I'm with you there, but who do you like particularly?'

'Oh, I could name dozens, but the chap who's never lost his appeal is The Bard himself.'

'It's true love, is it?'

'Yes, I even annoy my crew by quoting him on long, boring searches. He has a *bon mot* for every occasion.'

'I can see how that might become wearing after a while.'

'Oh, I don't do it all the time, and I certainly don't do it in the wardroom.'

'Don't you?'

'Not with two celebrated actors in the place.'

She frowned. 'Who are they?'

'Laurence Olivier and Ralph Richardson.'

'You're joking.'

'Scouts' honour. They've been there for ever. Between them, they constitute Hitler's secret weapon.'

'Go on, I'll buy it.' She was still in a state of disbelief.

'They've written off more of our aircraft than most enemy fighter pilots. Richardson is known as "Pranger", and Olivier doesn't need a nickname. He's just a law unto himself.'

'I'm amazed.'

'If you come to the next wardroom party I'll introduce you to them. Vivien Leigh should be there too.'

Laura was shaking her head in continued disbelief. 'Are Wren ratings allowed in the wardroom?'

'I'm afraid not, but they hold these things in a place in the city centre and send out a blanket invitation to Wrens, who come in civvies, and no-one's any the wiser.' Seeing that she'd finished her soup, he asked, 'Shall we dance?'

'Let's.'

The band was playing 'I'm in the Mood for Love.'

As they stepped on to the dance floor, Laura said, 'They seem to specialise in old favourites. It's rather nice.'

'It's a quiet hotel that caters for people who don't want to jitterbug and jive. You only need to look at the musicians. They're all over fifty.' He added with only a hint of apology, 'I like it.'

'You're full of surprises, Cliff, but so do I.'

A Chance Sighting

In fact, they enjoyed the number so much that it ended all too soon, at least from their point of view. As she said, and he had to agree, the pleasant things in life frequently did.

Back at their table, Laura asked, 'Is it very boring, searching for survivors?'

'It can be. Sometimes I'm reminded of Winnie the Pooh and Piglet. Are you familiar with *The House at Pooh Corner*?'

'Yes.' She looked mystified but waited for him to go on.

'If you recall, at the beginning of the book, Pooh calls on Piglet. He finds the door open but Piglet isn't there, and the more Pooh looks, the more Piglet isn't there. Well, the sea is like that. There are lots of places for ditched airmen not to be.'

She smiled and nodded understandingly.

'But sometimes, and it happened recently, we get a chance sighting. We look down, and there they are.' He asked, 'Am I boring you?'

'Not in the least.'

'That's a relief. Have you heard Arthur Askey sing that song about a bee?'

'I'm afraid so.'

'It's pretty awful, isn't it? Some wag brought the record into the wardroom and it wasn't long before everyone was sick of it. Eventually, an order came from on high, that the next crew to become airborne had to take the offending record and bury it at sea. As it happened, the task fell to us.' He checked that she was still listening and, satisfied that he'd not lulled her to sleep, he continued.

'Now, we'd been searching for the pilot of a Thunderbolt – that's an American fighter – and the search had gone on for ages. One man is a tiny object against a seascape, you see, frequently hidden by waves or lost in the dazzle of the sun reflected off the surface.'

'It sounds impossible.'

'There are times when it seems impossible, believe me. However, at some stage, I remembered the record, so I opened the side panel of the canopy and ditched the wretched thing. As I did so, I suddenly gaped, because there was the American airman bobbing up and down beneath us. He was the one man who had cause to be grateful to Arthur Askey for the "Bee Song", although it's doubtful he'd ever heard of him or the song. It really was a Chance Sighting.'

She was shaking her head. 'You tell a good story, Cliff.'

'Nevertheless, it's true.'

'I'll believe you. What were you looking for when you sighted Doris and me in Winchester Bus Station?'

'The way home, actually. I was lost.'

She smiled. 'You just need to fly over the city a few times, the way you learned the route to *Flowerdown*.'

He could only agree.

The pheasant and the Bordeaux were all they expected, and they danced twice more before Laura looked at her watch and announced regretfully that it was time for them to leave.

Cliff managed to find the way back to *Flowerdown* with only a few directions from Laura, who was most encouraging.

'You just need to keep practising,' she told him.

'So you think we might do this again?'

'I meant generally driving in the blackout.'

'But do you think we might do something like this again?' He hadn't time to play games. By the light from the dashboard, he could see the time on his wristwatch. It was twenty-three fifty-five and she had to be back on board by twenty-three fifty-nine.

'My next night off is Saturday the fifteenth.'

'It's the day after your birthday. Aren't you doing something special?'

'Don't you think meeting you and guiding you through the blackout might be a bit special? I do. At the very least, it'll be amusing.'

'I must confess, I hadn't really thought about it like that.'

Her hand was on the door catch. 'Shall we meet at half-past-six again?'

'All right, but don't eat. We'll do that later.'

'Where are we going, or don't you know yet?'

'I think we'll go to the Awdry Restaurant. The food won't be quite as good as we had tonight but it won't be bad either, and the band should be pretty good.'

A Chance Sighting

'I'll look forward to it.' She inclined her head so that he could kiss her on the cheek. 'Thank you for a truly lovely evening. Drive carefully.'

And then she was gone. Cliff watched the glow of her tiny flashlight mark each jolting footstep until it came to rest at the main gate. He checked the time and relaxed. It was twenty-three fifty-eight.

5

Since leaving school, Laura had never met anyone like Cliff. His relaxed modesty and easy manner were new to her, and the matter-of-fact way he acknowledged his woeful sense of direction only counted in his favour. Also, she wondered how many men might have used the pheasant and wine to make an impression on a first date, rather than treating those things, as he had, simply as an enjoyable bonus to be shared with a friend.

He spoke with a slight accent, presumably a legacy of his northern upbringing, modified by years away from home. He'd mentioned Scarborough, which she recalled vaguely as a resort on the Yorkshire coast, and she wondered if modesty were a regional characteristic, or if, as she suspected, she really had met an unusual and remarkable man.

As she conjectured, she turned the tuning knob slowly and smoothly, searching for enemy transmissions.

Suddenly, she caught something and raised her hand to attract the chief Wren.

'Groups on four six oh eight,' she reported.

The chief Wren picked up a phone to start the direction-finding process while Laura continued to read the coded groups of letters. When she'd filled half a page or so, the chief Wren returned to her side and took the headset from her.

'The DO wants you,' she said, sliding into Laura's chair. 'Good luck.'

The Duty Officer, Lieutenant-Commander Simmonds, a man of about forty, long-since passed over for promotion, sat in a glass-fronted office that gave him a view of the entire room and its occupants. Laura knocked on the door.

A Chance Sighting

'Come in.'

She opened the door and stepped inside but remained at a distance from Lt-Cdr Simmonds, whose reputation for tactile behaviour was well known among Wrens and female civilians.

'Come over here, PO.'

Laura crossed the floor and stood in front of his desk. 'You sent for me, sir.'

'Yes, I did. We've intercepted a plain-language transmission.' He handed her a message form. 'Translate it as quickly as you can.'

'Aye-aye, sir.'

'Good girl.' He rose from his chair, but Laura beat him to the door and, closing it behind her, looked around for a spare bench.

Having located one, she sat down to translate the signal, grateful for another of Cliff's qualities, that he didn't take liberties. With characters like Lt-Cdr Simmonds around, there was too much of that already.

Cliff's next diversion was the dinner party at which Worthy Down, or *HMS Kestrel*, to give the air station its official name, was host to the officers from Bisterne, an air station recently taken over by the US Air Force.

It was a lively gathering, although Cliff found himself seated at dinner between two serious and critical guests. On his left, sat Lieutenant William Hollins, who declared early in the proceedings his post-war ambition to run for election to Congress. On Cliff's right, Lieutenant Wilbur Burns declared his whole-hearted support for his colleague and all that the Republican Party stood for.

'Now, that's interesting,' said Cliff, who was out of his depth where American politics were concerned, but who was nevertheless determined to be hospitable. 'You see, you talk about "running" for election, whereas we – if we really feel that we have to go in for that kind of thing – use the word "standing".'

'That makes sense,' said Lt Burns. 'We run and you stand. We are dynamic and forward-looking, but you guys are somehow stuck in the nineteenth century. We see it all around us.'

'That's right.' Lt Hollins lent his weight to the argument. 'You have only to look at the farms in this state. They are *tiny*. What can they produce?'

'Oh, be fair,' urged Cliff. 'Look at the size of this country. How big can a farm be? By the way,' he added, 'Hampshire is a county, not a state. We don't have states. Even if we had, we'd struggle to find room for more than one or maybe two.'

'I'm surprised there's enough room for anything,' said William.

'Ah, but I am a citizen of the largest county in Britain.'

Wilbur gave him a doubting look and asked, 'And just where is this county?'

'Yorkshire is in the north of England. It extends from the River Tees in the north to the Humber in the south, and westward, almost to the west coast. Only Cumberland and Lancashire get in the way. My home, by the way, is in Scarborough, on the east coast.'

William asked, 'What do they do there?'

'It's a holiday resort.'

'A *holiday* resort?' William looked baffled, but then realisation dawned. 'You mean people take *vacations* there?'

'Yes, but they don't call them that. The locals wouldn't know what a vacation is. No, this side of the Atlantic we call them "holidays".' Then he remembered something else. 'Oh, and it's a fishing port as well.' He thought he'd better throw that in for added weight.

'Well,' said Wilbur, 'I'm from Kennebunkport, Maine, and that's what I *call* a coastal resort.'

'How grand. I imagine children grow up learning to spell its name.'

Wilbur ignored the observation, adding importantly, 'And it's got history.'

William nodded approvingly.

'It was founded in sixteen-fifty-nine,' said Wilbur, determined to establish his home town's credentials. 'Yes, sir, it sure has history. Let me tell you, in eighteen-ninety-one, the schooner *Empress* ran aground on the Fox Rocks and was smashed to smithereens. It was a terrible disaster. It was so terrible,' he said grimly, 'that every year, on October twenty-eighth, the cries of drowning sailors can still be heard miles away.'

A Chance Sighting

It was a harmless game, but Cliff felt that he'd been passive for too long. It was time to fly the flag for Scarborough.

'In the fourth century AD,' he told them, 'the Romans built a signalling station where Scarborough now stands, to warn the occupying forces of the presence of marauding Saxons.

'One night, the Saxon ship *Aethelred* was wrecked in the approaches, and there were no survivors. Naturally enough, stories have been told over the centuries, and fact has become inevitably interwoven with the product of fertile imagination. However, in recent years, divers have reported strange goings-on, things being moved around and so on. Only a few years ago, a diver descended on the poop deck and found that the lamp was alight.'

'No, surely not.'

'You can't expect us to believe that.'

'All right,' said Cliff. 'If you'll muzzle the drowning sailors, I'll blow the lamp out.'

After dinner, he found company of a more genial kind in Colonel John E. Schafer, who was interested in the Walrus.

'It's been around for nine years,' Cliff told him. 'It looks like a museum piece, being a biplane and with the "pusher" propeller, but it's proved its worth repeatedly and it's rescued countless ditched airmen.'

'Is that your area of responsibility? Air-sea rescue?'

'That's right, sir.'

'That's interesting. One of our boys was picked up recently.'

'What was he flying?'

'A P-47. He was shot down by an FW 190.'

Cliff had to give in. 'I'm sorry. What is a P-47?'

'Of course. You guys use names, don't you? The P-47 is the Republic Thunderbolt.'

'That's a coincidence, sir. I picked up a Thunderbolt pilot on New Year's Day.'

'You don't say.' Looking around the room, he called, 'Hey, where's Muratore? This is the guy who fished him out of the sea.'

A tall man with dark, Mediterranean features broke away from a group by the bar, and Cliff recognised him immediately.

Muratore saw him and grinned. 'You're the guy with the seaplane,' he said, offering his hand.

'Amphibian, actually, but yes. It's good to see you again. My name's Cliff, by the way.'

'Alfredo. Call me "Al".'

'I'll leave you guys to talk,' said Colonel Schafer, moving off to circulate.

'Cliff,' said Al, 'I'm more than glad to see you. You saved my life, and I'm not going to forget that in a hurry.'

'It was all in a day's work,' Cliff told him, a trifle embarrassed. 'No trouble at all.'

'No, Cliff, I insist on thanking you properly.'

'You already have. Honestly, there's no need to thank me again.'

It was as if Al hadn't heard him. 'Cliff,' he said, 'I owe you my life. If there's anything I can do for you, you have only to ask.'

'All right, I will.' Cliff hoped that would bring the conversation to its close. He could understand Al's compulsive need to thank his rescuer. Alone on his stretch of the sea, and fearful that he might never be found, he must have been overjoyed when he saw Agatha make her descent, but Cliff felt he'd been thanked enough. Al's offer was most certainly genuine, although Cliff had no intention of taking advantage of the situation. At least....

'Now I think of it, you could help me with something.' He moved him further away from the bar. 'Of course, you mustn't feel that you're under any obligation. I'm only talking about a favour between friends.'

'What do you have in mind, Cliff?'

'There are some things I want to buy that are hard to find over here.'

6

Her dress was in French navy; it buttoned down the front from a split neck and had box shoulders with short, puffed sleeves.

'I'm glad you like it,' she said, 'because you've now seen the extent of my wardrobe.'

He waited for her to take her seat at the table before joining her.

'Happy birthday, Laura,' he said, placing a box in floral wrapping paper in front of her.

Her hands went to her cheeks and she stared at the box. 'Cliff, there was no need.... Where did you find wrapping p...?' She continued to stare, open-mouthed.

'Oh, I'd better give you this as well.' He handed her an envelope. 'Everything came from the same place.'

She opened the envelope and took out a card, which appeared to be from the Ministry of Food.

' "Rationing Means Fair Shares For Everyone",' she read. 'Why are you telling me this, Cliff?'

'Open the card.'

She read his handwritten message

But I want you all to myself, especially on the 15th. Happy birthday. Cliff.

'That's really sweet. Thank you, Cliff.' She squeezed his hand. 'There really was no need for this, you know.'

'But I enjoy a birthday. Anyone's birthday. Aren't you going to open the parcel?'

'I hardly like to. I haven't seen wrapping paper since nineteen-forty.'

'I would if I were you.'

'All right.' She untied the bow and slid the ribbon aside to open the wrapping. Inside was a cardboard box, so she opened the lid and, for the second time that evening, gasped with surprise. 'I don't believe it,' she said, taking out two pairs of nylon stockings and holding them as if they were treasure trove.

'There's more.'

Delving further, she took out two lipsticks, a powder compact and a quantity of eye make-up. She shook her head, still in a trance-like state.

'I hope the colours are all right. I did it all by proxy.' Then, not wishing to be at all dishonest, he said, 'Actually, I didn't ask for the make-up. It just came as sort of bonus.'

'Thank you, Cliff. It's a lovely present.' She reached across and kissed his cheek. 'But how did you find these things?'

'We had some Americans over for dinner last week and one of them was the chap I told you about, the Thunderbolt pilot we found when I was ditching the Arthur Askey record.'

'So the story was true after all.'

'Of course it was. Anyway, the Americans have a shop that's bigger and posher than the NAAFI, and it's full of things we can't get, so I asked him to find me a card, some stockings and some wrapping paper. He threw the make-up in as a goodwill gesture.'

'How wonderful. Will you thank him for me?'

'I'll drop him a line,' he promised.

A waitress was hovering beside their table with her pencil poised. 'Have you decided yet?'

'No,' said Cliff. 'It's this lady's birthday, and we got side-tracked. Just give us a few minutes, will you?'

'Of course, sir. Happy birthday, madam.'

'Thank you. Actually,' said Laura, 'I think I'll have the chicken, please.'

Scanning the menu briefly, Cliff said, 'So will I.' He handed the menu back to the waitress and asked, 'Is wine a possibility?'

'It is, sir.' She opened the wine list and pointed to the remaining options, which were inevitably at the expensive end of the cellar.

'They have a *Chablis*,' he told Laura by way of a suggestion.

'Only if it's not too expensive.'

'No, not at all.' He turned to the waitress and said, 'Right, we'll have a bottle of the *Chablis*, please.' It was expensive, but a birthday was a birthday after all.

'Certainly, sir.' She made a note and left them.

As if in response to a sudden decision, Laura asked, 'Will you excuse me, Cliff? I'm going to change into a pair of these.' She picked up one of the cellophane packets and headed towards the ladies' room.

For the first time, Cliff was able to listen properly to Bert Osborne's band, who were playing 'How About You?' He couldn't help wondering how many of those present had actually experienced 'New York in June', but that wasn't the band's fault. They were playing well, and the lyrics were incidental. He listened until he felt Laura's hand on his arm, and he rose to his feet and delivered his verdict.

'You were lovely in artificial silk, but in nylon you are sublime.'

'Don't overdo it, Cliff, but thank you anyway.' She kissed him again, and he suspected that a pattern was emerging. He hoped so.

She took her seat again. 'What do you think of the band, Cliff?'

'They're good. Would you like to dance?'

'This number's just finishing. Shall we wait and see what they do next?'

He sat down again. 'You've got one of those organised minds I've heard about,' he observed.

'You're impressed. I can tell.'

The bandleader announced a request. It was 'I'll Be Seeing You,' and the embarrassed couple received a round of applause as the band began the number.

Laura caught Cliff's eye and asked, 'Shall we?'

'Let's.' He took her hand and they walked on to the dance floor.

'When I hear this,' said Laura, 'I always imagine someone getting a draft to some faraway place. It's very sad.'

'I don't think they're likely to send me anywhere far away.'

'It's just as well,' she told him gently. 'You'd never find it.'

'I was going to say I'm too valuable where I am.'

'Yes, you are. That's another reason.'

A singer emerged to provide the vocal refrain, and they enjoyed the rest of the number without speaking. The singer was very good.

They returned to their table in time for Cliff to taste the wine, but Laura's thoughts had reverted to an earlier conversation.

'My headmistress,' she said, 'told me I had a *dis*organised mind.'

'How could she say that?'

'She set very high standards.'

'Where was that?'

'A girls' boarding school near Tunbridge Wells.'

'Posh.' He was impressed.

'There was nothing posh about it.'

'Lady, where I lived, the grammar school was posh, at least until I arrived there and lowered the tone.'

'But at least you got there.'

The roast chicken arrived. They thanked the waitress, and resumed their conversation.

'I got to the grammar school eventually. The first time, you see, I didn't even try to pass the County Minor. All my friends were going to stay at the council school, and I wanted to stay with them.'

'So what happened then?'

He filled her glass and then his. 'My parents appealed, first to the County Council and then to me. They asked the council to take my school work into consideration and then they persuaded me that I could go to the grammar school and still be a plumber if that was my heart's desire.'

'And was it?'

'For a while. Plumbers, you see, were my heroes. It all went back to one winter when I was eight or maybe nine, and we had a burst pipe. It was the first emergency I ever experienced, and the dangers seemed to defy speculation. Set against the advantage of not having to wash, there was the prospect of death by thirst, not to mention my dad, who's a baker, rendered unable to make biscuits and gingerbread men.'

'You were a small boy, after all.' She seemed happy to make an excuse on his behalf.

'Yes, I was. So imagine, then, the scene when the plumber arrived with his canvas bass filled with mysterious implements.'

A Chance Sighting

'It's strange how men are fascinated by tools. My brother's the same.'

'I hope he's better with them than I am. The plumber certainly was. I watched him from a safe distance because I'd been told to stay out of his way, and I was enthralled. I wanted to be like this man who calmly went about his work, using his blowlamp like an angel's harp, to restore serenity after disaster and leave a family happy and relieved.'

'What happened to your idyllic dream?'

'It faded in time. When I got to the grammar school, I discovered Shakespeare, Dickens and Shelley. They became my heroes.'

She nodded as if it were a familiar story. 'Everyone has to grow up some time.'

'I suppose so, but how did we get on to this? We were talking about your school, weren't we?' He realised he'd been guilty of taking over the conversation.

'This chicken's not brilliant.'

'I think the bird was past its prime. Still, the band's good and the wine's even better.'

'I'm glad you brought me,' she said reassuringly. Then, on reflection, she said, 'There's not much I can say about my school. Those years were very uneventful.'

'Later, then. Did you go straight from school into the Wrens?'

'Good heavens, no, I was at university for two years. I only joined the Wrens in nineteen-forty, when things were looking bad.'

'More wine?' He picked up the bottle.

'Please.'

He refilled her glass. 'What did you do at university?'

'Modern Languages. I intend to go back and take my degree after the war.'

'Where?'

'University College, London. What about you?'

'Leeds. As a matter of fact, I've been thinking about making a change after the war. Much as I enjoy English literature, I fancy studying psychology.'

She gave him that engaged look that had impressed him so much on their first date. 'What made you think of that?'

'It was studying Shakespeare, basically. He's unbeatable on human nature.'

'He is,' she agreed, 'but I've never heard that as an argument for studying of psychology. Still, I wish you well with it.'

'Thanks. I suppose my one year at university was a kind of rehearsal. I've had two goes at most things. Leeds was my second choice.'

'Which was your first?'

'Cambridge.'

'Oh, well.' She gave him a sympathetic smile. 'Many aspire.... What else have you achieved the second time around?'

'Almost everything. There was the County Minor, as I told you, and I had to retake Latin at Higher School Certificate to get a better grade. I even had two goes at getting into flying training.'

'But you succeeded, and that's the main thing.'

'I'm glad you think so. My mother used to say I treated everything as a kind of rehearsal, knowing I'd always be given another chance.'

'Parents expect a lot, don't they?'

He noticed that she'd left the chicken breast at the side of her plate. 'I'm sorry about the chicken,' he said.

'Oh, don't worry. It's much better than the food we get at *Flowerdown*. I'm just not very hungry.'

'Maybe we can find something on the dessert menu.'

'Yes, there's no rush.' She waved the problem aside. 'Tell me about the people you work with, your crew.'

'All right, there's Marcus, my observer. We're very good friends.'

'I'm sure that's important.'

'Absolutely. Then there's Leading Airman Cyril Woodbridge, short title: "Woody". He's our telegraphist/air-gunner and a civilising influence on us both. He's a good hand.'

'Do you all get on well?'

'We have to. Of course, I try not to be too anchor-faced. I was a leading airman for two years before the Admiralty decided that all pilots must be gentlemen by definition, so I'm quite egalitarian, really.'

She squeezed his hand. 'You're a gentleman, Cliff, and not just because you're an officer.'

'I'm glad you think so. Have you never considered raising the tone of the wardroom?'

'No.'

'Do you mind if I ask why not?'

'No, I don't mind. I was put off from the start. When I joined in nineteen-forty, we could see immediately which of the girls had their sights on higher things. They treated the instructors like poodles and they couldn't wait to become involved with an officer who'd give them a leg-up with the interview board.'

Cliff nodded, recognising the type.

'And all that so they could enjoy the endless round of wardroom cocktail parties, or so they thought. Well, it wasn't what I wanted.'

'They're not all like that, Laura.'

'I know, but early experience dies hard.'

'All right, it's your decision. Would you like to dance?'

'Mm.' The band was playing the introduction to 'A Nightingale Sang in Berkeley Square.' 'Let's do that.'

Eyeing the crowded floor, he said, 'We weren't the only ones who thought this was a good idea. Let's shuffle.'

They moved closer and enjoyed the anonymous intimacy of the crowded dance floor. Nearby, a nasal voice asked, 'Who do we have to pay to make these guys wake up and play some real music?'

With his face blissfully in contact with Laura's, Cliff said, 'I anticipate an outbreak of jitterbuggery.'

'I didn't know there was such a word.'

'If there wasn't, there is now.'

'Let's just enjoy this while we can.'

'Mm.' It was a purr of contentment.

When the time came to leave, they walked just as happily to the car.

'It's been lovely,' she said.

He opened the door and held it for her. 'In spite of the chicken?'

'I'd forgotten about that.'

He swung the handle and the engine caught, coughed and settled into a steady rhythm. He took his seat behind the wheel and asked, 'You mentioned Tunbridge Wells. Is your home in Kent?'

'Yes, not in Tunbridge Wells itself, but close by. I just went to school there, but I couldn't see myself living anywhere but in Kent, and when I get my degree I'll probably find a teaching post there.'

'In a girls' boarding school?'

She laughed. 'Good heavens, no. It's a peculiar and precious world. I'm more inclined towards something less exclusive.'

'Good for you.'

'You know where you are now, don't you? It's almost a straight line to the Andover road.'

'Yes, but don't bale out yet. I may need you.'

'You can depend on me, Cliff. By the way, dare I ask how you find the petrol for this car? I've been wondering.'

'Horse trading.'

'What?'

'Barter. It's as simple as that. There's always someone with spare petrol coupons wanting something I've got, and the tiny drop I use isn't going to lose us the war.'

She seemed to consider his answer before saying, 'I know what you are, Cliff. You're a survivor. Whatever happens, you'll get through, even if you have to make two attempts at it. Does that make sense?'

'No, but keep talking to me anyway.'

'Why?'

'I like the sound your voice makes.'

She continued to talk until eventually he parked at a discreet distance from the main gate of *HMS Flowerdown*, secluded by the blackout.

'Cliff, thank you for a lovely evening and a wonderful birthday present.'

'You're very welcome.' He half expected another peck on the cheek and he moved closer to receive it, but she remained motionless, leaving the next move to him.

'It's our second tryst,' he announced solemnly. 'Am I allowed to kiss you?'

'Oh, I think I can allow that.' She laughed, leaning forward so that he could slip his arm round her shoulders. 'Is counting assignations an item of protocol I've missed?'

'Evidently, but you're a southerner, after all. In the coy North

A Chance Sighting

Riding, no respectable girl would permit herself to be kissed *aux lèvres*, as it were, on a first rendezvous.'

Still amused, she asked, 'Does everyone in Scarborough speak French?'

'Only the cultured few,' he murmured, touching her lips lightly before descending into a long and sensuous kiss.

7

Laura had to concentrate, firstly on the waveband allocated to her, turning the condenser knob minutely to detect enemy traffic, and then on the monotonous task of reading coded groups. When summoned by Lt-Cdr Simmonds, she had to remain alert to receive his orders, at the same time evading his unwelcome attentions, a precaution that also required concentration.

She knew her work was important; she'd been told that many times, and she knew that the results of her work were dispatched swiftly, either to Bletchley Park in the case of coded groups, or to Portsmouth if they were in plain language, but she had no idea how they were put to use, and no one was prepared to tell her. It seemed that job satisfaction, like most desirable commodities, was rationed. As for dodging Lt-Cdr Simmonds, that was merely self-preservation, a sordid fact of life.

So much for concentration. What she really wanted was to relive the events of the previous evening, from getting into Cliff's car to the last, lingering kiss. She wanted to recall everything about him: his silly story about wanting to be a plumber, the self-effacing way he spoke about having two goes at everything, making fun of himself and his upbringing, his distinctive cleft chin and those clear, brown eyes that made him look playful or soulful according to his changing disposition.

All that was out of the question, of course. *HMS Flowerdown* was a 'Y' Station, a listening station in the front line of naval intelligence, and to daydream about a new romance or about anything else would be criminally irresponsible. That was why she had to concentrate.

A Chance Sighting

It was easier for Cliff. The nature of his duties meant that he could discharge them quite adequately without closing out the memory of that Saturday evening. In fact, he thought compulsively and often about Laura, and counted the days until their next meeting.

The day eventually came, and they made the journey into Winchester to see 'When We Are Married' at the Royal Cinema in Jewry Street. They discussed the film on the way home.

'I couldn't believe how they could all be so stuffy and self-satisfied in the first place,' said Laura.

'Couldn't you? Priestley knew his characters, you know. Those solid, middle-class non-conformists are a feature of the north.' He added, 'Not that I have anything against non-conformists, of course. Or the middle-class, for that matter. My mother's family are Wesleyan Methodists, and my dad's a member of the Rotary Club.'

She laughed at his affected discomfiture. 'And you're an officer and a gentleman.'

'Well, a temporary gentleman.'

'You're hard on yourself, Cliff.'

'Let's say I'm unpretentious.'

'To a fault,' she agreed. 'By the way, we're coming to where we turn left.'

'Thanks, but I'm getting the hang of this journey now.' He proved it by taking the left turn without hesitation and driving to their usual stopping place.

'Thank you. I really enjoyed the film. Supper too.'

'So did I. We must do it again and again.'

'I certainly hope so.' She moved closer to him, and he put his arm round her, hesitant as yet to confess the extent of his true feelings.

'I think sometimes,' she told him, 'this is the best part of the evening.'

'I'm glad you told me that. I could save a small fortune just by parking here. Of course, it could be a trifle embarrassing when the days lengthen and daylight intrudes. Still, your people are good at keeping secrets, aren't they?'

'There's a world of difference between maintaining security and resisting the urge to gossip.'

'I never thought I'd say it, but thank goodness for the blackout.' He bent to kiss her.

Emerging eventually from a lengthy embrace, Laura looked at her watch and said, 'If only we had more time together.'

'My feeling exactly.'

'What are the chances of our getting leave at the same time? I only had forty-eight hours for Christmas, so I must be in line for something.'

'I should say so. Put a request in. It'll probably be easier for me, so I'll wait and see what happens before I do anything.' He felt in his inside pocket and took out a photograph of Agatha with Marcus, Woody and him standing beside her. 'I've been meaning to give you this,' he said. 'You asked me earlier about Agatha, and that's her behind those three impossibly handsome men.'

'Oh, wonderful. Are you sure you can spare it?'

'I think so.'

'Thank you.'

'Right, let's see what happens when you put in your request.'

'Just forty-eight hours would be wonderful.'

'Truly wonderful,' he agreed.

Suddenly, the future was filled with promise.

8

Laura's next evening off watch came eight days later. Cliff had booked a table again at the Cavendish, as it suited them both, and he was looking forward to meeting her as usual at six-thirty. He was still thinking about her when he took off on a search.

As he levelled out at 2,000 feet, Woody appeared at his shoulder to ask, 'What are we looking for, sir?' It was an unfortunate hangover from an unequal past that although pilots and observers were fully briefed it was deemed unnecessary to accord TAGs the same courtesy.

'A Typhoon pilot, Woody. He was hit by flak during an interdictory raid. He limped as far as the French coast, but then had to ditch. We have to find him before the home team does. They don't take kindly to our blokes beating up their airfields and their aircraft.'

'Most unreasonable of them, sir.'

'Quite. Anyway, keep a sharp look out. We don't want to go the same way as the Typhoon.'

'Aye-aye, sir.' Woody made his way aft, and Cliff flew on, ever watchful.

'Meanwhile,' said Marcus, 'rescue is on its way, albeit at a snail's pace.'

' "Wisely and slow; they stumble that run fast." '

Marcus groaned good-naturedly. 'Go on. I'll buy it.'

'*Romeo and Juliet*.'

'I might have known. Was there a subject on which that chap Shakespeare didn't have an opinion?'

'None whatsoever, Marcus, but you should remember that they

weren't necessarily his opinions, but those he put into the mouths of his characters.'

'Well now, that's a relief.'

'I detect a trace of irony in that sentiment. By the way, you will tell me when we need to lose altitude, won't you?'

'Affirmative, Skipper.'

Twenty minutes later, Woody shouted a warning. 'Aircraft fine on the starboard quarter! It's gaining on us.'

'Right, Woody. Keep me informed.'

'Aye-aye, Skip.... It's a Lizzie, Skipper.'

'Good oh. It must be joining in the search.'

As the Lysander drew level with them the pilot gave them a friendly wave before gaining altitude and turning east.

'They're at least sixty knots faster than this thing,' observed Marcus.

'But we have one big advantage over them. I mean, just imagine ditching in a kite that won't float. Speed wouldn't help you then.'

'Your loyalty does you credit, Cliff.' Marcus checked his calculations and said, 'We'll be over the last reported position in five minutes.'

'Good. The poor bugger's been afloat long enough.'

'Fighter, Skipper!' Woody's voice banished thoughts of sympathy. 'Above and astern. It's an F W 190!'

'Hold on tight, folks. We're going to dive.' Cliff knew it was the only option for an aircraft as slow and unwieldy as the Walrus.

'He's coming for us, Skipper.'

'Okay, let's see if we can tempt him into taking a cold bath.' He pushed the stick forward, putting the Walrus into a steep dive. As he did so, he heard the rattle of the Focke Wulf's machine guns followed more ominously by the slower, rhythmic thud of the twenty-millimetre cannon. For the time being, Woody's machine gun was silent. It would be impossible for him to return fire without shooting the tail off the Walrus.

Cliff could now hear nothing above the scream of Agatha's engine as the Walrus hurtled towards the sea. Marcus sat beside him in the second pilot's seat, bracing himself. He could only hope Woody was all right, because communication with him was impossible.

A Chance Sighting

There were three loud explosions and Agatha shook violently in a way that could only mean she had been hit by cannon shells. Marcus looked upward and yelled through the noise, 'The bastard's got the engine! There's black smoke pouring out of it.'

The noise receded as the stricken engine gave up the struggle.

'Bugger!' Cliff hauled laboriously on the stick, gradually pulling the Walrus out of its dive. The Focke Wulf flew past them, mocking them with an exuberant victory roll.

'So much for taking him down,' said Marcus.

'He was too good for that.' Cliff put the Walrus into a shallow glide.

'Let's hope the hull's still watertight, Cliff.'

'We'll soon find out.'

The aircraft hit the waves three times before settling into a level run and generating a wall of spray. With no power, however, it soon lost speed and hove-to. As it did so, Cliff and Marcus heard the sound of running water further aft. Marcus left his seat to investigate.

'We're holed beneath the waterline,' he reported, 'and Woody's injured.'

'Right, do what you can for him. See if you can get him out through the hatch. I'll see to the dinghy and ditching gear.'

It took less than two minutes for Cliff to inflate the dinghy and load the essential equipment. Even so, by the time he'd paddled as far as the after cockpit, the hull was almost under water.

'About time too,' said Marcus. 'I dressed Woody's wound while we were waiting for you. It helped pass the time.'

Cliff shook his head. 'The lowest form of wit,' he said, 'and at a time like this. What's the injury, Woody?'

'A splinter, I think, sir. I seem to have a piece of Agatha's hull lodged in my leg.' His face was white and he was clearly in a great deal of pain.

'Can you ease yourself into the dinghy? You're nearly there.'

Seated on top of the hull, Woody pushed himself forward with his hands until his feet were in the dinghy.

'Come on, Woody. Can you shove him from behind, Marcus?'

'Sorry if it hurts, but here goes, Woody.' Marcus pushed, and

Woody fell into the dinghy with a loud cry of pain. Marcus boarded after him, casting off the line that had secured the dinghy to the half-submerged aircraft.

They paddled away to a safe distance to avoid being dragged into the void that would be created when the Walrus sank. Then, as they watched her slip beneath the surface, Cliff said soberly, 'Goodbye, Agatha, and thank you for everything. I'm sorry it had to end like this.'

'I think we all are,' said Marcus. 'How's the leg, Woody?'

The TAG bit his lip and said, 'It's been better, sir.'

Marcus asked, 'Is there any morphine in the first-aid kit, Cliff?'

'I don't want to give him morphine. He's obviously lost a lot of blood, and we don't want him losing consciousness. It's the last thing he needs.'

'I suppose so.' Marcus busied himself by winding the handle of the 'squawk box', the equipment that sent an automatic signal enabling receiving stations to plot their position. 'I don't know how effective this contraption is,' he said, 'but anything is worth a try.'

'It is,' agreed Cliff, soberly taking stock. They had lost Agatha, they had an injured crew member, and he would not be meeting Laura after all.

More than six hours later, Laura stood at the place where Cliff always parked. He was twenty minutes late, and that troubled her, because he'd always been punctual. She tried telling herself that anything could happen in the blackout, but that was silly. *Flowerdown* was only a few miles – three or maybe four – from Worthy Down. What could possibly happen over that distance? She put the thought hurriedly out of her mind, preferring not to conjecture.

After another fifteen minutes she decided that something serious had happened. Consequently, she was disinclined to exchange banter with the sentries on the main gate.

'What's the matter, darlin'? Didn't he turn up? Never mind. I'll be off watch in an hour.'

His fellow sentry found that extremely amusing. Laura advised

A Chance Sighting

them both to grow up. She needed to get to a public telephone, and the nearest was outside the junior ratings' canteen.

When she got there, she had to wait for what seemed a ridiculous length of time while a wireless mechanic spoke to his parents. Common sense told her that private calls usually lasted no more than two minutes but it seemed much longer.

Eventually, he ended his conversation, and she was able to pick up the receiver.

The operator responded promptly. 'Number, please.'

'Will you connect me with *HMS Kestrel*, please? I don't know the number.'

'*HMS Kestrel*? Hold the line, please.'

After ten seconds or so, there was a click, and then the operator's voice said, 'Connecting you now.'

'Thank you.'

A woman's voice came on the line. '*HMS Kestrel.*'

'Good evening. Will you put me through to the wardroom, please?'

'The wardroom. Who's calling?'

'Laura Pembury. I'd like to speak to Lieutenant Stephens.'

'Hold the line, please.'

Laura waited rather longer this time, and she was beginning to wonder if she'd been forgotten, when a man's voice came on the line.

'Wardroom. Commander Watkinson speaking. Who is calling?'

'PO Wren Pembury, sir. I wonder if I might speak to Lieutenant Stephens, please.'

'I'm afraid he's not here. Is it an official matter?'

There was no point in denying it. 'No, sir, we arranged to meet this evening, but for some reason he didn't turn up.'

There was a worrying silence, and then Commander Watkinson spoke again. 'I'm afraid Lieutenant Stephens is missing. He went on a search this morning and failed to return.'

'I see.' Her voice was no more than a whisper. She was completely stunned.

'You know, my dear, there's every chance he and his crew will be picked up. The search will be resumed at first light, so try not to worry too much.'

'Thank you, sir.'

She walked to her accommodation, a corrugated steel Nissen hut, thinking about Commander Watkinson's final words.

Try not to worry too much.

It was a ridiculous thing to say, unless he really believed Cliff and the others stood a good chance of being found in the morning. Her thoughts turned one way and then the other, but without finding a trace of comfort.

Fortunately, the hut was empty. Distractedly, she undressed and climbed into bed.

'We just had to ditch in mid-bloody-winter.' Marcus beat his arms repeatedly in a bid to improve the circulation.

'That's a good idea,' said Cliff. 'We all need to exercise. Come on, Woody. Join in.'

'I can't, sir.'

'Yes, you can. You mustn't fall asleep. Now, buff your arms.'

They did that for several minutes until it lost its appeal. At that point, Cliff said, 'You're a musician, aren't you, Woody?'

'I was a music student before I enlisted, sir.' His voice was weak.

'What instrument do you play?'

'Piano and French hor....'

'Stay with us, Woody. You've got to stay awake. Tell us what music you like to play.'

'Beethoven, Chopin, Rachmaninov... lots more.'

Cliff reached out and shook his arm. 'Tell us about Chopin, Woody. Let's hear his life story.'

'I'll do my best, sir.'

'That's the spirit.'

'Right, sir.' With an effort, Woody began. 'Chopin was born either in eighteen-oh-nine or eighteen-ten. No one is certain, and I'm struggling to remember, now, with the pain in my leg.'

'Concentrate,' Cliff urged him.

'He was born in Poland.'

'I thought he was French,' said Marcus. 'His name sounds French.'

A Chance Sighting

'His father was a Frenchman, sir. His name was Nicolas Choppen, but Chopin changed it, for some reason.' His eyelids were drooping.

'Come on, Woody,' said Cliff. 'Stay awake.'

'It's surprising what you can learn if you hang around long enough,' said Marcus, 'even if it entails being shot down and cast adrift on a rubber raft.'

'Don't let this philistine distract you, Woody. Go on.' Cliff motioned Marcus to keep quiet.

'He moved to Paris, where he was soon in demand as a salon pianist.' Woody saw Marcus open his mouth to speak, but forestalled him. 'He was very delicate. He had consumption, and he wasn't strong enough to fill a concert hall with sound.' Woody hesitated and said, 'I have an idea of how he must have felt.'

'Bear up, Woody.' Cliff squeezed his arm again.

'His ideal venue was the fashionable salon. Female aristocrats vied with one another for his services.'

Marcus appeared to be missing the essential point. 'If he was weak and consumptive,' he said, 'he wouldn't be much use to them in the boudoir.'

'Lieutenant Rhodes has a salacious mind,' explained Cliff. 'He's also a stranger to culture. We must make allowances for him.'

'He did have a romantic association with a lady called Georges Sand, sir.'

'But that's a chap's name,' objected Marcus.

'Yes, sir. Her name was actually Aurore Dupin, but she was a novelist, and to be published in those days a woman had to adopt a man's name. George Eliot was another example.'

'Did he have her as well?'

'No, she was an example of a lady novelist taking a man's name,' explained Cliff. 'Now, do try to keep up.'

The lesson continued, albeit with frequent interruptions, until the two officers knew considerably more about Chopin; at least, Cliff did. It was difficult to tell with Marcus. More importantly, however, Woody was still awake when they heard the rhythmic pounding of a ship's engine.

'Listen,' said Cliff, 'it's getting closer.'

They peered through the darkness until a shape became discernible.

'It's a fishing vessel of some kind,' said Marcus. 'A trawler, maybe.'

'Keep quiet,' warned Cliff. 'We're too close to the French coast for it to be one of ours.'

'They're coming towards us,' said Marcus. 'I think they've seen us.'

Confirmation came in the form of a searchlight beam that swept the water ahead of the trawler and finally settled on the dinghy.

'Now we've had it,' said Marcus.

The trawler drew inevitably closer and reduced speed until it was alongside. By now, it was clear that the vessel was an armed trawler in the service of the *Kriegsmarine*.

A voice said, '*Ich werde eine Leiter senken.*'

'He says he's going to lower a ladder,' said Cliff. Cupping his hands to his mouth, he called in reply, '*Ein Mitglied meiner Crew ist verwundet.*'

The voice assured Cliff that a line would be lowered for the injured man.

'Well,' he said, realising that his hopes of rescue by friendly forces were now dashed, 'at least, Woody will be cared for.'

9

Laura rose early, simply because it was something to do. She needed to be busy, even if the activity only amounted to reaching the heads and ablutions block before anyone else. Pulling her greatcoat on, she picked up her sponge bag and towel.

If she were barely awake before she left the hut, the icy wind roused her to full consciousness so that she was thankful when she reached her destination.

She stood for a while in her coat and pyjamas, enjoying the warmth before running a bath and undressing.

When the water reached the regulation five inches, she lowered herself into it and used her imagination and the last of her precious soap ration to create a fleeting sense of luxury. It was pay day, after all, and she would receive her new ration of toilet soap with her fortnight's pay.

For several minutes, she lay in the shallow water, wondering what the day might bring. She would make a phone call to Worthy Down after lunch, but only if she could make herself wait so long.

Maybe they would have good news, and she would be happier than she had ever been. After the shock of learning that he was missing, the relief would be too wonderful for words.

She couldn't bring herself to imagine the worst. Fate would never have allowed her to meet such a lovely man, only to lose him after less than a month. They must surely find him. After rescuing so many ditched airmen, he *deserved* to be rescued.

After a while, she realised that the water was no longer warm. Those five inches gave up their precious heat all too quickly. She pushed herself reluctantly to her feet and reached for her towel.

She was due to go on watch at 0800. Until then, if she were lucky, she might avoid contact with people she knew. She really couldn't face talking about Cliff.

The captain of the armed trawler, *Oberleutnant zur See* Franz Neumann, shook hands formally with Cliff and Marcus.

'My orders are to hand you over to an armed guard that will escort you to *Kriegsmarine* headquarters,' he said.

The ship was now tied up alongside the mole at Le Havre, and it seemed their real captivity was about to begin.

'What about the leading airman, *Herr Oberleutnant*? What will happen to him?'

'He will receive treatment for his injury. After that, he will be taken to a *Stammlager*. As officers, you will both be held at Marlag Nord "O", the camp for naval officers.'

'We are grateful to you, *Herr Oberleutnant*, for treating us well.'

The captain smiled briefly. 'We are not all monsters, *Leutnant* Stephens.'

'I never imagined you were, but thank you anyway. I wonder if I might be allowed to speak to Leading Airman Woodbridge before we are taken ashore.'

'Yes, speak with him now. It will not be possible after you have left the ship.'

'Thank you.' Cliff saluted and left the bridge.

He found Woody lying on a bunk. His leg was dressed with a clean bandage.

'Hello, Woody.'

'Hello, sir.'

'How's it going?'

'It still hurts like hell, sir. They say I'm going ashore to a hospital.'

'That's right. The Germans have a reputation for caring for the sick and wounded. Let me remind you, though, that when the intelligence blokes get to you, you tell them your name, rate and official number. No more than that.'

'Of course, sir.'

A Chance Sighting

'Fine.' Cliff shook his hand. 'Good luck, Woody. We'll see each other again.'

'Good luck, sir, and thank you.'

'You've nothing to thank me for. I got you into this mess.'

'It wasn't your fault, sir. Anyway, thanks *are* in order.'

'If you say so, Woody.' It seemed wrong to argue with him when he was in pain.

'I know this isn't exactly original, sir, but it seems to me that a skipper has the power to render the lives of his crew members happy or unhappy; to make their service light or burdensome, a pleasure or a toil, and flying with you has never been a toil.'

'I don't think Dickens would have resented the allusion or the rewriting, and thanks for telling me that. I've appreciated your contribution as well.' He shook his hand again. 'Take care, Woody.'

'You too, sir.'

Cliff returned to the bridge, where he found Marcus and two armed sailors of the *Kriegsmarine*.

The intense concentration required of a special telegraphist in a 'Y' Station such as *Flowerdown* necessitated watches being divided into four-hour spells alternating with four-hour rest periods. Officers as well as ratings had been known to fall victim to nervous tension; some had even succumbed to complete breakdown, and supervising officers were ever watchful for the signs. On this occasion, however, Laura welcomed the need for concentration, because it was the only relief she had from the worry that had tormented her since her conversation with Commander Watkinson.

When her rest period came, instead of going to the mess for lunch, she went straight to the public telephone and called *HMS Kestrel*. This time she asked for Commander Watkinson and after a brief silence he came on the line.

'Commander Watkinson.'

'Good afternoon, sir. It's PO Wren Pembury again. I'm sorry to be a nuisance, but I wondered if there was any news about Lieutenant Stephens and his crew.'

'Hello, PO. You're not a nuisance at all. I'm afraid there's no news yet; they're still searching, so there's still a chance they'll find them.'

'I see, sir.'

'Look, where are you based?'

'*HMS Flowerdown*, sir.'

'And who's your divisional officer?'

'Second Officer Denham, sir.'

'You're PO Wren Pembury. I've got that. I just need your Christian name and official number.'

'My name is Laura, sir, and my number is nine four two three seven six.'

'Right, as soon as we know something, I'll get a message to you via Second Officer Denham.'

'That's very kind of you, sir. Thank you.'

'Not at all. Now, you run along and wait until you hear from me.'

'Aye-aye, sir, and thank you.'

'You're welcome, my dear. Goodbye.'

Cliff and Marcus were escorted to what looked like a large hotel in the centre of Le Havre. It turned out to be *Kriegsmarine* Headquarters, and the two officers were quickly separated on arrival. Cliff found himself in an office with a desk and two chairs. The walls were lined with files and folders, and the room reeked unpleasantly of pipe smoke.

After a while, the door opened and an officer bearing the same insignia as Neumann entered the room. Out of politeness, Cliff rose to his feet. Taking the other chair, the officer told him curtly to remain seated.

'What is your name?' His manner continued to be brusque.

'Clifford William Stephens.'

'Spell it.'

Cliff obliged, and the officer wrote his name at the head of a form.

'Your rank?'

A Chance Sighting

'Lieutenant RNVR.' He thought that would have been obvious from the rings on his sleeves, but it was perhaps inadvisable to say so. The Oberleutnant seemed decidedly unfriendly. Instead, Cliff asked, 'What's your name, *Herr Oberleutnant?*'

'You are here to answer questions, not to ask them.'

'Okay, you're the boss.'

The officer pointed to the wings on Cliff's sleeve. 'You are a pilot, I see.'

'I can't deny that.'

'Were you shot down or did you fall from the sky for another reason?'

'Clifford Stephens, Lieutenant RNVR.'

'What aircraft were you flying?'

'Clifford Stephens, Lieutenant RNVR.'

The officer shrugged. 'What harm is there in telling me? We know every detail of your naval aircraft, both British and American.'

'So, why are you asking me what aircraft I was flying?'

'Because I want to know. Answer my question.'

'Under the terms of the Geneva Convention, I'm required to give you only my name and rank.'

'You had with you one other officer and a *Matrosen-Obergefreiter*, which suggests that you were flying one of four types of aircraft.'

'What are the chances of a meal, *Herr Oberleutnant*? We haven't eaten for over twenty-four hours.' It wasn't strictly true; they had eaten on board the trawler, but several hours had elapsed since that meal.

'You will eat after we have had a little chat, as you Englanders say.'

'Can we make it quite a quick chat? We're very hungry.'

The officer went on, ignoring Cliff's entreaty. 'Your aircraft may have been the American Grumann TB-F Avenger.' He paused. 'Was it?' The question came out sharply, as if to shock Cliff into being indiscreet.

'Clifford Stephens, Lieutenant RNVR.'

'It may, of course, have been the Fairey Barracuda.' Suddenly, he smiled and said, 'An English joke, *nicht wahr?*'

Not if you're a U-boat crew under attack, thought Cliff.

'Perhaps it was that museum exhibit, the Fairey Swordfish.'

Cliff wanted to remind him that the Swordfish had crippled the Italian fleet and had been instrumental in the sinking of the battleship *Bismarck*, but he resisted the impulse.

'Could it have been the Supermarine Walrus?' The officer was teasing him again. 'Another English joke, I believe.'

'Clifford Stephens, Lieutenant RNVR.'

'Would you care for a cigarette, Lieutenant?' The officer opened a box and offered it.

'Thank you, but I'll stick to my own.' Cliff took a packet of Player's from his pocket and lit one.

'Yes, I believe English cigarettes are surprisingly good.' He looked wistfully at the packet that Cliff returned to his pocket. 'Where were you based, Lieutenant?'

'Clifford Stephens, Lieutenant RNVR.'

'We know there are no aircraft carriers in the area, so you must have flown from either Eastleigh or Lee-on-Solent.'

'Clifford Stephens, Lieutenant RNVR.' It was a tiresome game, but it was good to know that the enemy believed there were only two naval air stations in the south of England. He still recalled with amusement Lord Haw Haw's claim that *HMS Kestrel* had been sunk with heavy loss of life; in fact, he'd enjoyed the joke for some time afterwards, whenever he drove through *Kestrel*'s main gate.

'We shall see what your navigator has to tell us,' said the *Oberleutnant*, picking up his papers.

Cliff was confident that Marcus would stonewall his interrogator just as he had. He'd never worried about that, just as he was convinced his captors would tire of asking questions that didn't seem important. The rest of his fortunes as a prisoner-of-war he would face when they occurred. His main concern now was to find a way of letting Laura know he was still alive.

By 16:45, it was completely dark outside and rain was hammering against the windows of the hut. Even the tight-fitting blackout boards failed to muffle the noise completely.

A Chance Sighting

It was Laura's rest period and she had been trying to read, solely as a means of driving her current preoccupation, however temporarily, from her mind, but she was finding it impossible to concentrate for longer than a few lines.

Fretfully, she grabbed her coat and set out for the NAAFI canteen. If a mug of tea failed to provide a distraction, it would be no worse than staring uncomprehendingly at a printed page.

Holding her coat over her head to shield herself from the worst of the rain, she ran along the concrete path, avoiding as far as she could the shallow puddles, and finally reached the canteen. As a PO Wren, she was entitled to use the Chiefs' and Petty Officers' mess, but she would have risked running into people she knew, and she couldn't cope with that.

Opening and closing the outer door to the canteen and pushing her way past the blackout curtain, she stepped abruptly into the meagre comfort of light and warmth.

Ignoring the inquisitive looks of some of the junior ratings around her, she went to the counter and asked for a mug of tea. The NAAFI assistant served her without appearing to notice that she was a senior rating. It was doubtless one of those things she regarded simply as none of her business.

Laura took the tea to a free table and waited for it to cool. She was in no hurry.

Minutes passed by without her noticing anything around her, and she was taking a tentative sip, when a voice by her side said, 'So here you are. I've been looking for you all over the place.' It was Eileen Goodall looking drenched but relieved.

'I just wanted some peace and quiet.'

Eileen looked around her quite unnecessarily and said, 'This is a funny place to come looking for it.' Then, dismissing the subject with a shrug, she said, 'Second Officer Denham wants to see you in her office. She didn't sound as if she was in much of a hurry, but I'd be inclined to get a move on if I were you.'

'Second Officer Denham? Right.' She must have heard from Commander Watkinson. Hurriedly, she put her mug of tea on the counter and left the canteen with Eileen.

'What have you been up to, anyway?' Eileen would never remain in ignorance for want of a direct question.

'Nothing at all. I don't think it's a disciplinary matter.'

'What can it be, then?'

Laura decided there was nothing to be gained by evasion. 'Cliff's been missing for more than twenty-four hours,' she said.

'Oh, no.' Eileen stopped suddenly.

'Keep going. They said they'd let me know when they knew something. They were going to phone Second Officer Denham.'

'Maybe they've found him.'

'I hope so. I've been going frantic. I hardly dare hope.'

They ran the rest of the way without speaking. When they reached Second Officer Denham's office, Eileen waited in the corridor while Laura knocked on the door.

'Come in.'

Laura opened the door. 'You sent for me, ma'am.' Her heart was pounding, and not solely because she'd been running.

'Yes, come in and close the door. Don't stand on ceremony, PO. Take a seat.'

Miss Denham was a woman of about thirty, and quite attractive in a severe kind of way, but her next words held no hint of severity.

'PO Wren Pembury, I received a phone call about half-an-hour ago from Commander Watkinson at *HMS Kestrel*.' She referred to a note on her desk. 'It was about Lieutenant Stephens. I believe you two have been seeing each other recently.'

'Yes, ma'am.' Laura suddenly felt hollow. Had it been good news, Second Officer Denham would have told her already.

'You should prepare yourself, although you mustn't fear the worst at this stage.' She drew a deep breath as if bracing herself to speak. 'The fact is, they've been unable to find Lieutenant Stephens and his crew, and this awful weather that's set to persist for at least twenty-four hours has led to the search being called off.'

'But why?' She could feel tears forming beneath her eyelids. 'I mean, why have they called it off? I don't understand.'

'The weather in the Channel is even worse than this.' She pointed vaguely with her pen towards a window. 'The sea is too rough for anyone to survive in an open dinghy. I'm sorry.'

10

Cliff lay on a straw palliasse in his cell, shivering in spite of the two blankets in which he'd cocooned himself, and cursing the Focke Wulf pilot responsible for his predicament.

Since his interrogation at *Kriegsmarine* Headquarters, he and Marcus had been obliged to undergo, separately, a slow journey across France and part of Germany, stopping frequently for no obvious reason, and occasionally because of an air raid, although that afforded him a perverse kind of pleasure.

After several days, the train had halted at a place called Hüttenbusch, where he and Marcus were thrust into a utility vehicle and driven to their current place of incarceration, Dulag Nord, which was apparently a holding camp.

Cold and anger apart, his chief preoccupation was his inability to communicate with Laura. By this time, she would probably think he'd been killed, and that was too awful. He knew he'd be allowed to write home once he was in the main camp, but her home address was a mystery; he only knew that she lived somewhere in Kent, and he couldn't write to her at *Flowerdown*. The Germans would know it was a shore establishment and very likely one that was worth a visit from the *Luftwaffe* once they'd discovered its whereabouts. Air raids had become desultory of late, but it wasn't worth the risk.

Neither could he write to her care of *HMS Kestrel*, the ship they claimed to have sunk, and the only other person who knew about Laura was Marcus. He continued to turn the problem over repeatedly, until fatigue overcame anxiety, and he fell into a fitful sleep.

Laura was still trying to come to terms with the situation. There was a chance, she was told, that an enemy ship might have picked up Cliff and his crew, and that she might yet learn that they were prisoners-of-war, but she rejected the idea as a chance in a million. She had no wish to live in a fool's paradise only to suffer the tragedy afresh when the facts became known.

She slept when she was off-watch because that was the only panacea available to her, and any relief was better than none. Even then, she had to cope with her waking moments, when she would open her eyes and, just for one halcyon second, all was well. And then realisation came like a stab wound and she sobbed silently into her pillow until it was time to get up and go on watch.

Second Officer Denham had offered to arrange leave, but Laura had turned that down, preferring to remain fully occupied.

She was on watch when Lieutenant-Commander Simmonds sent for her again. Accordingly, she made her way to his office and arrived as a steward was taking his morning coffee in to him. Laura waited in the open doorway.

'Come in,' he called. 'Come over here.'

She let the steward make her exit and then approached the officer's desk.

He swung in his swivel chair to face her. 'This side,' he said, inclining his head towards his left. 'That's unless you're skilled at reading upside-down.'

She approached him warily, still leaving a safe distance between them.

'Come closer. I don't bite.'

Reluctantly, she edged closer.

'Now, this particular station,' he said, tapping a signal form on his blotter, 'seems to be guilty of more indiscretions than any other, and I find that intriguing.'

Laura leaned forward to see what he was talking about. As she did so, she felt his hand slide purposefully up the back and the inside of her thigh. Hurriedly, she stepped backward, taking with her his hand, which was momentarily trapped, engaged as it was in exploring the area above her stocking. This caused him to

A Chance Sighting

swivel towards her, and his right hand to knock over the coffee cup, showering his lap with scalding coffee.

With a roar of agony, he leapt to his feet, endeavouring to hold his trousers away from his vulnerable parts, and then, failing in this expedient, he hobbled, still howling and clutching his trousers, in the direction of the officers' heads.

Cliff was taken into an office and given pen and ink and a form bearing the Red Cross insignia. He was told it would ensure that his next-of-kin would learn of his whereabouts promptly and that it would facilitate the delivery of Red Cross parcels. He dipped the pen in ink, and was about to begin, when something struck him as odd. He read further and his suspicion was confirmed. He laid the pen on the desk and folded his arms.

After ten minutes or so, a senior rating came in and took the form. Cliff could hear a muffled conversation taking place outside the office, and then a *Korvettenkapitän*, a lieutenant-commander, entered the room. He was clearly displeased.

'Stand.'

Cliff stood obediently at the desk.

The officer held the form so that Cliff could see it, and asked, 'Why have you not completed this form?'

'Because it's a bogus form.'

'What is the meaning of "bogus"?'

'*Falsch. Dies ist ein falsches Dokument.*'

'Why do you say this?'

Cliff shook his head in sorrow for the simple mind behind the ploy. 'It didn't come from the Red Cross,' he said, 'any more than it came from outer space, sliding down a moonbeam.'

The *Korvettenkapitän* took his seat behind the larger of the two desks. 'It is the official Red Cross form,' he said. 'I advise you to forget your foolish ideas and complete it.'

'Tell me this, then. Why does the Red Cross want to know about the range and bomb-carrying capacity of the aircraft I was flying? Why does it want to know my squadron, my ship or air station, its whereabouts, and the name of my commanding officer?'

'So you refuse to co-operate.'

'I refuse to fill in a form designed to procure intelligence.'

The officer shrugged. 'Have it your own way. You can answer my questions instead.'

'You already have my name and rank. I am Clifford Stephens, Lieutenant RNVR.'

The *Korvettenkapitän* ignored his reply and went on to question him about military activity in the south of England. Had he seen landing craft? Was there an increase in troop movements? What was the appetite for an attempted invasion?

To all his questions, Cliff gave his stock answer, until the *Korvettenkapitän* tried a new approach.

'You must have family who are worried about you. Your wife must be wondering what has happened to you.'

Cliff shook his head. 'Absolutely not,' he said confidently.

'Why?'

'I'm not married.'

'In that case, perhaps there is a girl who is waiting to hear from you.'

That struck an uncomfortable note, but Cliff maintained a straight face. 'There's always that possibility.'

'Lieutenant, we could arrange your repatriation. Transport could be provided to a neutral country and your passage to England could be easily arranged.'

'Don't tell me you have a branch of Thomas Cook here.'

Clearly irritated, the officer said, 'It is not a good idea to make jokes, Lieutenant. I am saying that, in exchange for your co-operation, we could arrange your return to England.'

'Wouldn't that look fishy?'

'Fishy?'

Cliff objected to having to translate for the man, but he did so in the interests of politeness. '*Verdächtig*. Someone would be sure to wonder about my speedy return.'

'A medical certificate would be obtained.'

'I see, but that's not playing the game, is it? And what do you mean exactly by "co-operation", *Herr Korvettenkapitän?*'

A Chance Sighting

'You could achieve all this by telling me all you know about the Allied plan to attempt an invasion of Europe, Lieutenant.'

'If I told you everything I know about that, you would be no wiser than you are now, but in any case....'

'What?'

'I'm going to tell you no more than my name and rank. I am Clifford Stephens, Lieutenant RNVR.'

The officer sat back in his chair and nodded. 'In that case,' he said, 'we will give you another opportunity to enjoy your own company.' He pushed a bell on his desk. When an orderly appeared, he said, 'Return this officer to his cell. He will remain there until he decides to co-operate.'

'Take a seat, PO.' Second Officer Denham opened a box of cigarettes and offered it to Laura.

'No, thank you, ma'am. I don't smoke.'

Miss Denham lit hers and said, 'I want you to tell me exactly what happened in Lieutenant-Commander Simmonds' office.'

'Very well, ma'am. He ordered me to stand beside him. He said he wanted to show me something to do with a station that's been transmitting in plain language. When I stood as close to him as I dared, he told me to stand closer.'

'Why did you say as near as you *dared*?'

'Lieutenant-Commander Simmonds has a reputation among the Wrens and female civilians in this establishment ma'am.'

Miss Denham shifted uncomfortably. 'A reputation for what, PO?'

'I was about to say that he's known for his wandering hands, ma'am, except that's not an accurate description, as his hands usually take the most direct route.'

'Oh, good grief.'

'He put his hand up my skirt, ma'am.' She wouldn't normally have been so ready to describe the offence but, in her current state, she simply didn't care what her divisional officer thought about her complaint.

'And this has happened before, you say?'

'Yes, ma'am. He finds the contents of Wrens' blackouts irresistible. Anyway, on this occasion, I stepped backwards, and that caused him to swivel in his chair. In doing so, he swept the coffee off his desk and into his lap.'

'I'm sorry, PO. I hadn't realised. How long has this been going on?'

'It was happening when I was drafted here three years ago, ma'am.'

'But no one has said anything about it.'

'We don't make complaints about officers, ma'am, especially regular RN officers.'

'Quite.' She stubbed out her cigarette firmly. 'Well, I'm going to make sure this kind of thing doesn't happen again, although this morning's incident must have gone some way towards cooling his ardour.' She considered that and said, 'Maybe "cooled" isn't quite the word I'm looking for.'

'Not from where I was standing, ma'am,' agreed Laura, 'and certainly not where he was sitting.'

'No.' For the first time, Second Officer Denham allowed herself a half-smile. 'I suppose he'll be nursing his grievance now.'

'They say cold water is the best thing,' said Laura, also smiling for the first time in several days.

'At all events, it wasn't your fault. You can rest assured that you won't be disciplined.'

'I don't care,' said Laura. 'Naval discipline is one thing, but I'm not going to submit to the attentions of a lecherous bully.' She was aware that she'd probably said too much; he was an officer, after all, but suddenly she felt reckless.

'Of course you're not.' She lit another cigarette and asked, 'How are you coping generally?'

'Generally, ma'am, I'm coping as well as I can.'

'It must be awful for you, doing a demanding job at a time like this.'

'I'm all right, ma'am.'

Miss Denham looked at her apologetically. 'It's been decided, in view of your current problem, that you should go on draft.'

'I know what they're thinking.' Laura looked down at her hands. 'They don't want someone with an emotional problem working with sensitive material.'

'It's as much for your sake, PO. You do need the change, and you've been working under a lot of pressure.'

'In that case, I'll just have to accept it.'

'Not long ago,' said Miss Denham pointedly, 'you wanted a draft to somewhere where you could make better use your languages.'

'And now I just want to hit back at the people who killed Cliff.' In spite of herself, she felt her eyes filling with tears.

'There is a way you can do that. It's an appointment that's already been suggested for you, and you'd certainly be using your German. There's just one tiny fly in the ointment.'

'What's that, ma'am?' It was odd that the officer had used the word 'appointment' rather than 'draft'. Suddenly, Laura was keen to know more.

'The appointment is for a third officer.'

'Oh.'

'Listen, PO. I have an idea I want to put to you. It could sound a little odd, considering all you're going through, but hear me out.'

'I'm listening, ma'am.'

'I want you to apply for a commission.'

'What?'

Miss Denham waved her hand dismissively. 'I've heard your objection and, frankly, it no longer holds water. I certainly hope you don't see me as a simpering debutante.'

'Of course not, ma'am.'

'Good, because things have moved on since nineteen-forty. The service needs intelligent, educated women like you. Listen, PO, I want you to put in your application and then go on a much-needed leave. Where do you live?'

'I'm sorry, ma'am?' Her mind was elsewhere, considering the ramifications of life in the commissioned ranks.

'I asked you where you lived.'

'Oh, in Kent, ma'am.'

'Good. It shouldn't take you long to get there. We'll go through the application this afternoon and by the time we've done that your leave documents should be ready. In the meantime,' she said, looking at her watch, 'you'd better secure for lunch. I don't know what we're having today. Do you?'

'Shepherd's pie, I believe, ma'am, and I think the dessert is stewed prunes.' Recalling the morning's drama, she was struggling to keep a straight face.

'Off you go,' said Miss Denham, also trying not to laugh.

After another week in the 'cooler', Cliff satisfied his captors that he was no nearer to co-operating with them. He was escorted accordingly to Marlag 'O' and allocated a bunk in a long hut divided into eight rooms, each with either two or three tiers of bunks. He was welcomed to the camp by the Senior British Officer, and he used the opportunity to air his problem.

'I met a girl, a Wren, just a few weeks ago,' he said, 'and I have to say we both became extremely involved. It's very difficult to explain, sir, but, even after so short a time, everything about it seemed right.'

'And now you're separated from her.' The captain lit his pipe. When he spoke again, his voice was sympathetic but pragmatic. 'It was a cruel thing to happen, but you're not the only one, Stephens.'

'I realise that, sir, but most of these blokes can at least write to their wives and girlfriends.'

'Can't you?'

'I'm afraid not, sir. She's at a high-security wireless station. I wouldn't dream of addressing a letter there, and I don't know her home address.'

'I see.' The captain drew thoughtfully on his pipe and asked, 'Is she an officer?'

'No, sir, she's a PO.'

'Do you know her official number?'

'I'm afraid not, sir.'

The SBO thought again. 'The words "needle" and "haystack" spring frustratingly to mind, but there is one thing you could try.'

'Really, sir?' Suddenly, Cliff sensed a glimmer of light.

A Chance Sighting

'You could write to her care of the Admiralty. Some kind-hearted writer there might take the trouble to locate her. It's certainly worth a try.'

'It is.' Cliff was suddenly excited. 'Thank you, sir. I'll get on to that as soon as I can lay my hands on some writing paper.'

'You'll have to use the official *Kriegsgefangener* letter form, Stephens, now that you're officially a "Kriegie", and your first job must be to send the regulation postcard to your next-of-kin.'

11

About four weeks later, Commander Watkinson had something to celebrate. He shared the news with the officers currently in *HMS Kestrel's* wardroom.

'Gentlemen,' he announced, 'I've just heard officially that Stephens, Rhodes and Woodbridge have been taken prisoner.'

There was a loud cheer, and several officers headed for the bar so that the company could drink the health of the unexpected survivors. The news was particularly welcome as Cliff and Marcus had been popular with their brother officers. One of them asked him, 'Are you going to join us in a drink, sir?'

'Thank you. No, I have to do something important that can't wait.' He left them to celebrate. He could have used the telephone in the wardroom, but it was far too noisy in there. Instead, he returned to his office, referred to a note he'd made a month previously, and asked for an outside line.

When the operator answered, he asked, 'Will you get me *HMS Flowerdown*, please?'

'*HMS Flowerdown*. Connecting you now, sir.'

A switchboard operator, presumably a Wren, answered promptly.

'*HMS Flowerdown*.'

'Good morning. Commander Watkinson at *HMS Kestrel* here. I'd like to speak to Second Officer Denham.'

'I'm afraid Second Officer Denham is no longer here, sir. She was posted two weeks ago.'

'I see. In that case, can you put me through to the officer who's taken on Second Officer Denham's divisional duties?'

A Chance Sighting

'That'll be Second Officer Phillips, sir. I'll try her office.'

He waited for a short time, and then another, somewhat deeper, voice came on the line.

'Second Officer Phillips speaking. Who's calling?'

'Commander Watkinson at *HMS Kestrel*. Good morning. I have a piece of welcome news for a senior rating in your division: PO Wren Laura Pembury.'

'Good morning, sir. What was that name again?'

'PO Wren Laura Pembury, official number nine four two three seven six.'

'I've got that, sir. What would you like me to tell her?'

'Just say that Lieutenant Clifford Stephens – she probably knows him as "Cliff" – has been taken prisoner and he's being held at Marlag Nord "O".' He spelt it for her. 'She'll be delighted, I'm sure. Like the rest of us, she'd probably given him up for dead, but it seems an enemy ship must have picked them up.'

'I see, sir. Are Lieutenant Stephens and PO Wren Pembury related?'

'No, I gather they're romantically involved.'

'Really, sir?' The second officer's disapproval was apparent from her tone. 'Wrens are actively discouraged from forming relationships with officers.'

'I've no doubt they are, Miss Phillips, but boys will be boys, and girls will be girls; especially so in wartime, I'm told. I have both a son and a daughter, so I speak from bewildering experience.'

'Well, it's too late for me to tackle her about it now, but I'll pass on your message.'

'Thank you.'

'You're welcome, sir.'

The letter had been in the 'IN' basket for two days, just long enough to make Wren Mary McIntyre experience a measure of guilt. It was true that the letter was a nuisance, having found its way to an office where people were busy enough with official matters, but the anxious and thrice-underlined entreaty *Please Forward* seemed to appeal to Mary personally. It was addressed to *PO Wren Laura Pembury, c/o Postal Section, The Admiralty, London SW1*, and it was an official prisoner-of-war letter, with German words on it that meant nothing to Mary. All she knew was that this unfortunate Lieutenant C. W. Stephens was probably desperate to contact the girl, although she couldn't help wondering why he didn't have her address or even her official number. She pondered that briefly. Maybe they had met only once or twice; long enough to fall in love but before they'd had time to learn the everyday details about each other. It might have been the beginnings of a whirlwind romance, and now he was a prisoner in something called *Marlag Nord 'O'*. Just the sound of it was chilling.

Mary was a Highlander from Wester Ross, and a romantic soul. It seemed wrong to her that two people were separated, first by enemy action, and then for want of vital information. She knew there was work waiting to be done but it would have to wait a while longer. She began searching the lists for PO Wren Laura Pembury.

She tried the PO Wren list and found the name almost immediately, but it had been struck off, and she had no idea why. After some thought, she wondered if maybe Laura Pembury had been promoted. It happened frequently. She opened the list of Chief Petty Officer Wrens and ran her eye down the pages, but there was no CPO Wren Pembury. Mary was so puzzled that she never heard the approach of PO Wren Driver. The first she heard was the voice behind her.

'Wren McIntyre, what are you doing with those lists?'

There was no point in lying or prevaricating. 'I was trying to trace this person, PO.' She held up the letter to show her.

PO Wren Driver examined it and snorted. 'You can leave this with me, Wren McIntyre, and get on with what you're supposed to be doing.'

'But, PO, I was only trying to help these people. I felt sorry for them.'

'Nonsense. If some foolish girl's got herself involved with an officer, it's her look out, and he's no better than he should be.' After a final glance at the address, she tore the letter in half and dropped it in the basket marked *Non-Classified Waste*, before leaving the office.

Mary looked at the torn letter form in the basket with dismay. It

A Chance Sighting

was an awful shame and all because PO Wren Driver disapproved of Wrens and officers having relationships. On reflection, Mary decided there was little chance of PO Wren Driver having any kind of relationship. Maybe that was the problem and, in any case, she didn't deserve one. If it came to that, Mary couldn't imagine any man wanting to be lumbered with her.

Second Officer Phillips had only been at HMS Flowerdown less than a fortnight, and she didn't yet know all the Wrens in her division. Because of this, she had to rely on CPO Wren Hartley. She spoke to her after lunch.

'Chief,' she said, 'tell me about this girl who was adrift at the weekend.'

'Wren Roberts, ma'am? She's usually very reliable. She missed a train connection because of disruption on the London line. I don't think any disciplinary action is necessary.'

'I suppose not.'

'Will that be all, ma'am?'

'I think so. Oh, there is one other matter. What do you know about PO Wren Pembury?'

'She was an excellent telegraphist, ma'am, very good at her job, but she left *Flowerdown* a couple of months ago. Is there a problem concerning her, ma'am?'

'Not really. I received a message for her this morning, concerning an officer she'd been seeing.'

'Oh, that would be the pilot from Worthy Down.'

'I see. Well, it seems he's been taken prisoner.'

'Oh, that's good news. She was convinced he'd been killed.'

Miss Phillips gave her a stern look. 'If I'd been her divisional officer at the time, Chief, I'd have given her a piece of my mind.'

'Quite so, ma'am. Still, she hasn't exactly got away with it scot-free. The poor girl was suffering torment when she left us.'

'Really? And where was her draft?'

'To Greenwich, ma'am, for officer training.'

'Good grief. What will they take next?'

'I'd back her against most candidates, ma'am, and I must say, I wish her well.'

'Very well.' Miss Phillips was still unimpressed. 'Thank you, Chief.'

'Not at all, ma'am. Good day.'

As Chief Wren Hartley left the office, Second Officer Phillips screwed up the note she'd received about Wren Roberts. Life was difficult enough without Wrens missing trains. She would telephone RN College Greenwich with the message for PO Wren Pembury in the morning. Meanwhile, matters of greater importance awaited her attention.

It was 0310. Second Officer Phillips had just returned from a call of nature and was settling beneath the bedclothes when the noise began that she knew would keep her awake for at least the next hour. It was the relentless drone of the bombers returning from their raids on Germany. Irritably, she held the pillow to her ears in an attempt to muffle the sound of their engines.

She had drifted into a state of half-sleep when her senses were reawoken by a much louder roar from an aircraft that must be flying especially low. The din was increasing, too, so the aircraft was evidently approaching.

She slipped out of bed and pulled the blackout board away from the window to peer outside. It was very dark; very few stars were visible between the clouds and the new moon was similarly obscured. She was about to replace the blackout, when a huge shape, darker than the night that surrounded it, loomed overhead, close enough to make her flinch.

There was a deafening crash followed by several explosions in quick succession that lit up the landscape and sky momentarily as if it were daylight. Then the fire was partially obscured by thick smoke. Realising that the crash had occurred in the region of the Wrens' quarters, she pushed back the blackout and dressed hurriedly.

She had just reached the door when she heard the pipe.

A Chance Sighting

'D' you hear there? D' you hear there? Fire in the Wrens' quarters! Fire, fire, fire! Fire-fighting and Sick Bay parties to the Wren's quarters at the rush!'

There were voices and the sound of footsteps coming seemingly from
all directions and Second Officer Phillips reached the path that led to the Wrens' quarters in time to see sick berth attendants leading a party of Wrens in night attire away from their quarters. A chief petty officer barred the approach to the accommodation block.

'Just you leave it to us, m' dear' he told her. 'The fire's under control.' A fire engine of the National Fire Service had arrived, but the fire, as the chief petty officer had said, was clearly under control. In the neighbouring field, the almost burnt-out aircraft lay smoking beneath its own deluge of water.

'Is anyone hurt?'

'There's a few been affected by the smoke,' he said. 'Horrible stuff, but we got them out pretty much in time.'

The smoke was awful, and so was the reek of charred and wet timber.

'Is everyone accounted for?'

'All alive and kicking,' he reassured her.

'Thank goodness for that.' The fire appeared to be out, and the men with hoses were damping down. Curiosity made her ask, 'How did it happen, Chief?'

'It was a bomber, most likely returning from a raid, and badly damaged, we think. We have to be thankful that the pilot managed to avoid *Flowerdown* and put it down where he did. It was the blast that set fire to the Wrens' huts.'

It was a sickening thought, but she had to ask, 'Has anyone seen the pilot and crew?'

'No, but they're beyond help now.' In a kinder tone, he said, 'Listen, m' dear, why don't you go to the Junior Ratings' Canteen? Your girls will very likely need calming down or maybe bracing up. You can never be sure unless you go and see them.'

It was good advice, and she felt guilty that she'd needed the prompt. 'You're quite right, and when I've done that, I'll go to the Sick Bay. Thank you, Chief. Good night.'

'Good night, m'dear.'

She followed the path to the canteen, partly thankful for men of resource and quiet professionalism, such as the CPO, but in some way resentful of their attitude. She feared it would be a long time before Wren officers were accorded the respect and deference that naval officers had enjoyed for centuries.

As she approached the canteen, she heard the hectic chorus from within. The voices sounded strangely excited and restrained, as if they were unsure just how to behave in the circumstances.

She opened the door and looked around the room at the multitude of girls in pyjamas and greatcoats. They were all drinking something, probably cocoa, and the NAAFI manager had evidently been dug out of bed to dispense buns.

A PO Wren spotted her at the door and called the gathering to attention, but Miss Phillips waved them down.

'No, as you were.' Her first inclination had been to call them to order, to remind them that they were not a disorderly mob, but now it was different. They'd been through a terrifying experience, and a reprimand wasn't what they needed.

'Just a quick word,' she said, 'and then I have to go up to the Sick Bay to find out about the casualties.' She looked around her again, taking in their dutiful expressions. They were probably expecting a lecture about putting the incident behind them, perhaps, and remembering their duty. She couldn't blame them for that. Events had taken her rather by surprise too.

'I just want to say that I saw you leaving your quarters and I felt proud. I'm still proud of you, that you behaved in such a calm, disciplined way. Well done, everyone. Now, carry on and relax. Good night, all of you.'

'Good night, ma'am.' It was a genuine, wholehearted response, and she doubted that she deserved it, but it was no less welcome.

It was little wonder, after the events of that early morning, that the matter of PO Wren Pembury slipped her mind.

12

May 1944

Newly commissioned and self-conscious in her third officer's uniform with the single blue ring on each cuff, Laura reported to Wellsted Priory in Surrey. She learned that her new place of work was part of the Combined Services Detailed Interrogation Centre, a place where German prisoners-of-war were processed before being sent to their respective camps. She learned that, as well as formal interrogation, the centre used bugging devices and 'stool pigeons', a term that was new to her but one, she was assured, that originated in 19th century America, where it described a type of decoy bird used in shooting. The other kind, those employed at Wellsted, were German speakers, who mingled with prisoners and encouraged them to talk. Lieutenant Armstrong RNVR, her senior officer, described to her the process and her duties.

'You'll be required to integrate intelligence gathered from various sources,' he told her, describing each of them. 'From those sources, you'll prepare reports for our customers.'

' "Customers", sir?' It seemed an odd title to use.

'Yes, the various branches of the service that depend on us for the intelligence that keeps them one jump ahead of the enemy.'

'What kind of information are we looking for, sir?'

'Anything at all. We want to know about technical developments, tactics, how well or badly the war at sea appears to be going for them; we want their opinions on everything, the state of morale in the *Kriegsmarine* and at home, and whether or not they are expecting an allied invasion. Also, when and where they believe it will happen.'

'I expect a great many people here would like to know that, sir.'

'I imagine they would. Hopefully, neither they nor the enemy will know anything about it until it happens.'

He left her to read copies of existing reports and their contents soon fascinated and intrigued her.

As she came to know her new male colleagues, she realised that they were all either RNR or RNVR. It was a little world untouched by the Royal Navy.

Lieutenant Armstrong explained that they were all 'Special Service', which meant that, whatever their route to naval service, they possessed special skills essential to intelligence gathering, that were not readily found in the professional service.

With officers from such diverse backgrounds, she found the wardroom a convivial place, and the adoption of a new and attractive Wren officer hadn't passed the notice of its younger occupants. Laura, however, was indifferent to their approaches. Cliff had left a void that was so far impossible to fill. She remembered once calling him a survivor, but that had been just playful nonsense. She was convinced he was dead.

Cliff's first inclination was to escape, and he put his case to the escape committee, who advised him to formulate a plan. His hopes and everyone else's were dashed, however, when news came late in March, that a mass breakout from *Stalag Luft* III had culminated in the execution of a large number of British prisoners. On Hitler's orders, future offenders would be dealt with similarly. Senior British Officers across Nazi-occupied Europe were therefore obliged to discourage further attempts.

Cliff could only wait and hope to hear from Laura, although more than two months had passed since his appeal to the Admiralty. Fellow kriegies told him that letters could take as long as that and sometimes even longer, but he fretted nonetheless. He'd already received letters from his parents and his brother and, welcome though they were, it was Laura's he waited for. He remembered his own letter in minute detail, so eager he'd been to tell her of his

A Chance Sighting

feelings. He still tried to imagine her opening the letter, happy and relieved to know he was alive. For the time being, imagination was all he had.

There were diversions, however. The camp held cricket, football and hockey matches as well as supporting an orchestra and a theatre. The kriegie population included some professional actors as well as keen amateurs. Marcus gravitated naturally towards sport, whilst Cliff was drawn to the instructional classes, and it was at one of these that he met Reginald Sims, a ditched observer and sometime lecturer in psychology at London University. He was slightly built, with prematurely-thinning hair and an engaging manner. He was impressed by Cliff's enthusiasm for his subject.

He asked, 'What drew you to my class in the first place?'

'Shakespeare.'

'What?'

'I was at Leeds University for a year before I joined up, studying English, and I became fascinated by Shakespeare's characterisation. He had an uncanny grasp of human nature.'

'I suppose he had. I must confess you're the first person who's offered that to me as a reason for becoming interested in psychology.'

'I'm more than interested. I intend to change courses after the war.'

'Well, good for you. What's your name?'

'Cliff.' He offered his hand.

'Call me "Reg".' They shook hands. 'Listen, old son, if you'd like to make a start while you're here, I'm more than happy to guide your footsteps. We can get the books we need through the Red Cross and, depending on how much time and effort you put in, you might easily get a year or so knocked off the degree course.'

'Really?'

'Absolutely. Kriegies are taking courses in all manner of subjects nowadays. This place is like a university in itself.'

It was good news to Cliff and it went some way towards compensating for the loss of his freedom, although he knew things might have been worse. In conversation with one of the chaplains, he'd learned that officer prisoners were generally well treated, whereas junior ratings and other ranks were required to work for their captors, sometimes in appalling conditions and for long hours. The chaplain had spent some time at Stalag VIIIB in Silesia and seen the results first hand. Cliff thought immediately of Woody and wondered how he was faring.

The Centre had compiled an extensive dictionary of German technical terms, largely to do with U-boats, and Laura had to refer to it repeatedly, although she'd memorised much of the vocabulary. Most of the reports were about weapons, engines and performance, all of which were vitally important to the allies, but it was the personal, human revelations that interested her most.

One man had said in conversation, 'There are towns and villages here that have been untouched by war. Our bombing seems to have been futile, and when I think of what those murderous bastards are doing to our cities, I could only wish them all the torments of hell.'

Another asked, 'What does the *Führer* know about our fate? He knows nothing about being depth-charged and rammed by destroyers, U-boat crews drowning and being blown to pieces. He is probably having a glorious time, hosting parties at *Berchtesgarten* while we suffer. I hope the allies win this damned war, and then they can hang Hitler for all I care.'

Laura had little sympathy for the Nazis; they'd killed the kindest and gentlest man she'd ever known, and she resented that passionately, so it was odd that one scrap of pitiful dialogue aroused in her an element of concern.

'I don't know how my wife will cope,' a prisoner had said. 'It's bad enough when I'm away at sea, but this is worse by far. She is partially crippled, you know, after she was hit by a car. The driver was drunk and they dealt with him very severely, but that didn't help my wife. She can hardly walk, but she has to work in the factory, making uniforms for the *Wehrmacht*. She shouldn't have to do that. They just don't care about ordinary people.'

Laura was collating similar conversations when she received a visit from one of the junior officers, a sub-lieutenant called George

A Chance Sighting

Dickinson. She'd met him in the wardroom, and he seemed entertaining enough, but she was nevertheless on her guard.

'Good morning, Laura,' he said, rather like someone bringing good news.

'Good morning, George.'

'Are you getting the hang of these things now?' He indicated the transcripts on her desk.

'Oh, I think so. There's nothing difficult about it.'

'Well, if you're not sure about anything, say the word and I'll be over.'

Laura wondered if he had any work of his own. He seemed remarkably at a loose end. 'I think I'll be all right,' she said.

George took the empty seat by her desk and said, 'I was wondering if we might meet up one evening and maybe go for a drink. I could give you a few helpful tips.'

She looked at him in mock surprise. 'I hope you don't talk about work when you're ashore,' she said.

'No, of course not. We could still go for a drink, though.'

'Thank you for asking me, but no, I'd rather not.'

'Oh dear, I've put my foot in it, haven't I? I imagine you're already seeing someone.'

'You could say that.'

'Oh well, I'd best be off, then.'

'Yes.' She picked up another transcript and studied it, saying, 'The job won't do itself.'

All she wanted to do was work, because there was little else left in her life. Her mother had advised her to draw the curtains on the episode with Cliff and to get on with her life, but it was one pair of curtains that refused to be drawn.

13

Red Cross parcels were the Kriegies' greatest blessing, providing a much-needed supplement to the camp diet as well as reminding its inmates that they had not been forgotten.

Typically, a parcel contained a tin of powdered milk, sometimes a tin of condensed milk, a tin of butter, cocoa powder, tea, tinned meat, fish and vegetables, a bar of chocolate and fifty cigarettes or the equivalent in pipe tobacco. To ensure fairness, the Senior British Officer at Marlag 'O' insisted that the contents were pooled, so that each officer received an equal share. Otherwise, the trading of cigarettes was commonplace among smokers and non-smokers alike; such was their value as currency. It was a lesson that Cliff was grateful to learn.

He had been awake for most of the night with a raging toothache and, as soon as roll-call was over, he made a request to see a dentist. He was told that there was no British dentist, but that he might be treated by the German *Zahnartzt*. For some undisclosed reason, the suggestion caused the guards unbridled amusement, but Cliff was beyond caring. All he wanted was to be relieved of the agony in his upper jaw.

After a great deal of form filling and waiting, he was taken eventually to the German sick bay and left in the company of a single guard to await the dentist's services.

An hour passed by before the door opened and an orderly ushered him into a spotless surgery, where a dentist of mature years sat writing in a large book. After blotting his entry, he closed the book and gave Cliff his full attention.

'Good morning, Lieutenant.'

A Chance Sighting

'Good morning, *Herr Doktor*.' Cliff was being as polite as he could be, considering the dentist's badges of rank were concealed inside a white coat.

'How may I help you?'

'I have a severe toothache, *Herr Doktor*.' He pointed to the rear of his right upper jaw.'

'Open your mouth and let me see.' The dentist examined the area and inserted a probe, causing Cliff to jerk backward as the pain shot through his head. 'Ah, I see that the tooth is badly decayed. I shall have to remove it.'

It was welcome news; at least, that was what Cliff thought until he saw the dentist pick up a pair of forceps.

'Aren't you going to give me anaesthetic?'

'Regretfully, no, Lieutenant. Because of bombing by the Royal Air Force, there is a severe shortage of anaesthetics, which must now be reserved for *Kriegsmarine* personnel.'

'I'm Fleet Air Arm, *Herr Doktor*,' he protested, 'not RAF. I've never bombed an anaesthetics factory in my life; in fact, I've never bombed anything.'

'But the principle is the same, Lieutenant. I am sure you understand.'

Cliff understood well enough, and he braced himself as the dentist leaned forward, open-mouthed in concentration, to make the extraction. For Cliff, it was a moment of inspiration, because, scenting tobacco smoke on the dentist's breath, he said hurriedly, '*Herr Doktor*, I have twenty cigarettes in my pocket.' He waited for a reaction.

'English cigarettes?'

'John Player's,' confirmed Cliff.

'And you have them on your person?'

'In my pocket, as I told you.' In spite of his pain, he was enjoying the dentist's dilemma. 'For a whiff of gas,' he prompted, 'they could be yours.'

The dentist looked around the room, ensuring that the orderly was nowhere about, before saying, 'There must be no mention of this to anyone, Lieutenant.'

'None whatsoever, *Herr Doktor*.' He took the cigarettes from his pocket and handed them over.

'Thank you, Lieutenant.' The dentist placed a mask over Cliff's nose and mouth and opened a valve.

Later that day, sore but relieved, Cliff decided to stop smoking, reasoning that he would die of shame if he thought his breath were even remotely as unpleasant as the dentist's. In any case, cigarettes were infinitely more useful as currency.

14

Lieutenant Armstrong caught up with Laura as she made her way back to her office after lunch. He seemed eager to speak to her.

'Laura,' he said, 'have you anything lined up for this evening?'

'Well, I... not really, sir.' Only recently, she'd had to disappoint two sub-lieutenants but she hadn't been expecting an approach from her superior. It was very awkward.

'This is strictly business,' he assured her, following her into her office. 'The thing is, we are entertaining two of our German officers, and I thought a little feminine reinforcement might oil the wheels a little.'

'Entertaining, sir? I don't understand.'

'Sit down and I'll explain.' He waited for her to be seated before taking the chair George had occupied only a week or so earlier. 'Every so often, we take a prisoner or maybe two out to dinner,' he told her. 'We ply them with good food and drink – well, as good as we can find in these straitened times – and the conversation flows. There'll be two chaps present; that's Lieutenant Duncan and I, and we thought you might come and add to the sparkle of the evening, so to speak.'

'Where exactly do I come in, sir?'

'Can you drive?'

'Yes, sir.'

'Good, then you can drive us tonight. You'll also be one of the party. It's surprising how indiscreet a U-boat commander can be when there's an attractive young woman at the table.'

'Ah.' She was beginning to understand.

'You'll enjoy it. We used Simpson's in the Strand until we were caught out.'

'What happened, sir?'

'Well, when I say "we", I'm talking about a party from Latimer House, but we're all part of CSDIC. Anyway, there they were, putting away the oysters and having a high old time, when who should walk into Simpson's but the Old Man himself.'

'Not...?'

'Complete with cigar and bulldog expression.'

'And he caught them entertaining a German prisoner?'

'Two of them, actually. He was furious that they were treating the enemy to the good life, and basically ordered the practice to cease.'

It was sounding more ridiculous all the time. 'So, where are we going this evening, sir?'

'The Ritz. That's the one we use nowadays.'

Laura could scarcely believe it. She'd never imagined herself dining at the Ritz. She heard herself ask, 'Is it safe, sir?'

'Safe as houses. Churchill thinks it's frequented by theatricals and homosexuals.'

'Is it?'

'Bless your heart, no. They prefer the West End clubs. No, the Ritz attracts a more genteel class of diner.'

It was beginning to sound less ridiculous and more like fun. One question remained. 'What do you want me to wear, sir? I have some civilian clothes with me.'

'Perish the thought. No, wear your number five uniform. The Germans love that.'

'If you say so, sir.'

'I do, and don't look surprised when you see that Lieutenant Duncan and I have received unexpected promotion.'

She blinked. 'You've lost me again, sir.'

'The officers we're entertaining hold the rank of *Korvettenkapitän*. That's the equivalent of lieutenant-commander, so Duncan and I will be wearing an extra half ring.' He added by way of explanation, 'We have lots of spare uniforms. It helps with interrogation if we can match the prisoner in rank.' He looked about to leave, and then

A Chance Sighting

he remembered something else. 'By the way,' he said, 'as far as this evening is concerned, you're on the paymaster's staff and you don't understand a word of German.'

It was sounding stranger every minute but she nodded her acceptance. 'Roger, sir.'

'That's not a term I've heard them use in the pay office, Laura.'

'No, sir. I'll remember not to use it.'

CSDIC had been described to Laura as an 'irregular establishment', and it had so far lived up to that description.

One of the prisoners was quite good-looking in a dark, heavy-browed way. His name was Klostermann, and he merely nodded when he was introduced to Laura. The other, whose name was Stark, was the physical opposite of his companion. His hair and complexion were fair and his features were more finely drawn. Laura imagined him playing the violin and living with a maiden aunt.

The two Germans got into the back of the Wolsley with Lieutenant Duncan, a pleasant Highland Scot with an easy manner. Lieutenant Armstrong took the front passenger seat. He asked, 'Do you know the way, Laura, or do you want me to navigate?'

'I need all the help I can get, sir.'

'Consider it yours.' It all felt very strange. It was the first time Laura had worn her best doeskin uniform and she felt quite self-conscious. The whole thing seemed bizarre: the two prisoners in the back, and the British officers wearing the insignia of an assumed rank, but she played her part as well as she could, taking directions from Lieutenant Armstrong and joining in the general conversation.

The road to London was almost devoid of traffic, a fact that Stark was quick to notice.

'The road is ours, I believe, gentlemen. There must be an acute shortage of fuel in England.'

'There's no shortage,' Duncan assured him. 'It's the end of the day and people have gone home.'

'But your oil comes from America. Surely your ships are being sunk all the time.'

'Not nowadays. There was a problem at one time but things are much easier now.'

Lieutenant Armstrong turned in his seat to say, 'There aren't as many U-boats about as there were at one time, you see. Things have become easier for us.'

Laura could see what was happening. The idea was clearly to convince the prisoners that things were nothing like as bad in Britain as they'd been led to believe, and that the U-boat menace was no longer the threat it had been.

The conversation went on, with the Germans eager to know more about life in Britain, and the British officers playing down wartime hardships as if they had ceased to exist.

Presently, it was time for Lieutenant Armstrong to guide Laura into London's West End. As he did so, *Korvettenkapitän* Stark asked Armstrong, 'How are we to address the *Fräulein*, *Herr* Lieutenant-Commander?'

'Strictly speaking, she is Third Officer Pembury, but I'm sure she won't mind your addressing her by her Christian name, which is "Laura".'

'Thank you, *Herr* Lieutenant-Commander.' The German tried out Laura's name several times, but failed to enunciate it correctly. His compatriot also tried it with equal lack of success. The 'r' was proving to be a problem.

'Perhaps you should settle for "*Fräulein*",' suggested Armstrong. 'What do you say, Laura?'

'I'm happy to be called "*Fräu*..." what you said, sir.'

'Good girl. Now, turn left at the next junction.' He directed her into Piccadilly and the Ritz. 'Just park at the roadside, Laura.'

'Aye-aye, sir.' She brought the car to a halt outside the entrance, and everyone disembarked. A member of the hotel staff appeared as if from nowhere and took the keys from Laura.

'Allow me to park the car for you, madam,' he said, noticing from her badge of rank that she was no mere driver.

'Thank you.'

A Chance Sighting

'They're very good here,' commented Duncan. 'They always make us feel at home.'

They entered by the revolving doors, and Armstrong gave his name. Their host then relieved them of their coats and showed them to a cocktail lounge. Throughout the process, Armstrong and Duncan behaved as if they frequented the Ritz every night, the Germans looked a little less confident, and Laura kept her eye on Armstrong for prompts and signals. When he ordered cocktails, she asked for tomato juice, as she had to keep a clear head.

Armstrong asked, 'Won't you have something in it?'

'Just Worcestershire sauce, please, sir.'

'Of course.'

The Germans followed their captors' lead and asked for pink gin. Laura wondered how they would fare during the evening, drinking alcohol after a long period of abstention. Maybe that was part of Lt Armstrong's plan, that a generous supply of alcohol would loosen their tongues. Otherwise, she decided, any harmful effects were their problem. There was quite a difference between the Ritz and the Cavendish, but the music and the ambience took her back wretchedly to her last date with Cliff and, in her misery, she could find no sympathy for the two guests.

She took part in the conversation, remembering not to register surprise at sirloin steak being on the menu, and being careful to appear unfamiliar with the German words and phrases that were used. Klostermann's English was limited, so Stark and the two naval officers had to translate for him frequently.

Presently, the head waiter took them through to their table, barely appearing to notice the German uniforms.

After a while, Lieutenant Duncan leaned forward to speak to her. 'Laura,' he asked, 'may I have the pleasure of this dance?'

'Of course, sir.'

'As we're out of school, you can call me Alec.' He sounded rather like a schoolmaster, which was just what he'd been before the war.

'Likewise,' added Lieutenant Armstrong, 'my name is Brian.'

The two Germans exchanged a look of transparent disapproval.

The band was playing 'That Old Black Magic', but it might have been anything as far as Alec was concerned, because as soon as they reached the dance floor he was whispering orders in Laura's ear.

'At some point,' he said, 'Brian and I will leave you for a short time with our guests. Hopefully, they'll seize the opportunity for a private conversation. They won't include you – you are, after all, a woman of inferior rank – and, believing you to be ignorant of their language, they'll converse in German. I want you simply to listen and report back.'

It sounded very odd to Laura. 'How do you know they'll do that?'

'Experience, my dear.'

Laura absorbed all that, but one important doubt remained. 'Suppose they try to escape?'

'They wouldn't get past the door, and they know it.'

She had to accept his assurance. Meanwhile, the dance went on, and Alec proved to be an excellent dancer. It occurred to her that she might yet learn to enjoy music and dancing without the pangs of nostalgia.

Later in the evening, coffee, cigars and, incredibly, cognac were served. At this point, Alec and Brian asked to be excused. It was to be Laura's moment. She was still feeling awkward in the company of Klostermann and Stark, who had so far spoken only a few words to her. Still, as Alec had told her, the object was to let them talk between themselves.

As if on cue, Stark addressed her. 'Forgive us, *Fräulein*, if we speak in German. *Herr Korvettenkapitän Klostermann* speaks some English, as you know, but his vocabulary is limited.'

'Please don't give it a moment's thought, sir.'

'Thank you, *gnädige Fräulein*.'

Klostermann was eyeing her speculatively.

'Relax,' Stark told him in German. 'She has no knowledge of German.'

'But she has certain qualities,' said Klostermann, 'and I would welcome an hour alone with her. She is most appealing.'

'An hour, Klostermann? You restrict yourself needlessly. Surely you would prefer to spend the night with her.' They both laughed, and Laura half-smiled politely, hoping that, having ascertained that she really didn't understand German, they would change the subject.

A Chance Sighting

'Her breasts are small,' observed Klostermann, 'perhaps a little small for my taste, but her legs are truly impressive.'

'Yes, Klostermann, let us not forget the two roads that converge on paradise.' They both laughed again, and then Stark changed the subject.

'I imagine you have drawn the same conclusion as I, Klostermann, that our English companions have brought us here in order to encourage indiscretion.'

'Yes.' Klostermann smiled knowingly. 'I wonder what interests them particularly.'

Laura opened her shoulder bag and pretended to search methodically for something. It was all she could think of to make herself appear oblivious to their conversation.

'Maybe,' continued Klostermann, 'they are keen to know more about *Schnorchel*. I know some of our fellow prisoners have been interrogated on the subject.'

'Possibly they think it is something wonderful,' said Stark. 'To be honest, I find it frustrating that our submerged speed must be restricted to six knots when charging the batteries.'

'Why is this?'

'It is to avoid breaking the *Schnorchel* tube.'

'Even so,' said Klostermann, 'the main advantage remains: namely that we can remain submerged for longer and so avoid detection.'

'Yes.' Stark laughed. 'But you say "we", Klostermann. I do not believe you and I will ever see *Schnorchel* in action.'

Klostermann gave Laura a quick glance and said, 'I doubt I shall ever see our female companion in action, Stark, but it is pleasant to think of it.'

'My friend, you will drive yourself insane by thinking such thoughts.'

'Maybe, but the uniform, you know, has special appeal.'

'What, all of it, in bed?'

'No, I should insist that she removes her tunic, skirt and shoes. Only the shirt and stockings would remain.'

While they laughed, Laura clenched her teeth, hoping the British officers would return soon.

Klostermann asked, 'What do you think of this place, Stark? It seems to have everything.'

'Yes, I believe the propagandists have misled us into believing that the Englanders are starving.' He looked around the restaurant. 'If that is true, it will be pleasant to starve with them.'

Klostermann held up one hand in warning. 'Enough, my friend. The Englanders are returning.'

Brian and Alec took their places at the table.

'I'm sorry we took so long,' said Brian. 'We were admiring the *décor* in the men's facilities.'

'It is of no consequence,' Stark assured him.

Laura said, 'Please excuse me, gentlemen.'

'Of course.' Brian, Alec and the Germans rose with her, and she walked gratefully to the powder room.

Leaning against the door of her cubicle, she took several deep breaths until the feeling of nausea had subsided and, with it, the immediate memory of Klostermann's loathsome remarks.

When she re-joined the others, she found them discussing cigars, a matter in which she had no interest beyond the relief of knowing that the topic was inoffensive.

Laura opened the office door and said, 'You sent for me, sir.'

'Let's stay with "Brian", shall we? It makes life easier.' He indicated a chair on the opposite side of his desk and said, 'Come in and take a seat, Laura. Coffee?'

'Yes, please.'

'Help yourself. It should still be reasonably warm.' He waited for her to pour a cup of coffee, and then came to the point. 'Thank you for your assistance last evening, Laura. I'm keen to know if you learned anything useful when you were alone with those two.'

'I did learn something, Brian, although I don't know how useful it might be. They imagined you were interested in something called "*Schnorchel*".'

'Indeed we are. As far as we can make out, it's a device for drawing air into a submerged U-boat so they can run the diesel engines to charge the batteries.'

'Apparently, their U-boats can do no more than six knots submerged, for fear of damaging the *Schnorchel* tube. Does that make sense? I'm assuming that their "*Knoten*" are the same measurement as our "knots".'

'It makes perfect sense, Laura, and you're right about *Knoten*. Knots are the same the world over.'

'That's a relief.'

He smiled. 'You did well. What else did you learn?'

'Nothing useful.' She looked down at her cup and it reminded her of something. 'Oh yes, they're quite envious of our lifestyle.' She grimaced. 'If they only knew.'

'The Ritz impresses them every time.' Seeing her empty cup, he motioned towards the tray. 'Have some more coffee and tell me about your general impression.'

'My overall impression, Brian, is that they are the enemy, and the sooner they can be defeated the better the future will be for mankind.' What else could she tell him? That her bust had failed to win *Korvettenkapitän* Klostermann's approval, but her legs had received their joint endorsement? She'd felt insulted and debased by their remarks, and the experience had reinforced her conviction that the enemy had killed a far better man than either of them.

15

The officer who entered the room Cliff shared with eleven others was a lean paymaster-lieutenant with an earnest expression. He looked about him carefully and, having checked that there were no Germans present, said, 'Gentlemen, the information I am about to read to you must not be discussed outside this hut.'

Realising that they were about to hear news received *via* the illicit camp wireless set, the assembled company became silent and gave their attention.

Taking a sheet of paper from his tunic and unfolding it, he began. 'This bulletin was broadcast earlier by the BBC Home Service.' He paused, and there were calls of 'Go on, "Scratch",' and 'Get on with it.'

The harassed paymaster, known to the irreverent majority as 'Scratch' in accordance with his calling, began.

'"Early this morning, allied forces landed on a number of beaches in Normandy. There was some opposition but the enemy were taken largely by surprise, and our forces are now making progress inland."'

Someone whistled softly. Elsewhere, there were muted exclamations.

'This is the one we've been waiting for.'

'Keep your fingers crossed they make it stick this time.'

'Of course they will. Dieppe was a raid, remember, not an invasion.'

'It was a disaster. Hopefully, this won't be.'

'There will be frequent bulletins,' the paymaster assured them, 'and I'll keep you informed. All you need to do is keep "mum".' With

A Chance Sighting

that modest quip, he returned the sensitive document to his inside pocket and left the hut.

Speculation and counter-speculation continued but, cheered though he was by the news, Cliff's thoughts were elsewhere. He'd arranged to spend some time with Reg that morning and he was keen to begin, such was the attraction psychology held for him. So far, his studies had been confined to basic principles, although, with several branches to the subject, principles abounded, presenting Cliff with a huge and fascinating challenge. They also provided a merciful distraction from the nagging question of Laura, at least for some of the time.

Everyone at Wellsted Priory had been ordered to muster in the refectory. It was the largest room in the building and the only one capable of accommodating the entire company, so it was a safe bet that a major development was about to be announced.

In the event, the news about D-Day took everyone by surprise, and there was much celebrating and conjecturing before Brian Armstrong could take Laura on one side and tell her she was due for leave.

'But I had a long leave when I left *Flowerdown*.'

'Nevertheless, you're due for seventy-two hours, and you can catch the ten o'clock train if you look lively.'

Unexpected as it was, a period of leave was welcome news, and Laura was happy to catch the next train into London.

After several delays and an unexpected detour and change at Sevenoaks, she arrived at her family home at a little after three o' clock. Her mother was at home to welcome her.

'Laura,' she said, accepting a kiss but casting a critical glance at her daughter's flowered dress, 'why on earth are you not in uniform?'

'I'm on leave, Mother. Don't you think I get enough of it when I'm at work? It feels good to change into civvies once in a while.'

'When Richard was here last month he wore his uniform. He has to wear it all the time.'

Laura nodded. Her brother was a meteorological officer in the

RAF, a man of serious interests and pursuits, who would never dream of relaxing and changing into casual clothes, even in the privacy of his home. She was very fond of Richard but their personalities could not have been more different. 'Wrens are not subject to the Naval Discipline Act,' she explained. 'We're allowed to wear civvies when we're ashore.'

'Well, it's a shame.'

Laura eyed her mother mischievously. 'You wanted to show me off, didn't you?'

'Don't be silly, Laura.'

'I remember when Richard got his commission, and you and he walked along the Pantiles collecting salutes.'

'He couldn't help it if they saw fit to accord respect to the King's commission, dear.'

'Well, I'm afraid naval ratings are not required to salute Wren officers. In any case, I wouldn't dream of doing that.'

Her mother adopted a resigned look as she said, 'You'll never change, Laura. You've always been argumentative.'

'If I were to go upstairs and change into my uniform, would you be more inclined to welcome me home?'

Resignation gave way to impatience. 'Don't be silly, Laura. You're always welcome.'

'I was beginning to wonder.'

'I'll put the kettle on for tea. It's Gloria's afternoon off.'

'Now, there we can agree. Tea will be lovely.'

'Good.' She glanced briefly at the window and ruled out tea in the garden. 'We'll have it in the drawing room. There are too many black clouds up there for my liking.'

Laura took her usual seat in the drawing room and waited for her mother to reappear with the tea things. It was a shame they had to quarrel, but it had become an established feature of their relationship. She sometimes tried to remember when it had begun, as if that might provide a clue as to its cause, but no pattern ever emerged, except that it had been particularly prevalent during the times Laura had been home from school.

Her mother brought in the tea things and asked, 'Did you hear the news this morning?'

A Chance Sighting

'About D-Day? Yes, they gathered everyone together for the announcement.'

'I should hope so. According to your father, it's the biggest thing to happen since El Alamein.' She poured the tea. 'Yes, it's only a matter of time now before that awful Hitler has to face the music.'

'A matter of time, yes.' She was determined not to provoke another argument, but the thought that had lingered in her mind ever since the announcement was for the thousands who would lose their lives as the Allies fought their way through France and Germany, and for their families, friends and girlfriends, because she knew all too well how that felt.

As if reading her thoughts, her mother said, 'You won't have heard yet. The Aspinalls' son-in-law was killed last week in Italy. It's bad enough for them, of course, but my heart goes out to their daughter and the little boy.'

'Oh, bugger.'

'That's not a nice word, Laura.'

'Maybe not, but it was used to good effect by someone else who was killed recently, and I use it in his memory. It's one tiny part of him that lives on through me, and when I hear of the kind of tragedy you've just described, I want to say, "Bugger", because I've lived through that.'

'I know. It must still be very upsetting for you.'

'Upsetting? It certainly is, although I should be inclined to describe it somewhat less euphemistically.'

Her mother lowered her eyes and said, 'It will take time, Laura, but you'll come through it and you'll find someone else, someone you'll want to marry.'

'I don't think so.'

'But surely you don't want to become an old maid.'

'Mother, if you can find me a man as good as Cliff, I may look him over, always provided he's of the same mind, but don't expect that immediately or for some time to come, because I really can't oblige.' It was an impossible subject to discuss with her mother, so she said, 'Look, I don't want to argue with you, so let's drop the subject. Tell me, instead, about the Aspinalls. I know I've met them. Don't they live in the house down the lane, just before the stables?'

'That's right.' Her mother seemed relieved by the change of subject. 'Their daughter was married about ten years ago. She has a boy of eight.'

'Poor little scrap.'

'Yes, I went to see them when I heard about their son-in-law. It was Mrs White, the draper who told me. Anyway, their daughter and grandson are staying with them for the time being, but it's not an ideal situation.'

'In what sense?'

'I mean it's not ideal for the little boy. He can't go to school while he's here, and I think he'd be better off if he could. Mrs Aspinall has taken over both of their lives, and while I was there, I heard her telling little Michael not to make a fuss for fear of upsetting his mother.'

Laura gaped. 'Not to make a fuss? And he's just lost his dad? That's inhuman.'

'She's a very stubborn woman.'

'That's not all I'd call her.'

'But we mustn't interfere, Laura.'

'Mustn't we? Well, I'll tell you what I'm going to do. I'm going round there tomorrow, and I'm going to take Michael out for the day.'

'Well, I suppose if they're agreeable....'

'They sound most *dis*agreeable to me, but I'll put it to them nicely. Don't worry. What that little boy needs is love and reassurance, and if I have to grit my teeth and be friendly to his grandparents to make it happen, so be it.'

'Of course,' said her mother, recalling an earlier incident, 'you know Michael, don't you?'

'We met once, when he fell off his tricycle. I brought him here because it was nearer than their place.'

'I remember now.' Her mother smiled in recollection. 'He screamed the house down, didn't he?'

'I'm not surprised. That was a nasty cut on his arm and an awful bump on his head. Still, we managed to patch him up, didn't we?'

Still smiling, her mother said, 'And you gave him your chocolate ration.'

It was good that Laura had been able to win her mother's approval on that occasion, at least.

A Chance Sighting

With her father for company, she found dinner enjoyable and free from contention. It was quite a relief, and she went to bed in a more settled frame of mind.

In the morning, she phoned the Aspinalls. Mr Aspinall answered.

'Good morning, Mr Aspinall. This is Laura Pembury. We have met.'

'Yes, I remember you. You helped Michael when he had an accident.'

'Yes, well, it's about Michael that I'm phoning.'

'Ah, in that case it's my wife you need to talk to. I'll go and find her.'

It struck Laura as odd that Mr Aspinall had to defer to his wife, unless she had organised something and needed to be consulted about it. She might never know, but she had little time to think about it before Mrs Aspinall came on the line.

'Yes? Edith Aspinall speaking.'

'Good morning, Mrs Aspinall. This is Laura Pembury. First of all, I should like to offer my sympathy for the loss of your son-in-law.'

'Thank you.'

'Also, I wonder if I might be allowed to take Michael out for the day. I think it would be good for him.' She added quickly, 'We do know each other.'

'Yes, I know you do.' After a few seconds' silence, she spoke again. 'I think that's a good idea.'

'Should I speak to his mother?'

'No, I don't want her disturbed. When will you come for him?'

'Is ten o'clock convenient?'

'Yes. Ten o'clock, then.'

Replacing the receiver, Laura said to her mother, 'She's very sharp, isn't she?'

Her mother nodded.

'I get the impression she wears the trousers.'

'Mr Aspinall's weak,' she agreed. 'Your father knows him through the Rotary Club. You wouldn't think he was a bank manager, would you?'

'I certainly wouldn't.' She had a mental picture of him referring overdraft and loan requests to Mrs Aspinall, and then a practical question occurred to her. 'May I bring Michael back for lunch?'

'Of course. Do you know what little boys like to eat nowadays?'

'I'm not sure, but my guess would be baked beans on toast.'

'I'm sure we can provide that.'

Laura and Michael left his grandparents' house at ten o'clock and walked up the lane hand in hand. Not surprisingly, Michael was quiet and withdrawn, and Laura was struggling to think of something to say that might entice him into conversation. She decided against mentioning the tricycle accident in case it caused him embarrassment, but when they reached the *locus in quo*, he looked up at her and said, 'This where I fell off my bike.'

'That's right.'

'You tied me up.'

'I dressed you and bandaged you,' she corrected him.

'Where are we going?' He sounded apprehensive.

'There's nothing to worry about. We're going to my house first of all, and then we're going to do lots of things.' They stopped for her to unhook the garden gate. 'We have to find out what you like to do.' She led him into the house, where her mother was waiting.

'Hello, Michael,' she said. 'Would you like a glass of cherryade? It's just been made.'

He stared at her uncertainly and then, slowly and wretchedly, his face crumpled.

'Michael,' said Laura, kneeling in front of him, 'come here.' She held him in her arms as he descended into huge, tearing sobs. It was the desperate outpouring of a child who had neither hope nor comfort.

'Go on, Michael,' Laura told him, 'Cry away. No one's going to stop you.'

'Poor little chap,' said her mother helplessly. 'I'll leave you two together.'

After what seemed a long time, Michael's sobs lessened, and he managed to articulate the words, 'Big... boys... don't cry.'

'Oh yes, they do.' She kissed him reassuringly. 'Big girls do too.'

'My dad's gone to... Heaven.'

'I know, Michael.'

'My Gran... says big... boys don't... cry. It only... upsets my... mum.'

'She won't always be upset,' she told him, giving him a handkerchief from her bag.

'Won't she?'

'No, and neither will you. It gets easier, you see. It takes time, but it does get easier.' She'd seen it happen. She knew it was true, even though she still needed reassurance.

'Why did... he die?' He was still holding the handkerchief, so she took it and held it to his nose.

'Have a good blow.'

When he was finished, she explained, 'Your dad was doing something very brave, Michael. He and a lot of other men were fighting so that the rest of us can be free. Because of them, the war will end one day, and we'll all be free to live our lives in peace. You should be very proud of him.'

'I am.' He was still shuddering, but his tears were stilled for the moment.

'Let's go and tidy up, Michael.'

'What do you mean?'

'We need to wash our faces.'

He looked at her curiously. 'Have you... been crying... too?'

'Yes.'

'For my dad?'

'No, for you and for another man who's gone to Heaven.'

'Did... my dad know him?'

'I don't think so.'

'Are you... proud of him?'

'Yes, I'm very proud of him. Come this way.' She took him to the downstairs cloakroom and ran water into the basin. 'There,' she said. 'Wash your face and you'll be as good as new.'

When they had both washed, Michael asked, 'What's your name?'

'Laura.'

'I haven't to call grown-ups by their Christian names.'
'Okay. Will you settle for "*Auntie* Laura"?'
'"Auntie Laura",' He tried out the new name and evidently found it acceptable.

Laura said, 'Come upstairs, Michael.'

'What for?'

'There are some things in my brother's room that I want to show you.'

He followed her upstairs and into Richard's room, which was still the shrine to boyhood that she remembered. There was a rugby ball and a pair of boots, a cricket bat and pads, a bag containing fishing tackle, and a sailing yacht. It was the last item that seized Michael's attention.

'Do you like it?'

'It's beautiful.'

'My brother's a generous chap. He won't mind if we borrow it, as long as we take good care of it and bring it back when we've finished with it.'

'Won't he?'

'Not in the slightest.'

They took the yacht to the boating lake in the park, where it attracted much attention and advice, for which Laura was grateful, having never sailed a model yacht in her life. It was an omission that was lost on Michael, however, who asked, 'Do you know all about boats 'cause you're in the Navy?'

She thought of the reports she'd had to write and the technical terms she'd learned relating to U-boats, and said, 'I know quite a lot.' It was better not to disillusion him altogether.

After lunch at home, she took Michael to the Plaza Cinema for the Saturday matinee. She found that the place had lost none of the features she remembered from childhood: the wine-red upholstery, the lantern-like lamp shades and the combined odours of hair cream and tobacco smoke. It was also a noisy, rowdy experience, but Michael was thrilled and diverted alternately by the cowboy Tom Mix, by Felix the Cat, a short film about a wagon train, and Popeye the Sailor Man.

Afterwards, in the café, he insisted on re-living his favourite

A Chance Sighting

sequence, when the wagon train was attacked by Indians, and just when all seemed lost, the cavalry arrived to save the wagon train and the lives of the settlers. It seemed odd to Laura that a boy who was mourning his soldier father should find such a thing entertaining.

Before she left him at his grandparents' home, he asked if she would write to him, so she wrote: *Michael Croft* in her diary with his address. Then, on a separate page, she wrote her name and address.

Tearing it out, she handed it to him, and he examined it carefully before taking it as if it were something precious, which it very likely was, up to his room, leaving Laura to confront Mrs Aspinall.

'He's a broken-hearted little boy,' she told her, 'and he needs his mother; in fact, there's every likelihood that she needs him as much as he needs her. If you'll only leave them to grieve together, they'll work it out between them. I know what I'm talking about, believe me.' She left the stunned grandmother to reflect on her actions and, hopefully, some unexpected advice.

It had been a successful day marred only when, on leaving the cinema café, Laura had spotted a dark-haired naval officer. She had only seen him from behind, but she'd noticed the two wavy rings on his sleeves and the pilots' wings above them. For one moment, her heart made a leap, and then common sense asserted itself.

16

The guards who ringed the compound were a study in incomprehension. From time to time, one would look inquiringly to another, as if his neighbour might know the key to this mystery that was being played out. A consignment of sporting equipment had arrived from the Joint War Organisation for the benefit of the prisoners, who were now taking advantage of it. Two of them were armed with a wooden club apiece and they wore protective padding on their legs. Each stood either beside, or in front of, three wooden stakes driven into the ground. Two smaller pieces of wood formed a bridge over the stakes. It was evidently a ball game, although the ball was made of hard leather and it was lobbed, rather than thrown, at the man in front of the stakes.

Cliff, who was fielding at cover point, kept looking at the nearest guard and laughed to himself. After the final ball of the over, he joined in the general applause for the bowler, a development that was too much for the guard.

'Why are they applauding this man?'

'Why not?'

'He has done nothing. He has not broken the stakes.'

'They are applauding him because he has bowled a maiden over,' explained Cliff.

'A maiden?'

Clearly, the man didn't understand, but Cliff saw no reason why he should be expected to explain the rules of cricket to a goon. He crossed the compound and took his place for the next over, which was more eventful, the batsmen scoring four runs.

When he crossed the compound again, the same guard

A Chance Sighting

demanded to know why batsmen sometimes made no attempt to hit the ball.

'Because they're not stupid,' Cliff told him. 'They could easily get themselves out by playing at every ball.'

'So they are afraid?'

'No, they just don't want to be bowled out.'

The bowler was about to walk back to his mark, when the umpire showed him three fingers. The guard was immediately inquisitive.

'What is this sign he gives to the baller?'

'*Bowler*,' corrected Cliff. 'He was telling him he has three balls left.'

'Why has he three balls?'

'I don't know. You've just got to blame nature. You have two and he has three.' To press home his point, he said, 'Don't take it personally, but George Bernard Shaw wrote a play about it: *Man and Superman*.' He continued to concentrate on the game.

At the end of the match, a hand descended on Cliff's shoulder.

'You are to report to the *Kommandant*,' he was told.

'Why?'

'Do not ask questions. Come with me.'

'Okay.' He followed the guard, who took him to the block where German officers were accommodated. They stopped outside the office marked *Kommandant*, and the guard knocked on the door, which opened promptly to reveal an *Oberbootsmansmaat*, whom Cliff judged to be roughly the equivalent of a petty officer.

'*Was ist los?*'

The guard explained that Cliff had been summoned by the *Kommandant*, and he stood aside to let them in.

After spelling his name and rank for what seemed the hundredth time, Cliff was pushed into an office, where a *Kapitän zur See* sat behind a large desk.

Eyeing Cliff with obvious displeasure, he demanded, 'Do you know why you are here?'

'I've no idea, *Herr Kommandant*.'

'I shall enlighten you. This afternoon, during your game of cricket, you said something to a guard about a girl, who, I believe, was assaulted by a prisoner. Where is this girl?'

'I know nothing about a girl, *Herr Kommandant*.'

'I advise you to search your memory, Lieutenant Stephens. Women and girls are not allowed in Marlag Nord "O", or in any *Lager* in the *Reich*. How did you bring her in and where is she now?'

Incredulous, Cliff answered him again. 'I haven't seen a woman since I was captured, *Herr Kommandant*. If there's one in the camp, all I can say is that someone has made a damned good job of hiding her.'

The *Kommandant* consulted a sheet of paper. 'The guard in question asked you why you were applauding, and you told him that this man had assaulted a girl. Make no mistake, Lieutenant, this man will be identified and questioned.'

Suddenly it made sense. 'This is not a problem of loose morals, *Herr Kommandant*, but of language. When the guard asked me why we were applauding the bowler, I told him it was because he had bowled a maiden over. To bowl is to project the ball, an over is a series of six deliveries, and a maiden over is one from which no runs have been scored. There was never any reference to a girl, *Mädchen, Fräulein, Frau, Dame* or anything remotely female. Does that answer your question?'

The *Kommandant* closed his eyes. 'So this is a word used in cricket.'

'Correct, *Herr Kommandant*.'

It seemed that Cliff was off the hook. That was until his interrogator consulted his sheet of paper again.

'You also insulted a sailor of the *Reich*.'

'Did I?'

'You told him he had only two *Eier* – I do not know the correct English word – but the *Englander* playing the cricket has three.'

'That was a joke, Herr Kommandant. The bowler had bowled three of the six balls of his over, which meant he had three left.'

'You accused a German guard of being inferior!'

This time, Cliff closed his eyes wearily and said, 'Whereas as everyone knows, The Master Race is superior in every way.'

'You will be silent! Always you joke. You take nothing seriously. It is not surprising you are losing the war.'

Cliff heard a little voice telling him to climb down, to apologise

A Chance Sighting

and to accept his punishment graciously, but he ignored it. The whole interview had been a farce, and his patience was almost spent.

'You may believe that if you wish, *Herr Kommandant*. On the other hand, I could remind you of many stories of equal substance to yours, and all of them collected by *Die Gebruder Grimm*.'

'*Silence!*' He called for the Oberbootsmansmaat, and ordered him to conduct Cliff with his kit to the place known to all kriegies as 'the cooler'. He was sentenced to fourteen days' solitary confinement.

Fifteen minutes later, the cell door was closed, and Cliff sat on his bed. Beside him were his washing and shaving kit and a copy of *A Source Book of Gestalt Psychology*, edited by Willis Davis Ellis. With the limited light that reached the cell, he would spend his time reading about Perceptual Organisation, and he would do it with minimal interruption. Some good had come of the incident after all.

Laura sat down with her letters. There was one addressed in her mother's handwriting, one from her brother and one addressed awkwardly in a childish hand. She opened the envelope and took it out to read.

Dear Auntie Laura,
I am writing to say thank you for a lovly day. It was so nice I will never foget it. The yot was good but my favarit was the pichers and the tea after it. I am with my mum alot more now she dosent cry as much in the night as she use to. You made me feel alot better. I hope you are well. Thank you.
Love from Michael X X X

She folded the letter and put it away. It was something she might return to when she, too, needed to feel better.

17

The arrival of new prisoners was always an exciting time because it meant news from home. Kriegies received regular bulletins, of course, via the camp wireless set, but official announcements always seemed to have an unreal, sanitised quality. By contrast, newcomers to the camp brought stories of everyday life, reminders that the world beyond the wire was still waiting, and news that was meaningful in a familiar way.

The latest arrival was Sub-Lieutenant 'Jimmy' Ellison, a Seafire pilot from Lee-on-Solent, who'd been shot down whilst attacking an armed trawler in the English Channel.

'It was always a dangerous business,' said Cliff sympathetically. 'Those things are armed to the teeth.'

'Don't I know it, sir? Opened up on me with everything they had.' He smiled ruefully. 'Wouldn't mind so much, but I'd only been operational for a month. Poor effort, really.'

Jimmy had to be told about D-Day, having been under interrogation when the announcement was made, but he still brought with him stories of home that ensured his popularity with the others.

Cliff saw little of him for a while, being heavily occupied with his studies, but they came across each other from time to time and had an occasional chat. Jimmy was outgoing and interested in his fellow kriegies.

He asked, 'What were you flying when you were shot down, sir?'

'A Walrus, and don't bother with the "sir",' Cliff told him.

'Right, er, Cliff. With the fleet?'

'Not by then. I served in *HMS Stranraer* until 'forty-two, but then I joined Worthy Down as an air-sea rescue pilot.'

'Oh, bad luck, being shot down yourself. Rotten sort of irony about that.'

'It wasn't the best day of my life,' agreed Cliff, 'and I think my observer and air-gunner are probably of the same mind.'

Jimmy nodded sagely. 'Main thing is we're safe,' he said. It seemed to be one of his characteristics that he seldom spoke in complete sentences.

'"Lend me a heart replete with thankfulness".'

'Say again, old chap?'

'We must count our blessings,' explained Cliff. 'Meanwhile, I must go. I have a meeting with my tutor in five minutes' time.'

It occurred to Cliff that Jimmy's apparent economy with words was likely to prove deceptive, as he was rapidly acquiring a reputation as a chatterbox. Still, tolerance was one of the qualities that made kriegie life bearable, and Cliff was as tolerant as most men.

His meeting with Reg was brief, as Reg had other demands on his time, but it was also encouraging.

'So far,' he said, 'we have looked on a descriptive level at the main branches of psychology. Now, at some time, you'll have to decide which is going to be your main area of study, and that brings up another question.'

'Oh?'

'What is your purpose in studying psychology? I mean, apart from intellectual curiosity.'

Cliff had already given the question some thought. In kriegie life, there was no shortage of time, and thought was a useful means of bridging one event and the next.

'I want to go into clinical psychology,' he said.

'Why? It probably sounds like a silly question, but it's an important one.'

'I want to help some of the poor buggers who are going to return from this war damaged in mind as well as body, having given everything.'

'I see. You do realise, don't you, that you'll never get rich doing that? The Beveridge Report proposes a welfare state with a free health service, as you're probably aware but, even if a general election takes us there, which is doubtful, there's no guarantee that there'll be funding for non-medical treatments, such as psychotherapy.'

It was as if Reg were playing devil's advocate, but Cliff was not to be deterred.

'I realise that, Reg. I said I wanted to help those people, not make a fortune out of them.'

'Quite. Now, is there a branch of psychology that interests you particularly at this stage?'

'Yes, I feel drawn towards *Gestalt* psychology. My fortnight in the Cooler was a great aid to study.'

'I see. What excites you about *Gestalt* theory?'

'The subject's experience in the present, the environmental and social facets of the subject's life, and the adjustments the subject makes because of his overall situation. It all makes sense.'

Reg was nodding, a sign that he was about to take the argument further.

'I asked you about *Gestalt* theory,' he said, 'and you've spoken about *Gestalt* therapy.'

'Precisely because that's the direction in which I want to go.'

'Hm.' Reg nodded sagely. 'You left out an important element.'

'Oh yes, the relationship between the subject and the therapist.'

'Quite right. And you'd better start referring to the "subject" as the "client".' He added, 'Subjects are the focus of theory, but clients are people.'

'I shan't forget that.'

'Good.' The two men shook hands and parted.

It had been a useful conversation for Cliff because it had crystallised his ideas about the future, and he was very concerned about his future.

That afternoon, he had an opportunity to catch up with Marcus. Remarkably, and for a brief spell, the latter was not engaged in any of the several sports he favoured.

'Cliff, old son,' he said in greeting, 'just what have you been up to? I haven't seen you for ages.'

A Chance Sighting

'At least a week,' agreed Cliff. 'I've been studying.'

'Oh yes.' Marcus sounded like someone searching the nooks and recesses of his memory. 'The trick-cycling class. I remember now. It's all to do with sex, they tell me.'

'I don't know who told you that, Marcus, but don't get too excited. If you ever do read anything by Freud, I promise you, it won't be like leafing through *Health and Efficiency*.'

'How disappointing. I think I'll stick to golf. You know we have a putting green now, don't you?'

'That's much more your kind of thing, Marcus.'

'I should say so.' He leaned forward to offer a piece of avuncular advice. 'Study can be bad for your health, you know.'

'Surely not.'

'It's true. I broke my ankle preparing for School Certificate.'

'How on earth did you do that?' Good manners meant he had to ask.

'It was in the library. I was standing on a pile of books, trying to reach a high shelf. Unfortunately, I wobbled, and the pile of books collapsed. You can imagine the rest.'

'It must have been very distressing for you, Marcus.'

'Well, be warned.'

'I'll take great care,' promised Cliff.

Marcus looked at his watch. 'An hour before lunch,' he said. 'I'll see if I can get on to the putting green. It's excellent for honing the skills, you know.' He looked over Cliff's shoulder and said, 'Hello, there's that kid who never stops talking. Ellison, isn't it? He's coming this way.' Marcus made his exit.

Jimmy was as cheerful as usual.

'Hello, Cliff. How did your meeting go?'

'Pretty well. What have you been up to, Jimmy?'

'Auditioning for a part in the play. Seemed to go quite well. Fingers crossed, anyway.'

'Good luck.'

'Thanks, Cliff.' He looked thoughtful for a moment and asked, 'Didn't you tell me you were at Worthy Down?'

'That's right.'

'I was at Lee-on-Solent.'

'I know.'

Jimmy was rather more interested in Worthy Down. 'Is it true,' he asked, 'about Ralph Richardson and Laurence Olivier?'

'Is what true?'

'That they were both at Worthy Down?'

Cliff nodded. 'Quite true.'

'Knew them, did you?'

'Both of them,' he confirmed.

'It must have been smashing.'

'Yes, they both did a lot of that.'

'Wish I'd been there.' Still pursuing the subject, he asked, 'When were you there, Cliff?'

'October 'forty-two to last February.'

'You must have missed the crash.'

'What crash was that?' He was still thinking about Richardson and Olivier.

'Just before Easter. Lancaster returning from a raid crashed on Flowerdown.'

He tried to control the alarm in his voice. '*HMS Flowerdown?*'

'Partly, as it happened. It crashed just outside the perimeter fence but the blast hit the Wrens' quarters, I'm told. They say there was quite a fire.'

'What about... casualties? Were there any casualties?'

'Must have been. Stands to reason, really. We only heard about it, but they say it swept through the Wrens' accommodation in a matter of minutes.' He looked anxiously at Cliff. 'I say,' he said, 'have I said something wrong?'

For the next half-hour, Cliff walked alone around the compound with an awful feeling of desolation like an almost tangible void deep in his stomach. After four months, he'd heard nothing from Laura. He'd imagined the letter going astray. He'd thought about it a thousand times. Maybe Worthy Down had refused to talk to Laura. It was possible as she wasn't a relation. He'd agonised and conjectured for four months, and now... He had no way of knowing for certain that she was dead, but it sounded likely. If he could only bear to think about it.

A Chance Sighting

He had no appetite at lunchtime, unlike Marcus, who ate heartily, pleased with himself after two holes in one.

'Of course, the putting green is too flat and easy,' he said. 'We need something more challenging.' Then, as good manners prevailed, he asked, 'Was our young friend in good form this morning?'

'In good form? Yes, I suppose so. You're right about one thing, Marcus.'

'What's that, old man?'

'He does talk too much.'

18

The transcripts of interviews and other sources that Laura was required to collate before she could write her report had usually passed through several pairs of hands by the time they reached her desk. Some had scribbled notes in the margin; passages were sometimes encircled in pencil with a label that might read *A* or *CC*, meaning that the information must be relayed to the Admiralty and/or RAF Coastal Command. More often than not, however, passages were simply underlined as being important, and the significance and therefore the 'customer' were left to Laura's good sense. She was therefore surprised when she discovered a lengthy Special Report, a transcript of a bugged conversation, that was devoid of pencilled comments. It was so unusual that she began to read the content.

Reference was made to *Der Hof*, the courtyard of the Priory, a place where prisoners believed they could talk without being overheard. It was a dangerous assumption, the courtyard having been thoroughly bugged for some time.

It seemed that the two prisoners had gone there for a secure conversation. One of them, an officer called Kehrer, had lost his U-boat and several of his crew within hours of slipping from Brest and was clearly distressed by the incident. The culprit was a Lockheed Hudson with British markings and it had taken the U-boat very much by surprise. A thirty-seven millimetre M42 was only any good if its crew had time to fire it, it seemed.

His companion Rüdiger was sympathetic. If only they still had the U-flaks. Properly used, they would teach the damned Englanders a lesson.

A Chance Sighting

At this point, Laura made a note of the term 'U-flak' and read on. The conversation was very much about U-flaks and the woeful fact that they had been converted back to normal attack U-boats.

So a U-flak was a type of U-boat, and 'flak' suggested an anti-aircraft facility. She decided to take the transcript to Brian Armstrong, as it had clearly been overlooked.

When she arrived at his office, he was talking with Alec Duncan, so she waited politely until he was free and then knocked on his door.

'Come in. Hello, Laura. What can I do for you?'

'I have a Special Report, Brian, and I think I may have been the first to see it. I think it must have been transcribed by one of the German speakers and then overlooked.'

'Really? Let me see it.'

She handed over the file and its contents. 'It's about U-flaks,' she said. 'It was the first I'd heard of them. I imagine they were U-boats with extra guns?'

'That's right. Last summer, they equipped seven U-boats with one thirty-seven millimetre and four twenty-millimetre cannon as a means of protecting their attack boats against air attack as they went on patrol.'

Laura was intrigued. 'When you say "cannon", they sound like something from Nelson's time.'

'I'm sorry. You weren't to know. These are small-calibre automatic weapons that fire explosive shells.'

'Nasty.'

'Quite, but the U-flak boats weren't a success. They shot down a couple of aircraft, but they still lost too many U-boats, at least from their point of view.'

'So that's why they converted them back to attack boats, I suppose, but it sounds as if U-boats are being more heavily armed anyway.'

'That's right.'

'And they're equipping them with something called *Turmumbau Typ Vier*. That's a type of conning tower, isn't it?'

'Yes, it's designed to accommodate the thirty-seven millimetre and four twenty-millimetre cannon.' He read to the end of the transcript and said, 'Well done, Laura. It seems this was overlooked. Leave it with me and I'll mark it up.'

'I don't understand.'

'What don't you understand?'

'What use is an anti-aircraft gun when the U-boat spends so much of its time submerged?'

'Okay. Take a seat and I'll explain.' He waited until she was settled before going on. 'You see, when there's nothing in sight, they'll surface to charge their batteries and to make progress. They can move faster on the surface than they can submerged, but every now and again, a patrolling aircraft comes on the scene and spoils the party. Now, the U-boat can dive and be at the mercy of depth charges, bearing in mind the aircraft knows exactly where it is, or it can remain on the surface and fight it out. And why not, when it's better armed than the aircraft that's hunting it?'

It sounded pretty awful. She had to ask, 'What's the answer?'

'Rocket projectiles. They can be fired from beyond the U-boat's range, and one rocket can blast a hole in a pressure hull. The RP is a blessing for a Swordfish biplane, even if it has to fire them in a dive so as not to stall.'

'Are they still using biplanes?'

'Swordfish? Yes, they are. So far, the old Stringbag has sunk more shipping that any other aircraft in any theatre of war. It has an unassailable lead and its name will live for evermore, believe me.'

'Good for the Swordfish.' It had set her thinking. 'Do they still use the Supermarine Walrus?'

'Yes, it's still in service, and that's another name that's going to be immortal. What makes you ask about the Walrus?'

'Oh well, it's just that I knew someone who flew one, and he used to sing its praises, rather as you talk about the Swordfish.'

'Which aircraft did you fly, Cliff?' It was at Reg's suggestion that the two were strolling around the perimeter of the compound.

'A Walrus.'

'Air-sea rescue?'

A Chance Sighting

'Yes.'

'Just right for you.'

'You wouldn't have thought so when we were shot down. It was one of the few times a Walrus failed to float.' On reflection, Reg's remark puzzled him, so he asked, 'Why was it right for me, Reg?'

'War is a time that brings out hawks and doves, and you are unmistakably one of life's doves.'

Cliff smiled sadly. 'Someone once told me that air-sea rescue was a humanitarian calling and that it was as important as heroism.'

'Who was that philosopher, Cliff? I'd like to meet him.'

Cliff kicked at a dried rut, creating a shower of earth, and said, 'So would I. She was a girl, by the way, a Wren.'

'Have I opened a wound?'

'I was the one who mentioned her, Reg.'

'So we can either change the subject or talk it through. It's up to you to decide.'

'Why not?' Cliff didn't usually make a practice of unburdening himself to anyone, but Reg wasn't just anyone.

'Take your time.'

Cliff nodded. 'I met her in Winchester and gave her a lift to the wireless station at Flowerdown. She'd missed the last bus. Anyway, I decided immediately that I had to see her again. We met a few times, and the whole thing took off. We were even discussing going on leave together. That was just before we were shot down.'

'What's the situation now?'

Cliff sighed hopelessly. 'How can I describe it? She doesn't know where I am. It all happened so quickly that I never learned her home address. She was at a secret establishment. Chances are the enemy don't know it exists, so I wouldn't dream of writing to her there.'

'Have you tried the Admiralty?'

'Yes, the SBO suggested that when I arrived, and I did write to her care of them, basically throwing myself on their mercy, but I don't even know her official number, so the letter must have come as a trifling nuisance to them.'

'No reply?'

'Correct, and I heard only a few weeks ago from one of the new blokes that an aircraft had come down on the edge of *HMS*

Flowerdown and destroyed the Wrens' quarters.' He looked down at his feet in silence before continuing. 'This bloke only heard about it second-hand, but he reckoned there must have been a lot of casualties. He said the fire spread very quickly.' He added wretchedly, 'Frankly, I prefer not to think about it.'

They walked on in silence, until Cliff spoke again.

'I'm going round in circles, Reg. At first, I reckoned the letter hadn't got through. Then I wondered if it had, but she'd taken up with someone else, although I have to admit that seemed unlikely.'

'And now you're wondering if she was one of the casualties.'

'Yes.'

'What's her name, Cliff?'

Cliff looked at him strangely. 'Laura. Why do you ask?'

'If we're going to talk about her, I need to refer to her by name.'

'Is there anything to be gained by talking about her?' They were now level with Cliff's hut. He was thinking of making an excuse and slipping away.

'Don't you want to find a way of stopping the mental whirligig?'

'How do I go about that?' They had passed the hut.

'Let's just suppose you arrive home, whenever that happens, and find that Laura was one of the casualties. How will you deal with it?'

Cliff considered the question for a few paces before saying, 'At the risk of stating the obvious, death is final, isn't it?'

'Depending on your belief.'

'To all earthly intents and purposes, it is, and I suppose I'd deal with it in the usual way. There'd be a period of mourning, giving way eventually, I hope, to acceptance and recovery.'

They both saluted as the Camp Commandant accompanied by an orderly passed them *en route* for goodness-knew where.

'I must talk to you about the grieving process, but not just yet. Tell me how you would deal with the possibility of her having taken up with someone else.'

Again, Cliff thought about it. 'As I see it,' he said, 'it would be a less-extreme form of bereavement. I imagine I'd deal with it in the same way.'

Reg nodded slowly, giving the impression of neither agreement

A Chance Sighting

nor divergence. Eventually, he asked, 'In the here and now, what's your biggest problem?'

'My only problem is that I don't know what's happened. As I told you, I'm just chasing my tail.'

'You're ruminating.'

'You make me sound like a beast of the field.'

'Exactly. Chewing its cud. You're chewing over the little you know, and then bringing it back to chew over again. Does it help you at all?'

'Of course not.'

'In that case, let's discuss some triggers you can operate when rumination threatens and you want to stop it before it goes any further.

It was a useful conversation, and it led eventually towards alleviating much of Cliff's mental torment

At the same time, he continued with his studies until liberation and, eventually, demobilisation brought him to King's College, London, where he remained until 1949.

Part Two

1

August 1949
Folkestone, Kent.

Reg's new consulting rooms were in Manor Road, off Bouverie Road West. He shared the premises with a solicitor and an accountant, reasoning that they could turn out to be valuable allies, hopefully for the right reasons.

'This will be yours,' he told Cliff, opening an oak-panelled door to reveal a room of modest dimensions. One wall housed several bookshelves; the other stood bare, inviting adornment of some kind, and Cliff had the very thing in mind. In the days before demobilisation, when he was serving at Lee-on-Solent as an instructor on the new amphibian, he had asked a fellow officer, a talented artist, to paint a picture of a Walrus complete with the squadron and individual markings that would identify her as his beloved and lamented Agatha.

'It's perfect, Reg,' he said, visualising the painting on the wall.

'Are you glad you decided to come in with me?' Reg smiled as he asked the question, because he already knew the answer.

'I still can't believe my luck.'

'I invited you because I knew you were the man for the job, Cliff. I've watched you study through captivity and at university with unflagging commitment and when I decided on this venture I had to give you first refusal.'

'Thank you.' With his stoical northern upbringing, Cliff was unaccustomed to lavish compliments and, besides, he wanted to get on with the task of moving his personal belongings into his flat. He had turned down Reg and Jane's offer of their spare room in favour of a furnished flat in Bouverie Road West, not far from the consulting rooms.

'Let's get a pork pie or something,' suggested Reg. 'There's a pub I want to show you. We can eat there.'

'Okay, Reg.' His belongings would have to wait.

On the way out, Reg paused in the doorway to ask, 'Did you notice the brass plate on the way in?'

'No.' Cliff turned guiltily. 'I don't think I did.'

'It's very important.' Reg pointed to a new and shiny plate.

Cliff read:

R. G. Sims, PhD. (Lond.)
Psychotherapist.

C. W. Stephens, MSc. (Lond.)
Psychotherapist.

'Suddenly,' said Cliff, 'I'm feeling much more important than I should.'

As the two men drove off, Cliff remembered something.

'Reg,' he said, 'I need to go up to Scarborough again in a couple of weeks' time.'

'Summoned by the family?'

'In a way, yes. It's for my brother's wedding.'

'It's for you to organise your time, old chap.'

'Thanks.'

'Not at all. Did you get to see the chap you told me about, the air-gunner?'

'Woody, yes. He was much more settled.'

'How long had it been?'

'Three years. I looked him up after I was demobbed. He's a musician, you know.'

'I remember.'

'They put him to work in a stone quarry.'

'The bastards.'

Cliff nodded. 'It buggered up his hands for all time, but at least he's making a living now.'

'Doing what?'

'Teaching. He's a French horn player as well as a pianist.'

'Just as well, as things turned out.'

'It wasn't just his hands. He was emaciated when he came home. His mother said his ribcage was like a set of park railings, and the Nazis reckoned to give them extra rations for heavy work.'

'Like park railings were before they took them as scrap metal.' Reg appeared to reflect on that thought, and said, 'It seems an age ago that they did that.'

'Yes.' Cliff was more concerned with Woody's wellbeing than with wartime reminiscences. 'You know,' he said, 'our stay at Marlag "O" seems insignificant compared with life in the work camps.'

'That's very true,' said Reg, signalling right to turn into a pub car park, 'but life has improved for him, and it's good that you took the trouble to visit him.'

'I had to, Reg. I have a reputation to live up to.'

'Oh?'

'Apparently, I'm a modern-day Fezziwig, and that's quite a compliment.' He shrugged, as if the true reason should have been obvious. 'But, when all's said and done,' he said, 'he was one of the crew.'

'What was wrong with the job you had, Laura? Teaching is a secure profession, and with everyone being demobbed, safe jobs are at a premium.'

'There was nothing wrong with it, mother. I just couldn't settle there. I don't expect you to understand, but I'm not the only one who's finding it hard to adjust to civilian life.'

Her mother stirred the tea and replaced the teapot lid. 'But you've been out of the Wrens three years now. That should be ample time to settle down.'

'For some, maybe.' She accepted a cup of tea, hoping her mother would tire of the subject.

A Chance Sighting

'I can't keep track of you and your jobs. You seemed to be settled at the place in Surrey, and then you had to go to that awful seaside resort in Yorkshire.'

'I was posted, mother. Their Lordships said, "Go" and I went. My work at Wellsted Priory was done, and the wireless station in Scarborough needed an officer with... with my skills.'

'Oh well, I didn't know that.'

'There was no reason why you should, and, by the way, Scarborough is a charming town and so is Strasbourg, where I'm going next.'

Her mother shook her head in helpless acceptance. 'And what are you going to do there, or is it something else you're not at liberty to talk about?'

'No, it's not. I'm going to work for the Council of Europe as an interpreter. There's nothing secret about it.'

'Good. Now I think of it, I've heard Mr Churchill say something about it. I must say, I wish they'd call a general election soon, so that he can come back and sort things out. I'm sure the present government hasn't a clue.'

Laura finished her tea and put her cup down. 'You will have heard him talk about the Council of Europe,' she agreed. 'It was his idea.'

'Oh well, that's all right, then.' She lifted the teapot. 'More tea?'

'Yes, please.'

'Wasn't Scarborough where that unfortunate boy came from?'

'Do you mean Cliff? Yes, he was from Scarborough.' Her mother mentioned him occasionally, as if checking that her daughter really had put the matter behind her. It was true that the passage of time had taken the hurt out of her loss, but 'getting over him', as her mother had described the process, was a different matter, and one that Laura neither welcomed nor wanted to avoid.

The posting to Scarborough had troubled her at the time, coming as it did little more than a year after his death. She remembered going into town when she was off-watch, and finding the bakery owned by his family. At least, the sign above the window read: *J. Stephens & Son, Bakers and Confectioners*. The scent of freshly-baked bread issued from within, reaching the opposite side of the road, where Laura stood, transfixed by the sight of the shop that, with its upper storey, must have been Cliff's home.

After a while, a woman came out of the shop and asked her if she needed help. She had a soft, kindly voice.

'No, thank you,' said Laura, realising that this woman must be Cliff's mother. 'I'm just trying to get my bearings.'

'Haven't you been in Scarborough long, then?'

'No, I've only just arrived.'

'Oh, you'll be at the place with all the wireless masts on the old racecourse. Where are you trying to get to, love?'

Suddenly Laura felt ridiculous. Thinking quickly, she said, 'A haberdasher's, I suppose. I need some buttons and thread.'

'Doesn't the Navy supply those things?'

'No, they're for my civilian clothes.'

'Well, I suppose with the way things are going, you'll be needing them soon enough. Anyway, there's a haberdasher's down the hill, just after the barber's.' She pointed down the road. 'Can you see?'

'Yes, I see it. Thank you.'

'Is there anything else I can help you with?'

'No, thank you. You've been very helpful.'

It was as if she'd found a small part of Cliff and, as she walked away, it had made her quite tearful. Of course, she'd brought her feelings quickly under control. To appear emotional in public, and especially in uniform, was unthinkable.

She remembered wanting to go on talking to Mrs Stephens and maybe Cliff's father and his brother, but what could she say? 'Hello, I'm Laura Pembury and I knew Cliff...' That would have been a thoughtless intrusion. They must still be hurting; it had only been a year, and she knew she was.

The sound of the doorbell was a welcome interruption. A few moments later, Gloria, the maid, appeared in the doorway.

'There's a visitor for Miss Laura, Mrs Pembury.' She stood aside and let Michael into the room.

'Michael!' Laura hugged and kissed him before standing back to look at the transformation. 'You're nearly as tall as me,' she said, leaning forward to stroke back a lock of brown hair. 'Let me look at you. How old are you now?'

'Thirteen,' he told her shyly.

She imagined his shyness was at being kissed. Thirteen was a difficult age. 'Would you like something to drink?'

'We have lemonade,' her mother told him.

'Yes, please.'

'Gloria.' Mrs Pembury summoned the maid. 'Lemonade for Michael, please. Oh, and some more hot water for the tea.'

'Very good, Mrs Pembury.'

'I knew you were here, Auntie Laura,' said Michael. 'My gran saw you drive past her house.'

'Make the most of it, Michael,' Mrs Pembury told him. 'She won't be here long.' She added almost to herself, 'She never stays anywhere for long.'

'Today and tomorrow,' said Laura, conscious of his disappointment, 'and then I have to leave for Strasbourg. Shall we do something tomorrow? That's if I can square it with your mum and your gran. Would you like that? Or would you rather be with your friends?'

'I'd rather do something with you, if that's all right.'

'Okay,' said Laura, 'there's no time like the present. I'll phone your gran. Do you know the number?'

He shook his head. 'Sorry.'

'Don't worry, I'll find it.' She reached for the telephone directory, conscious of her mother's disappointed gaze and knowing what her next complaint would be.

Michael surprised Laura by opting to see The Paleface, starring Bob Hope and Jane Russell. It turned out to be an excellent film, which they both enjoyed.

Afterwards, in the cinema café, Michael said, 'My dad was like Bob Hope.'

'Do you mean he looked like him?'

'No, I mean he was always cracking jokes. He made me laugh, but my mum says he wasn't as funny as all that.'

'Ah well, a sense of humour is an individual thing, you know. We don't all laugh at the same things.' She picked up a menu and handed it to him. Would you like to decide what you're going to have?'

'Mm.' He studied the menu briefly and said, 'It's because of Mr Kendrick.'

'What is?'

'If I say my dad was, say, good at football, she says he wasn't all that good. It's because she wants me to forget my dad and start liking Mr Kendrick.'

'Who's Mr Kendrick?' She thought she already knew.

'He's her friend. They're going to be married.'

She picked up the menu again while she thought. 'Michael,' she said, 'if you're not keen on sandwiches made with the National Loaf, and I can't blame you, you could have it toasted with something on it. They have beans, toasted cheese, mushrooms, sardines, or you could have a boiled egg with toast. That's what I'm going to have.'

'Me too.' Then, remembering his manners, he added, 'Please.'

'Good, and what would you like to drink?'

'Lemonade, please.'

She attracted the attention of a waitress and gave her their order, conscious that this might be the last time she would take Michael for a treat. There came a time in every boy's life when he would be embarrassed to be seen in the company of an aunt, even an honorary one and, by her reckoning, Michael was approaching that age. Before that happened, however, she had a task to perform.

'Do you like Mr Kendrick, Michael?'

'He's okay, but he can't replace my dad.'

'Of course he can't, Michael. People can't be replaced. Your dad will always be the special person you remember.'

'But we'll have to live in Mr Kendrick's house.'

'I can see why that's troubling you.' She wondered for a

moment if she might be out of her depth, but she pressed on. 'It might not be too bad. In any case, it won't last for ever.'

'What do you mean?'

'Well, you're thirteen now—'

'Nearly fourteen.'

'That's even better. Before long, you'll be looking to start a career or maybe do some studying. Have you considered that?'

'I want to be a baker.' It was a confident, unqualified statement, and not at all what Laura had expected.

'Why do you want to be a baker, Michael?'

'Bakers make people happy.'

'Really?' The argument was new to Laura, but she was willing to learn.

'Yes, you don't see happy people in a butcher's shop. They're usually complaining about rationing and the price of meat, but the people you find in a baker's are happy and friendly.'

'In spite of the National Loaf and the usual shortages?' She couldn't resist playing devil's advocate.

'Yes. My granddad says rationing has to end sometime. In any case, it'll be years before I'm out of my indentures, and then I'll be able to bake proper bread – I can't really remember what it tasted like, but I know it was good – and I'll bake cakes and tarts and all kinds of things.'

Laura nodded approvingly. 'That's what I call taking the long-term view.'

'You're laughing at me.' He was blushing.

'No, Michael, I'll never do that. I think you've argued your case most effectively.' To lighten the mood, she said, 'You know, I knew someone years ago who was very much like you. He was a baker's son but, unlike you, he had little interest in baking. His passion was plumbing.'

'Plumbing?'

'Yes, he saw the plumber's function much as you see the baker's.'

'You're joking.'

'No, he told me how, when he was very young, his family called out a plumber to an emergency and, because the plumber made the repair and left everyone feeling happy, he decided to follow the same noble trade.'

'Did he become a plumber?'

'No, he was persuaded to stray from that path and go to university.'

'By his parents?' It was as if the story were all too familiar.

'No, by Shakespeare, Dickens and others. He went on to study English Literature.'

'And what did he do after that?'

'He joined the Navy, went to war and... failed to return.'

'Was he the man you told me about after my dad was killed?'

'Very likely. There have been depressingly few men in my life.'

'What was his name?'

'Cliff.'

'What happened?' He checked himself. 'That's if you don't mind talking about it.'

'No, I don't mind. It's long past the traumatic stage. No, he was a pilot, you see, and he flew over the Channel, looking for ditched airmen. He was probably shot down. At all events, they never found him.'

Michael studied her gravely. 'How old are you, Auntie Laura?'

'Oh, Michael,' she said with raised eyebrows, 'that's a question you should never ask. Some women would be mortified if you asked their age.'

'I'm sorry.'

'You weren't to know. I'm twenty-nine, by the way.'

'As old as that?'

'Yes, don't let me forget I have to call in at the Post Office on the way home to collect my old-age pension.'

'I didn't mean that. It just sort of came out. What I was going to ask was, well, will you ever get married?' He was completely flustered.

'It's always a possibility. Mind you, if you'd asked me that a few years ago, my answer would have been very different, but time works wonders.'

'So you might? It would be a shame if you didn't. I mean, you're pretty and kind and good fun....'

A Chance Sighting

'Oh, Michael, can I count on you for a reference? I think a word from you would clinch it with most men.'

'Well, you know what I mean.'

'Yes, I do, and I appreciate the compliment. I'll tell you what, though. Whoever I marry will struggle to measure up to Cliff.' Looking at him across the table made her think of something. 'You know,' she said, 'you and he had something in common.'

'What was that?'

'He wanted to do things for absolutely the best reasons, and so do you.'

2

'Are you going to hypnotise me?' Her tone suggested she'd been looking forward to it.

'No.'

'Oh, why not?' Cliff's new client was about forty, well-dressed and seemingly a woman of some substance. 'I thought that was what happened.'

'Only in films,' he assured her.

'Well, what are you going to do, Mr Stephens?'

'I'm going to ask you to tell me what the trouble is, and then we'll see how we can work together to alleviate it. First of all, though, I'd like you to call me Cliff.'

'All right.'

'And I should address you by your first name.'

'Oh, why?'

'It's to establish a working relationship between equals.'

'Oh, good heavens. In that case, I suppose you'd better call me Daisy.'

'Very well.'

She looked around the room and asked, 'Where's the couch?'

'There isn't one. I'd like you to sit in the armchair behind you and make yourself comfortable.'

'This isn't what I expected.' Nevertheless, she lowered herself into the armchair.

'Have you seen *The Seventh Veil*?'

'Yes, have you?'

'I thought you might have. Yes, it was the first film I saw after I was demobbed.'

A Chance Sighting

'Was it really? Wasn't Ann Todd wonderful?'

'She was, but, you know, it doesn't work the way it did in the film.'

'Oh.' She was clearly disappointed.

'No, I'm more interested in what's happening now than in the childhood secrets of your unconscious mind.'

'I see.' It was clear that her attention had wandered, and her next observation confirmed it. 'That's a very striking tie you're wearing, Mr... Cliff.'

Cliff looked down, having forgotten for the moment which tie he was wearing. 'Oh yes,' he said, 'it's the Fleet Air Arm tie.'

'Isn't that part of the Air Force?'

'No, it's part of the Navy.' It was time to be firm. 'Daisy, we really should make a start.'

'Oh, all right.'

'Now, you told me on the telephone that you lacked confidence.' There had been some evidence of that, and he was keen to hear more.

During the journey to his brother's wedding in Scarborough, Cliff studied his notes from the session with Daisy. The stretch between London and York was tedious and the process helped pass the time.

He'd noted her question about hypnosis, which was understandable, given her enthusiasm for *The Seventh Veil*, and he wondered how many cinemagoers must have formed similar expectations at around that time. The film had been very popular.

Daisy's frequent distractions he put down to nervousness, because, like many other clients, she was clearly uneasy about that first session.

He'd learned that she had a controlling husband and a critical mother-in-law. Dennis, her husband, was a commercial traveller and a 'stickler' for detail and precision, a dubious quality he ascribed to his having served in Aldershot, in the Pay Corps, for much of the war.

His one indulgence was that he allowed her to work part-time as a hairdresser, on the proviso that there must be no deterioration in the standard of her housework.

He was usually absent during the week and returned home on Friday evenings, when he expected to find her 'dressed up.' He disapproved of women who dressed casually for whatever reason, a prejudice he shared with his mother, who routinely criticised Daisy's appearance, her cooking, her housekeeping and anything else that sprang conveniently to mind. Daisy was clearly an easy target for them both.

Her greatest fear was that in falling short of Dennis's rigid, high standards and those set by his mother she might lose him to a rival. She had no knowledge that such a woman existed but her anxiety was no less real.

Cliff concluded that the case offered ample scope for his services. Daisy was a victim who needed help

He returned the file to his briefcase and considered what lay ahead.

He'd seen his family recently, so he would be spared another rapturous homecoming. The attention would, rightly, be on Ted and Vera, whose wedding it was.

Cliff's mother greeted him in her usual, cheery way.

'I thought you'd arrive soon,' she said. 'I said to your dad, 'Our Cliff'll be here any time now. That lad can smell tea a mile away.' She gave his hair a stroke as she poured his tea. It was a familiar and pleasing habit.

'It's good to be home again, Mum,' he said.

'Let me look at you.' She stood back a step to examine him. 'I still say you need feeding up. Those Germans have a lot to answer for. What do you think, Jim?'

Cliff's father looked up, half-amused by the familiar ritual, and said, 'I think you should leave the lad alone. He looks all right to me.'

'I'm okay, Mum, honestly. If you think I was starved, you

should have seen Woody. A gifted musician could have played a xylophone concerto on his ribcage when he came home.'

'Was he the lad who flew with you? His poor mother must have had a job on her hands feeding him up on post-war rations. I didn't get a chance with you. You weren't here two minutes before you were off to university again. It was as if the war had never happened, except you went to London instead of Leeds.'

'I wanted to stay with Reg Sims, Mum. He taught me a lot when we were POWs, and he was at King's College, London, so that was where I went to study.'

'I gather you're in business now,' said his father. 'How did you manage that?'

'Reg bought a practice in Folkestone and asked me to join him. I shan't be a partner for a long time yet but I'm first in line for it when the time comes.'

'I see.' It was still a mystery for Cliff's parents, because his father asked, 'What is it you do, exactly?'

'Psychotherapy. That's treatment for people who are emotionally troubled.'

'Oh,' said his mother, 'like Ann Todd in *The Seventh Veil*.'

'That kind of thing, I suppose. Just as an example, I'm treating a lady now, who's been made to feel worthless by her husband and mother-in-law. There'll be lots of cases like hers, I imagine, and ones in which people are troubled by other things.' Another, familiar, example came to him. 'You know Mr Edwards who lives next to the greengrocer's don't you?'

'I should,' said his father. 'He was in my platoon until it all got too much for him. They invalided him out with shell shock, poor chap.'

'Poor man.' Cliff's mother sighed. 'And there seems to be no end to his suffering.'

'Well, he's the kind of person I want to help. There must be hundreds of men whose minds have been affected by the war one way or another. They won't all come asking for help, but I'll treat those who do.'

'Well, I never,' said his mother, clearly taken aback. 'We're proud of you, aren't we, Jim?'

'Yes, we are,' agreed his father, adding dryly, 'mind you, we'd probably have been as proud if you'd been a plumber.'

'Oh, Jim.' Mrs Stephens picked up a cushion and threw it at her irreverent husband.

'Well, that's enough about me.' Cliff felt faintly embarrassed. 'This is Ted and Vera's weekend. Where is Ted, by the way?'

'He's minding the shop,' said his father. 'I'll go and relieve him in a minute.'

'You'll never guess what he did last weekend, Cliff.'

'No, but I'm sure you're going to tell me, Mum.'

'He went out to buy a pair of shoes for the wedding. You'd think it would be simple enough now that clothes are off the ration, but just guess what the daft article did.'

'I'll buy it.'

'He came back with brown shoes. Just imagine.'

'I've heard this story a dozen times,' said Mr Stephens, leaving his seat. 'I'll go and relieve young Ted.'

Cliff asked, 'What colour's the suit he's getting married in?'

'Dark blue.'

'I wish I'd known. I'd have brought my spare black shoes and he could have worn them. We take the same size.'

Mrs Stephens shook her head. 'It's all right, Cliff. He went out again and bought a black pair. And him getting married and needing every penny he has.'

'It sounds as if the poor lad can't do right for doing wrong.'

'You always did take his side, Cliff.'

'I just like to be fair.'

'Oh.' It seemed that something had suddenly occurred to her. 'Do you remember Ellison's grocers?'

'I think so. Their little girl used to come with the order for bread, and my dad spoiled her with gingerbread men.'

'Well, she's not such a little girl now. She's in the Wrens.'

'Never.'

'She came home on leave last month after passing out, and she looked ever so smart in her uniform.'

'Good for her.'

'She reminded me of something that happened towards the end

A Chance Sighting

of the war. I saw a Wren, an officer from the wireless station, standing across the road and looking at the shop front as if she was wondering whether or not to come in.'

'Surely, there'd have been no point in coming in unless she was registered with you.'

'I know, Cliff, but she looked lost, so I went out and spoke to her. She seemed very nice. She was looking for somewhere that sold sewing thread.'

'She wouldn't have found that in a bakery.'

'I know, you daft article. Anyway, I gave her directions. It's funny, though.'

'What is?' Cliff had never found his mother's thought processes easy to follow.

'She set me in mind of the girl you met just before you were taken prisoner, and I wondered, just for a minute, if it was her and she'd come looking for you.'

'The girl I knew wasn't an officer; in fact, she was determined to stay on the lower deck. In any case, I'm fairly certain she was killed when an aircraft crashed on *HMS Flowerdown*, where she was stationed.'

Later that evening, Ted suggested going to the pub.

Cliff asked, 'What? No stag night?'

'I can't afford one.'

'Not when you buy shoes two pairs at a time,' his mother reminded him.

'Honestly,' said Ted as they crossed the road to the 'Monk's Head', 'she's shown me no mercy since I bought them bloody shoes.'

'Just remember it's half in fun. A lot of mothers wouldn't be so ready to see a funny side to the story.'

'I suppose you're right.'

Most onlookers would be in no doubt that the two men were brothers. Ted looked younger – which he was – and he was also a little taller than Cliff, but the family resemblance was strong.

They walked into the lounge bar of the Monk's Head,

acknowledging the greetings of three regulars whom Cliff remembered from his last visit.

'What are you drinking?' Ted's hand was already in his pocket.

'No,' Cliff told him, 'I'll get these. Bitter?'

'Please.'

Cliff caught the landlord's eye and was rewarded with a welcoming grin.

'Na' then, young Cliff. Have they sent you back up north 'cause you're not posh enough for 'em?'

'No, Harry, I've got a return ticket.'

'I'll tell you what you won't get down yonder,' said Harry, reaching for the nearest beer pump.

'No,' agreed Cliff, 'I can't get Sam Smith's.'

'I reckon that's what brought you back to Scarborough.'

'Do you? Well, as soon you've pulled me two pints of bitter, I'll tell you.'

Harry obliged, setting the drinks down on the bar and leaning forward on his elbows. 'Go on then,' he said. 'Don't keep me in suspense.'

'All right, Harry. This young gadabout,' he said, patting Ted on the shoulder, 'is about to have his wings clipped.' He was enjoying Harry's bemusement, but he decided to end the suspense. 'He's tying the knot tomorrow,' he said.

'Getting wed, eh? It doesn't seem like two minutes since he were in short pants.' The thought evidently appealed to him. 'An' now he's getting wed. Well, I never. Love's a rum bugger, isn't it?'

Cliff nudged his brother and said, 'I think you've made his night, Ted.'

'Seemingly.'

'And who,' asked Harry, 'is going to be Mrs Bun, the Baker's Wife?'

'Vera Little.'

'A good choice, young Ted. She's a nice lass, an' I hope you'll both be very happy.'

A voice at the other end of the bar asked, 'Do I have to wait all night to get served?'

Harry gave Cliff and Ted a long-suffering look and went to serve his customer.

A Chance Sighting

Ted slumped back in his seat. 'It's all right for you,' he said.

'Why do you say that?' Cliff was puzzled by his brother's attitude on the eve of his wedding.

'You're the bright one. You went to university, served in the war and got made an officer.'

'That's nonsense, Ted. University doesn't mean a thing in the real world. I can't bake bread, and that's one of man's basic requirements. As for the war, you weren't old enough, and the only reason I was commissioned was that the Admiralty had decided that all pilots had to be officers.' It seemed a silly reason for argument. 'What's your problem, Ted?'

'Only that if you dropped a major clanger, you'd most likely survive it.'

'Because my stock is high at home?'

'Yes.'

'All right. Tell me about your clanger.'

'Oh, hell.' Ted braced himself before saying, 'It's just that it's all very well for Harry to talk about Mrs Bun, the Baker's Wife, but what he doesn't know is that the bun's already in the oven.'

'Ah.' Cliff thought quickly. 'When did it happen?'

'About two months ago.' He looked wretched.

'Has it been confirmed by a doctor?'

'Yes.'

Cliff picked up the glasses. 'Same again?'

'Please.'

He went to the bar and returned with two pints, having given Ted's problem some consideration.

'I'm sure babies have been known to put in an appearance at seven months.'

Ted shook his head. 'I'd never get away with it.'

'Not at home, I agree. You'll have to tell them, but it'll help your case if the situation's not obvious to outsiders.'

'No scandal, eh?'

'That's right.' Cliff felt sorry for his brother. 'I don't suppose Vera's parents know yet, do they?'

'No.' He toyed with his pint glass. 'We reckon on telling everybody after the honeymoon.'

'Go on, drink it. It'll do you good.' He watched as Ted took his advice, and said, 'I wouldn't wait as long as that.'

Ted looked at him in surprise. 'Wouldn't you?'

'No, I wouldn't. If you go away with this hanging over you, you might as well spend your honeymoon in sack cloth and ashes. You certainly won't enjoy it, and that's what it's supposed to be about, or so I believe. No, tell them before you go, and give them the week to get used to the idea, and then you can concentrate on enjoying yourselves.'

In his Best Man's speech, Cliff spoke about the bride and groom, listing a number of outstanding qualities, knowing that very soon they would need his advocacy. Naturally, he knew more about Ted than he did about Vera, but he made use of what he knew. Of his brother, he spoke of his readiness to enter the family business, his application and hard work in learning the trade, and how, on returning from two years' service in the army, he'd thrown himself once more into the bakery, knowing how important it was to the family as well as to himself.

In speaking about Vera, he'd found it necessary to restrict his accolade to abstract qualities, but he felt nevertheless that he'd given her an effective endorsement. He even went as far as to tell himself that his speech had put her father's in the shade.

As soon as the bride and groom had left the reception to change into their 'going away' clothes, Cliff's father leaned over to speak quietly to him.

'It wasn't a bad speech you made, Cliff. Mind you, if I were to criticise, I'd say you sounded as if you were in court, making the case for the defence.'

'That's what it sounded like to me.' Cliff's mother weighed into the conversation. 'Come on, Cliff,' she urged. 'What's he been up to?'

'It's not for me to say, Mum. He'll own up in his own time.'

Mr Stephens shook his head. 'They've rung the bell. I knew it would happen.'

'I've wondered about that too.'

A Chance Sighting

'I really can't say,' said Cliff.

'But you know more than you're letting on.' His mother's rebuke was mild enough. For all her righteous criticism, she probably approved of his brotherly loyalty.

Cliff looked around the room, wondering how much longer he would have to stall. He saw Vera's parents shaking hands with two of the guests, who were apparently leaving early. A member of the hotel staff was waiting to speak to them.

'I wonder what's happening over there,' said Cliff's mother, as Vera's parents made their way purposefully to the door.

'I think we're about to find out,' said his father. Another figure was emerging from the same door. Shamefaced, Ted approached them.

'Mum, Dad, I've got something to tell you.'

'We thought you might have,' said his mother. 'Sit yourself down. Cliff's going to leave us for a few minutes. You can have his seat.'

'All right, I'm going.' As a parting shot, Cliff said, 'I didn't tell them, Ted. They knew already.' He wandered off to speak to an aunt and uncle he'd not seen since before the war. Crises could come and go, but the niceties had to be observed.

After a while, Vera and her parents entered the room and joined the Stephens family. Vera was looking tearful, and her mother's arm was wrapped around her. Her father was shaking hands with Mr and Mrs Stephens and, incredibly, with Ted. Cliff decided to rejoin them.

'Hello, Cliff,' said Mr Little. 'It seems you're going to be an uncle sooner than you thought.'

'Hello, Mr Little, Mrs Little. Don't be too hard on them.'

'Nay, Cliff, they're not the first and they won't be the last.'

'At least,' said Mrs Little, 'they waited until knitting wool was off the ration.'

'Aye well,' said Mr Little, 'it's time for t' Going Away.'

'And you look lovely for it, Vera,' said Mrs Stephens.

'That's right.' Cliff felt free to speak again. 'Go and enjoy yourselves, you two.' He couldn't resist adding, 'You've got a licence for it now.'

His last remark earned him a smack on the arm from his mother.

'We'll have no more of that kind of talk,' she told him.

Everything was going to be all right; the errant pair were forgiven, the wedding had gone according to the highly-detailed arrangements, and his mother was in charge again. He couldn't help thinking, albeit briefly, that another wedding might have been on the cards had matters not taken the course they did in 1944.

3

The aim of the Council of Europe was to uphold human rights, democracy and the rule of law in Europe, all of which sounded highly laudable to Laura, although she would have welcomed just a little organisation as well, and particularly when she was searching the shelves of her office for a notepad. It was unfair of her, she knew; the Council had only recently moved out of the University Palace and into its own premises, and items of greater importance than interpreters' notepads had gone astray in the move. It was rather important, though, that she had something more practical than the back of her hand on which to make a note.

She was standing on a chair and searching the top shelf, when someone knocked confidently on the door.

'Come in.' Laura stepped down from her chair and back into her shoes, as a tall, fair-haired young man entered the room.

'Good morning,' he said, offering his hand. 'Gerald Pasco. "Gerry", actually,' he confided.

'Laura Pembury.'

'You're new, aren't you?'

'I thought we were all new.' The Council had only opened its doors that year.

'You know what I mean. You've just arrived.'

'Give or take a week,' she agreed.

'Quite, and I've been wondering if you have everything you need, or if there's anything I can help you with.'

'Not unless you know where the notepads are kept.' She indicated the unyielding shelves with a dismissive gesture.

'I'm afraid I haven't a clue, unless....' He opened the door a little wider. 'There's a box out here,' he said. 'I almost stumbled across it.'

'Let me look.' She crouched down and read:

50 Carnets
Taille D5 (135mm x 192mm)
Réglé 8mm

The box bore her room number: 114.

'These are what I've been looking for,' she confirmed.

'Good. Let me carry that in for you.'

'Thank you.'

'There,' he said, placing the box on her desk. 'Perhaps we can meet and I can give you the gen about the way things are done in Strasbourg.'

She wondered why men did that, why they had to offer an inducement in the form of advice or information. She knew from the way he'd been eyeing her just what he was after. Why didn't he simply ask her out?

'What do you really want?'

'As I said, I just wondered....' Rather than repeat himself, he spread his hands in mute appeal.

'Do you want me to go out with you?'

'Well, yes, that's the general idea.'

'All right.' She slit the adhesive tape on the parcel with her letter opener and took out a notepad, noticing that it was made from recycled paper. It seemed that paper was as scarce in France as in Britain, although it was hardly surprising. 'When?'

'How about this evening? We could eat somewhere.'

'Okay. This evening.'

'I'll pick you up if you like. Is seven all right?'

'Fine.' She wrote her address on the first leaf of the notepad and tore it out for him. 'Were you in the RAF?'

'Yes. How did you know?'

'You said "gen".'

'Of course. What about you? Were you in the services?'

'Yes, the Wrens.'

'Really? What did you do in the Wrens?'

'I'm afraid I'm not at liberty to say.'

'Oh well....' He waved the matter aside. 'I flew a Typhoon,' he told her, adding, 'ground attack fighter, you know. Lovely kite.'

'Really? I knew a pilot once.'

'What did he fly?'

'A Walrus. He was in the Fleet Air Arm.'

'A Shagbat?' He snorted derisively. 'I suppose someone had to fly the wretched things, and why not the Navy?'

Controlling her annoyance, Laura said, 'Before you sit in judgement, let me tell you that the pilot in question was one of the finest men I've ever known, and I have it on good authority that any ditched airman who was picked up by a Walrus would sing its praises for evermore. It's worth remembering if we're to stay on friendly terms.'

'Oh, quite. I meant absolutely no offence, I assure you. As a matter of fact, I was shot down in 'forty-five.'

'Over the sea?'

'No, over Germany. I was a prisoner for three weeks.'

'You were lucky.'

'Yes, I was. As a matter of fact, I was in a camp for naval officers, mostly Fleet Air Arm types. Nice chaps.' He was obviously keen to wipe out his earlier gaffe. 'I remember meeting a Walrus pilot, as it happens. He was a decent chap too.' He reflected on that for a moment. 'It was either a Walrus or a Sea Otter.'

'I'm glad to hear it.' She smiled at his discomfiture. 'All right,' she said, 'you're forgiven. I'll see you at seven, but I must get on with my work now.'

'Of course. Until tonight, then.'

Laura unpacked the remainder of the notepads and found a place for them on a convenient shelf. As she did so, she thought about Gerry Pasco. He seemed a pleasant enough chap, and she did demand rather high standards. She had to work at being less exacting where men were concerned, starting that evening.

She wore a blue, short-sleeved star print dress, her first acquisition since the end of clothes rationing, and she was delighted with it. Gerry was also impressed when the waiter took her coat and hat.

'You know, Laura,' he said, 'you're the best thing I've seen since I arrived in Strasbourg. You look a peach in that dress.'

'I'm sure that's an exaggeration, but thank you.'

After a brief conversation, it was established that, whilst Gerry's French was adequate for most purposes, it was very specialised, his role at the Council being on the legal side of things. However, Laura left him to order the food and the wine, although she had to enlighten him about one item.

'I've never had a decent steak in France,' he told her.

'I'm surprised. What did you ask for?'

'*Le steak*, I suppose.'

She couldn't help smiling. 'That probably explains it,' she said. 'You must have been eating horse meat.'

He gasped. 'Surely not.'

'They eat a lot of it. They had to when beef was in short supply.'

'So what should I have ordered?'

'*Le biftek*. You have to stipulate beef, you see.'

'And that's what they call it, *le biftek*?'

'That's right.'

'How odd.'

'Not really. They call us *les rosbifs*, at least when we're out of earshot.'

'Do they really? They're not at all grateful, are they?'

'Well, you know, maybe they believed Goebbels when he told them that Britain would fight to the last Frenchman.'

'I shouldn't be surprised. It's been an uneasy relationship for centuries, hasn't it? I've heard France described as Britain's oldest enemy and least-reliable ally. At least, it was something like that.'

'The relationship will be uneasier still if the waiter hears you, Gerry. He's coming this way.'

Gerry gave their order to the waiter and asked to see the wine waiter.

'I really believe,' said Laura when the waiter had taken their order, 'that we should set aside past differences. I find the French, by and large, a charming race, and the food's good as well.' She added, 'Of course, that's as long as you order the right thing.'

'*Touché.*'

'I'm sorry. I couldn't resist that.'

'That's all right.' He looked around the restaurant and saw the wine waiter taking a bottle to a nearby table. 'Hopefully, it'll be us next,' he said. 'I must say, when I arrived here, I was surprised to find that so many excellent wines had survived the war. I expected the Nazis to have rifled every cellar.'

'That's another great thing about the French. They're a nation of survivors. You only have to look at what they've experienced to realise that.'

'What do you mean?'

'Just that the occupation, horrible though it must have been, was the most recent of a whole series of catastrophes in their country's history, and they survived them all. Apparently, during the occupation, wine merchants, hoteliers and the like managed to conserve stocks of wine, sometimes by bricking up sections of their cellars, or by re-labelling bottles so that the Germans thought they were getting quality, and all the time they were being sold *vin ordinaire.*'

'I wonder how many of them realised they were being swindled.'

'I don't know, but the French were very successful on the whole.'

'You've only been here a short time.' He looked at her strangely. 'How do you know all that?'

She'd actually come by the information whilst working in Intelligence, but she couldn't tell him that. 'My father's a wine merchant,' she said, 'and he's heard things on the grapevine, if you'll allow the pun.'

'Right. That makes perfect sense.'

'I'm glad.'

'By the way, what *did* you do in the Wrens? Something with languages, I imagine.'

'I'm sorry.'

'Damn it, you can tell me. After all, I was a squadron-leader in the RAF.'

'It would make no difference if you were an air marshal. I couldn't tell you this morning when you asked me, and I still can't. It really is a subject best avoided.' She looked over his shoulder and said, 'Anyway, the wine waiter's here. That's something we *can* talk about.'

She sat back and relaxed as he ordered a bottle of the 1937 Nuits Saint Georges. It was an opportune interruption, and she hoped he would leave the matter of the war and her part in it alone. It was unfortunate when people took reticence personally, but she had no choice.

When the wine waiter was gone, she leaned forward, determined to take control of the conversation, and said, 'Now, tell me about your family.'

'All right, but it's not the most exciting of stories. My father and grandfather are both lawyers, as I am; in fact, the family firm goes back to eighteen-eighty. Oh, and I forgot to say that my brother is also a lawyer. He's with the family firm in Bury St Edmunds.'

'So there'd be no shortage of legal advice in your household, should the need ever arise.'

'None whatsoever, although I imagine life is livelier in your home, your people being in the wine trade.'

'Not really. No one in my family drinks an awful lot. The accent is on quality rather than quantity.'

'Will you take your place in the business?'

'No.' She could tell him that with confidence. 'I couldn't see myself in any business. It's just not me, I'm afraid. Fortunately, my brother's helping to run it now. He's much better qualified.'

'Has he a business background?'

'He had until the war intervened.' She added, 'He was in the RAF.'

'Aircrew?'

'No, he was a meteorological officer.'

'Ah, one of the "Never-Never types".'

Puzzled, she said, 'Go on, I'll buy it.'

'It's a little rhyme someone made up. It goes thus:

A Chance Sighting

"Never, never, never trust the man who reads the weather;
It's sure as sure is sure he'll drop a clanger.
When he forecasts bright and warm, just expect a full-blown storm,
And leave your kite parked safely in its hangar."

'I'll spare you the rest.'
'I've never heard that before.'
'There are lots more.'
'Do you disapprove of anyone who hasn't flown… what was it? Hurricanes?'
'Typhoons, actually. No, it's just harmless banter. You must have come across it in the Wrens when you weren't working hard at keeping secrets.'
'No, we had more important things to do.'
She decided he was quite entertaining, if a trifle dismissive of the efforts of others. It was good to spend some time in male company. She'd had so little of it in recent times.

4

'How have things been, Daisy?' Two weeks had elapsed since their last session, when Cliff had begun to anticipate significant progress.

'I'm feeling a bit more sure of myself. Not looking over my shoulder quite as much, you know.'

'Good. What's happened particularly to make you feel better?'

'I've started going to evening classes to learn dressmaking. I used to do a lot with my mother, and I think I was quite good, but I sort of lost the confidence to do it after we were married. It's all coming back, though. I've been wondering about maybe making things for other people as a side line.'

It was a major step forward. 'How has Dennis reacted to it, Daisy?'

'He doesn't seem to mind as long as it happens when he's away.'

'And your mother-in-law?'

'She hasn't had much to say. I think it's basically because she's not very good with a sewing machine, or any kind of sewing, really. It's the one thing I can do better than her.'

'Is it really, Daisy?' Suddenly, he saw an opportunity to make further progress.

'What do you mean?'

'Don't you think you have qualities that she hasn't?'

'What sort of qualities?'

'I went to a wedding recently—'

'Lovely.'

'It was. The bride wore a dress made from white silk and she looked amazing.'

Practical as ever, Daisy asked, 'Where on earth did she find silk for a dress?'

'It was from a parachute that someone had found, but the point is this, that I spent some time talking with the bridegroom's mother, and she told me something very interesting indeed.'

'What was that?'

'She said that dressmakers and hairdressers are special people. It's because women go to them and talk about things that we men don't understand.'

'I suppose that's true.' It was as if the concept had never occurred to her. 'I always enjoy getting my hair done and having a good old chat with my hairdresser.'

'And when women come to you to have theirs done, I imagine they talk to you.'

'Yes. You know, I've never thought about it before, but they do. They tell me about things sometimes that are quite private. I hear some very surprising things too, not that I'd ever say a word to anyone else.'

'Right.' It was time for a quick summary. 'So, you're a hairdresser and *confidante*.'

'What's that?'

'Someone people confide in.'

'In that case, yes.'

'And you're also very professional. You're told all these things in confidence and you respect that confidence. Doesn't that make you special?'

'I hadn't thought about it.'

'Could you see your mother-in-law in that situation?'

Daisy laughed. 'She hasn't a clue about hairdressing.'

'But if she had, do you think women would confide in her the way they confide in you?'

'Not if they'd any sense. She'd tell them how to live their lives, and nobody wants to be told that.'

'You know that, but she doesn't.'

'That's right.' It was another moment of realisation. 'She doesn't know, she doesn't even care when she's being unpleasant.'

'Right, Daisy.' It was time to summarise again. 'Women feel that they can confide in you, they know you'll keep their secrets to yourself, and they know you'll never say anything hurtful. It's a great quality, and one that your mother-in-law clearly lacks. How do you feel about that?'

He felt that Daisy was making excellent progress and it gave him a lot of satisfaction but, even so, there were times when he had to get away from the workplace. He enjoyed walking along the Leas in Folkestone, which, like Scarborough, had a funicular lift, although the Leas lift was still powered by sea water, whereas the Spa Lift in Scarborough had been recently converted to electricity. He imagined Folkestone would do the same before long.

Now that digging for victory was consigned to history, the Leas had an excellent show of flowers as well, and he enjoyed them, but the countryside beckoned and in the absence of a motor car he decided to visit the bicycle shop he'd seen in Cheriton High Street.

Because of government restrictions, new bicycles were impossible to find, but the shop had a varied stock of second-hand machines.

The proprietor asked him, 'What kind of bike are you looking for?'

'A touring bike. I want to get out into the country.'

'I don't blame you.' He cast his eye over the row of bicycles behind him and said, 'There's an Evans there that you might like.' He lifted the bicycle out for Cliff to see.

'I had one almost like this before the war,' Cliff told him, running his eye over the three-speed Super Champion derailleur gears.

'Yes, this is what we're reduced to: selling pre-war bikes because we can't get new ones.'

'I reckon this would serve me just as well.' He examined the saddle closely and said, 'Mind you, this is looking its age.'

The proprietor considered that for a moment. 'I haven't any new ones,' he said. 'That would take a miracle, but I can find you

A Chance Sighting

a good second-hand one.' He rooted through a box of accessories, eventually finding a leather saddle that looked almost new. 'I can sell you the bike and this saddle for six pounds, five and six, and I'll fit the saddle for you. How's that?'

'I'm happy with that.' Cliff counted out six pounds, two half-crowns and a shilling piece.

'Thank you.' The proprietor went to the cash register, recorded the sale and handed Cliff his sixpence change.

It was a while before Cliff was able to break-in the saddle, and he was obliged to anoint his hindquarters repeatedly with Zam-Buk before he was able to ride in comfort, but his excursions into the countryside around Folkestone became nevertheless an enjoyable habit.

He often met other cyclists and came to know some of them quite well. With others, he would exchange transient greetings as they continued on their way. One meeting, however, was to prove particularly significant for a fellow cyclist.

They met at Capel le Ferne on the coast road between Folkestone and Dover, where Cliff had stopped for a brief respite. He lay on his back, feeling the cool breeze on his face and enjoying the scent of the sea. The first indication that he had company was the squeal of rubber on steel as the cyclist braked and came to a standstill.

'D' you mind if I join you?' He was a young man, dark-haired like Cliff, but stockier.

'Feel free.' There was no shortage of space on the clifftop.

'Thanks.' The newcomer lowered his bike on to the grass and sat down beside Cliff.

'Have you come far?'

'Only from River.'

'Where's that?'

'Just outside Dover.'

'I've come from Folkestone but I'm feeling lazy. I'm Cliff Stephens, by the way.'

'Matthew Ingram. Call me "Matt".'

The two men shook hands.

Matt pointed to a large, white house along the road. 'Do you know what that place is? I've ridden past it a few times and wondered.'

'Some kind of clandestine wireless station, I imagine, judging by the antennae.' Secret wireless stations set him uncomfortably in mind of *HMS Flowerdown*, and he was relieved to learn that his new acquaintance had only a passing interest in the matter.

'Wherever you go,' he said, 'you see relics of the bloody war. It's not just Dover, but that's a bomb site in itself. It's as if it won't go away.'

'Maybe you have to let it go, Matt.'

'Easier said than done, old boy.'

Cliff was wondering about that. 'Which outfit were you with, Matt?'

'RAF Coastal Command. I flew a Lockheed Hudson for three years.' He added grimly, 'For my sins.'

Cliff merely nodded.

'Am I speaking a foreign language?'

'Not at all. I was in the Fleet Air Arm.'

'What did you fly?'

'A Walrus at first, but I was shot down in forty-four and taken prisoner. After I came home I was an instructor on the Sea Otter.' He smiled. 'There you have it. My war service in a nutshell.'

'So we have something in common.'

Cliff waited for him to enlarge on that observation but when Matt spoke again it was about something else.

'I see you have an Evans too. How do you find it?'

'I only bought it a month ago, but I've been very pleased with it.'

It was still on the subject of bicycles that their conversation ended, at least for the time being, because they saw nothing of each other until three weeks later, on the Warren, outside Folkestone.

'Hello again, Matt.'

'Hello, Cliff. Careful where you stand. There are adders hereabouts.'

A Chance Sighting

'In November? I imagine they're all under cover, trying to keep their teeth from chattering.'

Matt remained cautious. 'We're better sticking to the track.'

'Okay, we'll do that.' He dismounted and stood on the hard ground.

'How are things with you, Cliff?'

'Fine, thanks. And you?'

'Oh, fine.'

As a friendly conversation it lacked promise but Matt seemed uneasy, as if he had something important but difficult to say. Cliff suspected that he might have given further thought to their exchange at Capel le Ferne. He decided to keep the conversation ticking over.

'Do you know this corner of England well, Matt?'

'I've lived here most of my life. My folks are in the animal feed business. That's what I do.'

'Really? I wondered if you were local, you know, when you told me about the adders.'

'Oh, that.' Matt smiled self-consciously. 'You were probably right about them keeping their heads down. There's quite a nip in the air.'

'I know nothing about these things,' Cliff assured him. 'I'm dependent on locals like you to guide my footsteps.' He eyed the heathland beside them and added, 'Sometimes literally.'

They laughed together, and then Matt said, 'I've lived here all my life apart from during the war.'

Cliff had been wondering when Matt would mention the war. Casually, he asked, 'Where were you stationed?'

'Connel, Argyllshire.'

'Nice.'

'Well, I suppose so, but it's always good to come home.'

'It was good to come home,' agreed Cliff, 'after the war.'

Matt looked uncomfortable. 'Were you based on an aircraft carrier, Cliff?'

'No, a heavy cruiser to begin with, but then they posted me to air-sea rescue.'

'I see.'

'It was a welcome change. Spotting for the guns of the fleet imposes a hell of a strain after a while. It's all concentration.'

Again, Matt seemed lost in thought. 'You'd done your share of killing,' he said.

'Is that important?'

Matt made no reply, but it was clear that the matter was important to him. When he spoke, it was in the form of a confession. 'I flew anti-submarine patrols,' he said. His voice was low, as if he were afraid of being overheard. 'As far as I know, we only ever sank one U-boat.' He looked away, as if he were caught for the moment in the grip of that memory.

'Go on.'

Matt turned again to speak. 'It was more than enough.'

'It troubles you, doesn't it, that U-boat?'

'I've never spoken to anyone about it. I don't even know why I'm telling you.'

'Maybe it's the right time. You can talk to me, Matt. I may be able to help you.'

'How can you possibly help me?' The words came out as a challenge.

'I specialise in helping people cope with the emotional scars that war leaves behind. I'd like you to come and have a chat with me.'

5

Before long, Laura and Gerry were seeing each other regularly, eating out, dancing and going to the theatre, even though culture wasn't Gerry's main driving force. At the local cinemas, they saw *Les Derniéres Vacances*, *Les Parents Terribles*, *Impasse Des Deux Anges* and *The Red Shoes*, the latter overdubbed in French, which they found quite confusing. They also saw *Easter Parade* with French subtitles, which was downright distracting.

Otherwise, their relationship continued to develop. Laura still found it necessary to remind Gerry that his dismissive remarks were not universally appreciated, but she felt, on the whole, that he was beginning to grasp the basic principles of diplomacy.

One trait he already had in great measure was persistence. He was demonstrating the fact at her flat after a visit to the theatre.

'No, Gerry.' She arrested his hand in mid-travel and returned it to his lap.

'I can't help it, Laura. It's the effect you have on me.'

'There's nothing personal about it, Gerry. It's the effect most women have on almost all men.' She thought briefly, testing the validity of that assessment, and decided it was basically correct. 'I suppose there have to be exceptions,' she said, 'such as misogynists, priests, monks and so on, but it's generally true. You just need to restrain yourself and not always leave it to me to put the brakes on.'

'Go on, Laura, be a sport,' he pleaded.

She smiled good-naturedly. 'Is that the best entreaty a lawyer can muster? "Be a sport"? It's not about sport, Gerry. We'd be playing with fire, and you know it.'

'But there are ways to avoid... accidents.'

'I know. They say a cold bath works wonders. Otherwise, nothing is absolutely safe.'

'Except a cold and resolute woman.' He appeared to reflect on that gloomy fact before saying, almost to himself, 'And this is the woman I want to marry.'

'You must be desperate, Gerry. Marriage would be a drastic step just to get your wicked way with me.'

'No, seriously. I've been working up to asking you.'

'If this is a ploy to get me to—'

'No, not at all. You know I'm besotted with you, and you're quite keen. You have to admit that.'

'Keen?' She hesitated. 'Let's say I'm fond of you.'

'I'm serious, Laura. I really am asking you to marry me.'

Caught off-guard for the moment, Laura could find nothing to say. Until that moment, she'd associated Gerry's advances with nothing more noble than naked lust.

He continued to make his appeal. 'Will you, darling? Tell me you will.'

'Gerry, this has come as a complete surprise. You can't expect an instant decision.'

'I could pop in and see you tomorrow.'

'I need longer than that. I have to think about it.'

'Take as long as you like. A whole week, if necessary.'

'Leave me to consider it and I'll let you know.'

Laura considered Gerry's proposal at length and from a number of angles. She pondered his potential as a provider, as a parent and as a permanent companion and soul-mate. She also examined her feelings for him.

After two days, her thoughts were in chaos. She would readily give Gerry full marks as a provider but as far as the other qualities were concerned she had no idea. Her feelings for him were hopelessly confused. He was fun and entertaining, and she enjoyed his company, at least when he wasn't making demands, but was that the extent of his appeal? She wasn't at all sure. She was an intelligent, educated woman but she didn't know her own mind.

One thing she did know was that for too long she had been measuring men against Cliff, or at least against her memory of him. It was just possible that in almost six years, heartbreak and regret had caused her to see him through the soft focus of doting recollection, and that her memory of him had become to some extent idealised. That alone would make him impossible to follow.

She pursued that supposition for at least three hours and then, having slept on it, concluded that it was unlikely. She had spent so little time with Cliff that her recollection of him was as clear as ever. He remained impossible to follow, but only for as long she allowed him to be.

The truth as she saw it was that Cliff was dead and the past could not be revisited. It seemed that, since his death, she had been saving herself for him, and the absurdity of that had only just occurred to her. It was as if it had taken Gerry's proposal to make her see her situation for what it was. She was twenty-nine and still single, but only because of her preoccupation with a dead man.

After another night's sleep, which was always a good idea, she was ready to give Gerry her answer.

'Laura, I'm the happiest man on earth!' They were in the sitting room of her flat, and Gerry was just beginning to believe his good fortune.

'I doubt it, Gerry,' she said, teasing him. 'There has to be someone happier than you, or you've nothing left to strive for.'

'I have everything I could possibly want,' he insisted, taking her in his arms again. 'Now we can begin to make plans. I suggest that, as Christmas isn't far away, we make our announcement then, and we can spend Christmas with my folks in Suffolk.'

'What about my family?'

'We can go and see them later.'

'No, we can't. If you'll only think about it for a second, you'll agree with me that it's not a good idea.'

He looked puzzled. 'Do you mean you want to do it the other way round?'

'No.' She motioned to him to sit beside her. 'I'll explain.'

'Good, because I don't see how else we could arrange it.'

'You see, I always think it's a mistake to announce an engagement at Christmas. It's too much all at once, if you see what I mean. You're either celebrating Christmas or you're celebrating an engagement, but to do both is to over-egg an already rich pudding, even allowing for food rationing.'

'But how else can we do it?'

'I vote we keep mum about it over Christmas, and then, possibly later in January or maybe February, when our folks need something to lift them above the fog and the gloom, we can make two visits: one to Suffolk and the other to Kent. How does that sound?'

'I have to hand it to you, darling. You're amazing.'

'Not really, Gerry. It just calls for a little thought.'

It seemed that he was dazed by her organising prowess, because a full ten minutes elapsed before his next foray into the forbidden region.

'No, Gerry.' She seized his wrist and imprisoned it until she saw the look of glum acceptance on his face.

'But, as we're engaged, I thought....'

'I'm sure you did, but being engaged doesn't mean I'm going to surrender to your demands.'

'But we're engaged, Laura.'

'Yes, we are, and I don't want an extra panel let into my wedding gown because I allowed you to jump the gun. Some things are worth waiting for, Gerry.'

'But surely we need to practise for the great day. It would be awful if it got the slow handclap on our wedding night.'

'Are you thinking of inviting an audience?' She couldn't help showing her amusement.

'No, but I mean things have to be done properly, you know.'

'Gerry.' She spoke softly and as kindly as she could.

'What?'

'It was a wise decision you made.'

'When?'

A Chance Sighting

'When you elected not to practise in court as a barrister. Even without legal training I can see you would have been hopeless.'

'It's an indication of my state of mind when I'm with you. I'm so flustered I can't even mount a telling argument, never mind anything else.'

'Have patience, Gerry. See it as a challenge to be overcome.'

'I'm glad you find it funny. I certainly don't.'

'You will in time.'

6

Cliff felt that he and Matt were now making firm progress. After some initial reluctance to seek help, Matt was responding positively to new ideas, and Cliff was hopeful of a successful outcome.

Otherwise, he and Reg were attracting a growing number of clients. They had also secured the services of a secretary, whom they shared with the solicitor on the ground floor, so, with things going so well, they were able to approach the Christmas holiday in an optimistic mood. To improve matters further, Christmas Day fell on a Sunday, which created a longer than usual holiday. Christmas celebrations were to begin early for Cliff and Reg, however, as Widowsons, the printers, had invited them and other customers to a party that Friday. Cliff had intended catching the overnight train from London to York but, in the interests of goodwill, he postponed his travel plans until Saturday morning. He wasn't too disappointed; according to the latest weather forecast, the fog that had settled over Britain and northern Europe was likely to lift during the course of Friday night, and that would make travel easier.

As they approached Widowson's office, they were assailed with 'Rudolph, the Red-Nosed Reindeer', sung by Gene Autry. It was a new release for Christmas.

'It's popular already,' said Cliff.

'It won't last,' Reg told him. 'It's just a silly song for children.'

Harry Widowson greeted them at the door.

'Come in, you two,' he bellowed, 'and help yourselves to a drink.' Like many printers and others who worked in a noisy environment,

A Chance Sighting

he had succumbed over the years to hearing loss and the habit of stentorian speech.

They thanked him and made their way to the large, deal table that served as a bar. The gramophone, which stood beside the bar, was now playing 'Some Enchanted Evening', sung by Perry Como.

'Thank goodness for that,' said Reg. 'I'm sick of that bloody reindeer already.' He poured himself a light ale and went to speak to the local newsagent.

'Hello,' said a voice beside Cliff. 'I'm Gladys. I work at Day's, the estate agents. 'Who are you?' She had evidently arrived early at the party, because her speech was already slurred. Otherwise, she was quite attractive, with dark hair and limpid brown eyes that appeared to focus with difficulty.

'I'm Cliff. I'm a… psychologist.' He thought 'psychotherapist' sounded too serious at a party.

'Ooh. Do you psycholan…?' It was one of those words that didn't mix well with alcohol.

'Do I psychoanalyse people? No, I don't.'

'Why not?'

'I'm not an analytical psychologist.'

'Oh. Do you hypnotise people?'

'No, I don't do that either.'

'You don't do very much of anything, do you?' She regarded him through half-closed eyes, possibly as one of life's disappointments.

'What do you do at Day's, Gladys?'

'Typing, filing, showing people around houses….' She searched her memory, but gave up. 'All sorts of things.'

'Fascinating. Now, there are some people I should speak to.' He made to move away from her, but she grasped his arm.

'You can't leave me already. Do you like to dance?' The gramophone was playing 'Sentimental Me', and Gladys was already swaying, whether to the music or in response to an excess of alcohol, Cliff was unsure, but it was probably better to humour her than risk a scene, so he allowed her to tow him to the centre of the floor.

After a moment, she said, 'You dance properly, don' you?'

'I try.'

'I don', I jus' shuffle aroun'.'

'Okay.'

'Well, take hold of me. I'm not made of....' Once again, her memory failed her and she settled for, 'I don' fall apart.'

'All right.' He held her closer and swayed to the music.

'D' you know,' she said, 'you're a good-lookin' fella. It's that hole in your chin that does it.'

'Have I got a hole in my chin? I never felt a thing.'

'Silly.' She examined him more closely and said, 'It's a gash, really.'

'Is it?'

'No, it's a what-do-you-call-it.'

'That's a relief.'

'What do you call it, then?'

'I think you're trying to say I have a cleft chin.'

'That's right. D' you like Martini?'

'I can't say I've ever tried it.'

'I love Martini.'

'I've noticed.'

'Hah, you think I've had too much t' drink, don' you?'

'It's not for me to say, Gladys.'

'Well, le' me tell you I can drink a lot more than you think.' Her knees seemed to give way, because suddenly her nose was level with his bottom waistcoat button.

'Steady now.' He hauled her upright and she tottered for a moment, like a clumsy tap dancer, before steadying herself. 'Rudolph, the Red-Nosed Reindeer' was playing again.

'This is no good for dancing,' she said. 'Come with me.'

He was about to protest, but she grasped his arm again and towed him with surprising strength into a passageway.

'What do you want, Gladys?'

'You, you silly bugger. Come on, kiss me.' She seized his head with both hands and pulled it down until his mouth was in contact with hers. It was the wettest kiss he'd ever experienced, and he was almost afraid she might engulf him. At that point, however, she released her hold on him and said weakly, 'I don' feel very well. This room's goin' up an' up an' up all the time.'

A Chance Sighting

'Okay.' He had visions of her throwing up in the passage. 'Maybe you should go to the—'

'Yes, I need a…. Where is it?'

Mercifully, the ladies' lavatory was only a few feet away, down the passage. He managed to hold her upright until she reached the door. After that, she was on her own. He returned gratefully to the party, where the first person he encountered was Brian Day, the estate agent.

'You know,' he said, 'that girl Gladys is going to get herself into awful trouble before long.'

'And so say all of us.' Brian smiled almost guiltily. 'So you've escaped the clutches of "Good Time" Gladys. I should have warned you when I saw you drinking with her.'

'She's probably passed out by now. She'd put away almost a bottle of Martini when she staggered into the lavatory.'

'Only a bottle? She must be slipping.'

'Why on earth do you employ her, Brian?'

'Well, believe it or not, these drunken binges are only occasional, and she's actually quite good at her job when she's sober.' He smiled again as he recalled a noteworthy event. 'I once sent her to the station to meet someone who was interested in a flat we had for sale. She showed him the flat and brought him back to the office to make his offer. I couldn't help noticing that he looked very pleased with himself. I reckon they must have tried out one of the bedrooms.' He added, 'Not that I encourage that sort of thing, you understand.'

'I don't think she needs much encouragement.' He inclined his head towards the passage and said, 'I wonder if she's all right.'

'We'll give her another five minutes and, if she hasn't surfaced by then, I'll send in the girls.'

He was pre-empted after a minute or so, when one of his staff called out, 'Will someone give me a hand with Gladys, and someone get a taxi? She's passed out.'

After a while, Cliff and Reg left the party and stepped outside.

Reg looked about him with relief. 'The fog's lifted, thank goodness.'

Cliff stood on the pavement beneath a streetlamp, going through his pockets.

'I hope I haven't left the train timetable at the office,' he said.

'I say, Cliff—'

'No, it's all right. I have it here.'

'Did you see the woman in the taxi that just went by?'

'No, my mind was elsewhere.'

'She gave you a very strange look.'

'How odd. Mind you, women do stop and look at me. It's the hole in my chin that does it, you know.'

'You lucky man. Anyway, all the best for Christmas.' He offered his hand.

'Have a happy Christmas, Reg, and thanks for everything.' The two men shook hands.

7

'Miss Laura, you look exhausted. Let me take your coat and hat and then I'll take your case up to your room.'

'Thank you, Gloria. It's been an awful journey.'

'Would you like me to make some tea? I don't think Mrs Pembury will be long. She said she would call on Mr Pembury and they'd come home together.'

'No, thank you, Gloria. After that journey, I think I'll have something stronger. I'll help myself while you do all that.' Having asked after Gloria's health and that of her sister, she walked through to the drawing room and poured herself a gin and tonic before sinking gratefully into an armchair. Whilst she usually drank very little, she found the gin and tonic soothing and it wasn't long before she was asleep.

<hr />

'Wake up, Laura. We're back.'

Laura opened her eyes and blinked. 'I'm sorry,' she said. 'I must have dropped off. Hello, Mother. Hello, Dad.'

They exchanged kisses before her mother said, 'We expected you last night until you phoned to say you were going to be late.'

'So did I. I was going to fly from Strasbourg to Croydon and get the train from there, but then the fog came down and all aircraft were grounded, so I got the train to Calais. What a journey. Still, I'm here.'

'And we're glad to see you.' Her father gave her a reassuring hug.'

'So which way did you come across the Channel?' Her mother seemed to want the full story.

'To Folkestone. Believe it or not, there's only one sailing per day in winter.'

'And now, perversely,' said her father, 'the fog has lifted.'

'It means I should have a better journey back.'

'Well, let's enjoy the time we have together.'

'I'll go and see how dinner is progressing,' said her mother.

'A curious thing happened in Folkestone,' said Laura when they were alone.

'What was that, darling?' As ever, her father was a ready listener.

'I was in the taxi going from Folkestone harbour to Central Station, and suddenly I saw two men at the side of the road. It sounds ridiculous, I know, but I could have sworn one of them was Cliff, the pilot I was involved with, who was killed in nineteen-forty-four.'

'What was that?' Her mother came in towards the end of the conversation.

'Laura was just saying she'd seen someone who looked just like the chap she met in Hampshire.'

'Oh, nonsense, Laura. You know perfectly well he was killed. Anyway, how would you recognise him after so long?'

'I have a photo of him with his aeroplane and his crew.' She wished her mother hadn't come in when she did. It would only lead to another argument.

'You mean you still have it?'

'Yes.'

'Oh, Laura, isn't it time you forgot him? He wouldn't have been right for you, anyway. Do try to move on.'

Laura had no wish to argue on her first night at home, but her mother had a way of provoking anger. 'Why wouldn't he have been right for me?'

'Chalk and cheese, dear. I'm sure you said his father was a baker.'

'Whereas my father is a grocer. Are they like similar poles in magnetism or something?'

'Your father is much more than a grocer.'

'If I'm allowed to speak,' said her father, 'I think it will be better for all concerned if we call a halt to this pointless argument.'

A Chance Sighting

He rose from his armchair. 'I'm going upstairs to change. I hope you two will call a ceasefire. I don't want to come down to another commotion.'

In the last year or so, Laura's mother had taken to retiring at around nine-thirty, leaving her father to listen to the wireless or read. On this occasion, it enabled him to talk with his daughter, an opportunity they both welcomed.

'What are you going to drink, darling? I'm going to have a cognac.' He was a thoughtful, quietly-spoken man.

'I'll join you with that if I may.'

'Of course.' He poured the drinks and handed one to Laura.

'Thanks, Dad.'

'You're welcome.' He took his seat on the other side of the fireplace and said, 'You know, you and your mother are very much alike.'

'What?' She wasn't sure she'd heard him properly.

'I don't mean that you share the same views. Heaven forbid. No, I mean you're alike in temperament, and that's why you cross swords so readily.'

It was news to Laura. 'If you say so, Dad.'

'You'll take some convincing, I know, and it's just as difficult convince your mother of something she doesn't want to admit.'

Laura cradled her glass between her hands, inhaling the heady vapour from the cognac. She knew her father would go on without being prompted.

'I am a grocer, as you said. I began with one shop and I was fortunate enough to acquire several more as well as the wine business but, as far as your mother is concerned, I'm more than that. She sees me as a businessman and a member of the establishment.'

'That's what she wants to believe, I imagine.'

'Yes, it is.' He took a sip from his glass, savouring the taste and aroma of champagne cognac. 'When you find the man you want to marry, it won't matter to me whether his father's an engine driver or a stockbroker, as long as you're happy. That's what matters.'

For a second, she was tempted to let him in on the secret, but that wasn't part of the plan. In any case, she felt a vague unease about it that she wanted to explore in her own time. 'That's what matters to you and me,' she agreed.

'It'll take longer to convince your mother. In the meantime, you need to be circumspect.'

'What do you mean?'

'When she says something that annoys you, let it go. After a few tries, she'll stop doing it.'

Laura was sceptical. 'Really?'

'We've been married thirty-five years. I know your mother.'

Laura took her father's advice, and the Christmas holiday was all the more peaceful for it. Her mother was possibly as surprised as she was.

The journey back to Strasbourg was equally smooth, the fog having cleared completely, and she was able to fly from Croydon to Strasbourg, arriving fresh and ready for the work she enjoyed. She was also glad to see Gerry again.

Christmas with Cliff's family was the unqualified success it had always been. There was even a Dickensian touch on Christmas morning, when Ted came into the kitchen and said, 'You'll never guess what I've just been asked to do.'

'Paint your nose red and lead the sleigh,' suggested Cliff.

'No, Mrs Slater from number fourteen came to see me in a right old state. Her gas cooker's leaking and they've had to shut off the gas supply to it. She can't cook Christmas dinner and she's asked me to cook it for her. Pudding an' all.'

'I hope you told her you would,' said his father, 'otherwise you're no son of mine.'

"Cause I did. What do you take me for?'

'Good lad.'

The situation appealed to Cliff, who said, 'That's what they used

A Chance Sighting

to do in the olden days, you know. According to Charles Dickens, the poor folk, who didn't have ovens, used to prepare their meal and then take it to a baker, who cooked it for them. For some reason, it was usually a goose in those days.'

'Aye well, this is a capon,' said Ted. 'It shouldn't take as long as a goose.'

'I'll have a look at it directly,' said Mr Stephens.

In spite of rationing, their own meal was the best it could be, with no shortage of vegetables and roast potatoes. Vera's family were invited, which made it all the more embarrassing for her when she was bombarded with exhortations to 'tuck in' because she was 'eating for two.'

In all, it was worth the long return journey for Cliff, who enjoyed life in Folkestone but still relished a visit to Scarborough.

8
February 1950

'Gerry, what's wrong?'
'Nothing.'
'Something's obviously wrong.'
'Does something have to be wrong? Is it suddenly compulsory?'
They were on the train from Bury St Edmunds to Tunbridge Wells and were alone in the compartment, a situation for which Laura was currently thankful.
'I'll put it another way, Gerry. Why are you refusing to look at me, and why is your lower lip trying hard to resemble a doorstep?'
'Oh, for goodness' sake, if you don't know, there's something very wrong.' He continued to stare grimly at the disappearing countryside.
'I've really no idea. I wish you'd tell me, or at least adopt a more grown-up posture.'
'Damn it, Laura. Do you have to be so patronising?'
'Only when you behave like a spoilt child and indulge in guessing games.'
'All right.' He vented his anger by taking his folded newspaper and smacking it down hard on the seat beside him. 'My mother asked you a perfectly civil question and you refused to answer her.'
Laura narrowed her eyes in thought. 'Which question was that?'
'You know perfectly well. She was showing an interest in your life during the war.'
The memory returned. 'She asked me what I did in the Wrens.'
'And you repaid her polite interest with the curtest of replies.'
'There was nothing curt about it. I told her I wasn't at liberty to talk about it, and that's true. I'm not allowed to discuss it with you,

A Chance Sighting

your mother, your father, your brothers, or even the Man from the Prudential. I signed the Official Secrets Act and I'm bound by it.'

'That's ridiculous.'

'Didn't you have secrets in the RAF, or were you forever on the phone to Goering, giving him the dispositions of your squadrons?'

'Sarcasm is a despicable device.'

Laura decided it was time to adopt a softer approach. 'Look, Gerry,' she said, 'I hope this isn't a foretaste of married life. Let's declare a truce, anyway.'

Gerry was in no rush to climb down. 'I can't imagine that what you were doing was all that secret. If it had been so important, they wouldn't have given the job to a bunch of....'

'A bunch of what? Women? Honestly, Gerry, you must have been a by-word with the WAAFs on your station. They'd always know where to go to be insulted. You know, I'm tempted to stare through this window and push out my lower lip, but I shan't, because someone has to set you an example.'

For the remainder of the journey, Gerry read *The Times*, and Laura read Nancy Mitford's *Love in a Cold Climate*. It seemed appropriate.

By the time they reached Tunbridge Wells, however, normal relations were restored and after a short taxi ride, they were able to present themselves to Laura's parents as a devoted couple.

When the formalities had been observed, Laura's mother addressed the question of Gerry's suitability as a marriage partner for her daughter.

'What exactly do you do at the Council of Europe, Gerry?'

'I'm a lawyer, Mrs Pembury, actually a barrister, although I'm engaged more in an advisory capacity than in advocacy.'

'Splendid.'

Laura smiled to herself. Whether or not her mother could tell advice from advocacy, she would be in no doubt as to his social standing.

Switching his attention to Laura's father, Gerry said, 'I gather you're in the wine business, sir.'

'I have a small chain of groceries and wine stores.'

'High-class groceries,' added his wife.

'That's just an excuse for charging high prices,' said Laura.

Her father laughed heartily, and her mother glared at her.

'It's good that wine is no longer in short supply,' said Gerry lamely.

'Amen to that.' Mr Pembury was still smiling.

'Laura told us you were in the RAF, Gerry.'

'That's right, Mrs Pembury.'

'He flew a... Whirlwind, wasn't it, Gerry?'

'A *Typhoon*, actually.'

'I knew it was something to do with wind.'

'Really, Laura. Show a little respect.'

'Sorry, Mother.'

'Our son will be here soon, Gerry. He was a meteorological officer.'

'Oh, really?'

Laura recalled an early conversation with Gerry, and wondered how Richard might react when referred to as one of the 'Never-Never types'. It was sure to happen, just as boys would always be boys.

'Of course, we'll never know what Laura did in the Wrens, because she refuses to tell us.'

Laura said nothing, but waited for a change of topic. Happily, her father came to her rescue.

'Laura is bound by the Official Secrets Act, dear. A careless word could find her in prison.'

'Really, Harold. There's no need to make it all sound so dramatic.'

'But nevertheless, it is,' he assured her. 'Of course, we knew all about secrets in the last war.'

'My husband was in the West Kent Regiment,' said Laura's mother, still intent on furnishing everyone's military credentials.

'Yes,' he said, 'the PBI knew a great deal about secrets because the General Staff kept everything a secret from us: enemy strength, troop movements, their own intentions.... Of course, that's supposing the General Staff knew what their intentions were.'

'Yes, very funny, dear.'

'You wouldn't have thought so if you'd been there.'

'You mentioned the PBI, sir,' said Gerry. 'What was that?'

A Chance Sighting

'The Poor Bloody Infantry. You know, given what the General Staff inflicted on us, it still goes against the grain, if you'll allow the pun, that I'm obliged to sell a certain brand of whisky.'

Laura reached for his hand and squeezed it in thanks for his timely smokescreen. All the same, she still felt that Gerry would eventually tire of his resentment, and that her enforced reticence would cease to be a barrier between them.

Matt's problem was approaching a successful conclusion, and that was a source of great satisfaction for Cliff, but he wasn't complacent. New clients were emerging and they deserved the same commitment from him. One of them came to see him the next morning.

His name was Norman Fellows, he had served in the RNVR from 1941 until his discharge in 1946 at the rate of leading seaman, and he suffered from nightmares and disturbing memories of the Russian convoys.

'It's not about anything that happened to me,' he told Cliff. 'It was seeing blokes killed, ships sunk, survivors choking on fuel oil... that sort of thing.' He held up his hands in confusion. 'It sounds crazy, I know.'

'There's nothing crazy about it, Norman. It's often the case,' said Cliff. 'You're by no means alone.'

Norman's relief was tangible. 'I didn't know that.'

'Tell me more about those memories.' He sat back and listened to a semi-coherent attempt to describe the scenes that tormented Norman, but it was clear before long that the telling was proving to be a problem.

'D' you fancy a wet?'

Norman looked relieved. 'Not 'alf, sir.'

'Tea or coffee? By the way, I'm Cliff, remember? We're not in the Navy now.'

'Sorry, Cliff. It's a habit. Tea, please.'

'Okay. Take it easy while I put the kettle on.' He walked down the passage to the tiny kitchen and filled the kettle, taking his time. Norman needed that hiatus to organise his thoughts.

When the tea was brewed, Cliff put the tea things on to a tray and carried them into the consulting room.

'Help yourself to milk and sugar, Norman.'

'Thanks, Cliff.' He grinned self-consciously and said, 'It still feels odd, calling an officer by his Christian name.'

'I'm not an officer now. Just think of us as two blokes, equals.'

'I'll try.' Norman tried his tea but it was too hot. 'You know,' he said, 'after a few convoys, they rested us. It was a bit of a holiday, really, 'cept we had to wear uniform and take on some of the duties. The best place for that was *HMS Flowerdown*. What a draft that must have been for some blokes, telegraphists an' that. They had a swimming pool, playing fields, gyms…. They even had a ballroom. Did you ever go there?'

Cliff had been letting him talk, listening but regarding the process as one of relaxation, until Norman mentioned *HMS Flowerdown*. At that point, he was instantly alert.

'No,' he said, 'but I knew someone who served there.'

'There were parts of it we weren't allowed in,' Norman told him. 'Strict security and all that, but it was a good draft for all that.'

'When were you there, Norman?'

'Let me see.' He looked thoughtful. 'It was in forty-four. It was St Valentine's Day when we arrived. I do remember that 'cause I remember seein' all the Jennies an' getting excited. You know how it is. We were only there for three weeks though. Shame.'

'Were you there at the time of the crash?'

'The crash? Oh, you mean when that 'plane came down in the next field. Yes, I was there all right.'

'Were there many casualties?'

'Casualties? No, there weren't. I remember the padre makin' a point of telling us that. No, the Jennies' quarters were burned out, but they all got out in time.

9

'By this time, she could be married and have a houseful of kids, but I'd still like to get in touch with her.'

'If you don't, you'll never know.' Reg was trying not to smile.

'What's so funny, Reg?'

'You trying to play it down. You can't wait to get started.'

'Guilty as charged, but it's easier said than done. All I know is that her surname is Pembury, that she went to school in Tunbridge Wells and that she lived close by.'

'There's a village called Pembury. It's quite near Tunbridge Wells.' He reached for the telephone directory, but stopped. 'They wouldn't be in ours. Tunbridge Wells is a separate telephone area.'

'They may have one downstairs. Solicitors are always making calls to distant places. I'll go down and ask.'

The secretary was busy typing when he opened the door, but she looked up and smiled when she saw him.

'Joan,' he said, 'have you such a thing as a telephone directory for the Tunbridge Wells area? I've only the vaguest idea where it is.'

'It's about forty miles to the left of here and up a bit,' she told him, handing over the telephone book.

'You're my kind of navigator, Joan. Thank you.'

'Try telling my husband that. Are you taking it away or browsing *in situ*?'

'If you've got something I can write on, I'll have a quick look now.'

She tore a page from her notepad and handed it to him. 'You'll excuse me while I get on with this letter, won't you?'

'Of course.' He leafed through the book, coming to names

beginning with *Pa* and then *Pe,* and eventually he found *Pembury.* Excited, he made a note of the various numbers listed. There were several for *Pembury, H. R. and Son, Grocers and Wine Merchants*, and one domestic number. The address was in Bilshurst, near Tunbridge Wells.

Joan finished typing and pulled the letter out of the typewriter. 'Any luck with the number?'

'Thank you, Joan. Yes, I think I've found what I was looking for. It's an address in Bilshurst.' He closed the book and placed it on her desk.

'Nice,' she commented, 'but too pricey for the likes of us.'

'I believe they're people of substance. Thanks again, Joan.'

He was due to see a client, so it wasn't until mid-afternoon that he was free to make the call. When he did, the phone was answered by someone who sounded like a housekeeper or maid.

'Bilshurst three-four-oh.'

'Good afternoon. I wonder if I might speak with either Mr or Mrs Pembury, please.'

'Mr Pembury is at the office, sir, but I'll see if Mrs Pembury is available. Who shall I say is calling?'

'My name is Stephens.' Oddly, he felt nervous, like someone trying to make a date for the first time. He breathed deeply and waited.

'Alice Pembury speaking. Who's calling?'

'Good afternoon, Mrs Pembury. My name is Stephens. I hope I have the right number, because I'm trying to find Laura Pembury, who served in the Wrens during the war.'

'Oh, yes? Laura is my daughter. What's your connection with her?'

'We were friends at one time.' His heart was pounding. 'I've only recently arrived in Kent, and I thought I'd look her up for old times' sake.'

'I see. Well, Laura doesn't live here now. As a matter of fact, she's living in France.'

'Is she really? Of course, we haven't seen each other for some time, so I'd no way of knowing that.'

'Of course you hadn't, Mr... What did you say your name was?'

'Stephens.'

A Chance Sighting

'Well, Mr Stephens, I'm always interested to meet Laura's friends. As you're now in Kent, perhaps you'd like to drop in some time for a cup of tea and a chat.'

'Thank you, Mrs Pembury. I'd like that very much.' He hesitated and then said decisively, 'Look, I hate to appear forward, but I have a free afternoon on Wednesday. Would that be convenient for you?'

There was a pause, possibly while she reviewed her movements, and then she said, 'Yes, I suppose so. I shall be out until about three. Can you come at four o'clock?'

'Yes, I can.'

'And you have our address?'

'Yes, from the telephone book.'

'Very well. I shall expect you at four o'clock on Wednesday.'

'I'll look forward to it. Thank you so much, Mrs Pembury. Goodbye.'

'Goodbye, Mr Stephens.'

He put the phone down with a feeling of relief and achievement. In a little over an hour, he'd come closer to contacting Laura than he'd dared hope since he was taken prisoner.

Laura soon realised that the scene on the train had been exceptional. Certainly, Gerry had been on his most careful behaviour since then, albeit with one minor exception.

'I don't think your brother took to me,' he said over dinner in Strasbourg.

Laura smiled at the recollection. 'I don't think he took kindly to your remarks about his being a weather man. He'd always taken his work rather seriously. He's a serious kind of chap.'

'I got that impression.' Then, as if he felt he should make a positive comment, he said, 'I liked your parents.'

'Oh well, two out of three's better than nothing.'

'You're very irreverent.'

'That's me, Gerry. Take me or leave me.'

'I'm happy with you just as you are.'

'That's good.'

The house was large and imposing, built probably around 1930 and with sizeable gardens on each side. Cliff could only guess what lay behind the house as he brought the hired car to a halt on the circling drive.

He stepped up to the front door and rang the bell, feeling more apprehensive than ever.

The door opened and a middle-aged woman in a starched cap and pinafore said, 'Good afternoon, sir.'

'Good afternoon. My name is Cliff Stephens. Mrs Pembury's expecting me.'

'Of course, sir. May I take your coat and hat?' She relieved him of them and went to report to Mrs Pembury that he had arrived.

'Would you like to come this way, sir?' She led him into an opulent sitting room, where a lady, obviously Mrs Pembury, occupied an armchair beside the fire.

'Mr Stephens. How good of you to come.' She offered her hand. 'Do take a seat. Will you take tea with me?'

'Yes, please, Mrs Pembury. I should like that very much.'

'Gloria, we'll have tea now. Mr Stephens, do you prefer Earl Grey or English Breakfast?'

Cliff hadn't a clue, so he opted for the one that sounded more like tea. 'I should prefer English Breakfast if that's possible, Mrs Pembury.'

'By all means. A pot of English Breakfast, Gloria.'

'Very good, Mrs Pembury.'

'Now, Mr Stephens, tell me how you came to meet my daughter.'

'It was quite by chance, as it happened. I was struggling through the blackout in Winchester, when I came across Laura and a friend. They'd missed the last bus to *HMS Flowerdown*, so I gave them a lift. I was at the naval air station nearby.'

Mrs Pembury's mouth had fallen open, and Cliff feared that she might have suffered a stroke, but then she spoke.

'You are Cliff, then.'

'I am. Laura must have told you about me.'

'But we thought you were dead.'

'We were shot down over the Channel, Mrs Pembury. We were picked up by a German trawler and taken prisoner. I had no address for Laura and, because of the nature of her work, I was unable to write to her at *Flowerdown*. I had no way of telling her I was alive.'

'How extraordinary.' She waited for the maid to set down the tray of tea things and leave the room, before speaking again.

'And what are you doing in Kent, Mr Stephens?'

'I'm a psychotherapist. I work for an ex-tutor and fellow prisoner-of-war in Folkestone.'

She seemed puzzled. 'But what do you actually do?'

'I help people with their emotional problems. Some of them are mentally scarred by the war. Others are simply life's casualties.'

'I see.' She plied the teapot thoughtfully. 'Milk and sugar, Mr Stephens?'

'Milk, please, but no sugar.'

She added milk to his tea and handed it to him. 'I'll be honest with you. You've caused my daughter a great deal of distress.'

'I never intended that, Mrs Pembury.'

'Be that as it may, Mr Stephens, the damage is done. I'm not going to tell her about our meeting today, because I don't want to unsettle her at this special time in her life. As a matter of fact, in phoning when you did, you missed her by only a week. She was here with her fiancée.'

Cliff walked out on to the drive. Numbly, he felt in his pocket for the ignition key. As he did so, he realised he was being observed.

'Hello,' he said.

'Hello.' The boy was probably in his teens and his school trousers looked new. For all Cliff knew, they might have been his first pair of long trousers.

'Are you looking for someone?'

'I thought my Auntie Laura might be here.'

'So did I. Apparently, she's in France. I didn't know she had a nephew.'

The boy looked embarrassed, as if he'd been caught out. 'She's not really my auntie,' he said. 'I was only eight when I met her, and I hadn't to use grown-ups' first names, so I called her "Auntie Laura".'

'Sometimes,' said Cliff, 'a pretend auntie is better than the real thing.'

'Auntie Laura is. She's always been kind to me, like when my dad was killed in the war.'

'Oh, I'm sorry. What's your name?'

'Michael.'

'I'm sorry about your dad, Michael.'

'He was a hero, fighting for our freedom. That's what Auntie Laura said.'

'She was right, Michael.'

Five years after the war, the boy looked wretched. In the light of his own frustration, Cliff could sympathise with him.

'I wanted to tell Auntie Laura about my apprenticeship. I knew she'd be interested.'

'I'm sure she would, Michael.' Devastated as he was, Cliff wanted simply to drive away and leave his shattered dream behind him, but none of it was Michael's fault, and the poor lad had been buoyed up with his achievement. In Laura's absence, he clearly wanted to tell someone. He asked, 'Would you like to tell me about it?'

'All right. I'm starting at the Central Bakery after Easter. They're letting me leave school at Easter because my birthday's in November.'

'Are you going to be a baker?'

'Yes.'

'Good lad. It's a noble calling. My dad's a baker and so is my brother.'

'Yeah?' It was as if Michael had suddenly found the kindred spirit.

'Mind you, when I was your age, I wanted to be a plumber.'

'Are you a plumber?'

'No, I went to university and did something else.'

That seemed to strike a chord in Michael's memory. 'Auntie Laura told me about somebody like you. He was called Cliff, and he got killed in the war.'

'No, he didn't, Michael. I'm Cliff.'

Michael looked at him in alarm. 'But he was killed.'

'No, I wasn't.' For the second time that day, he told the story of his capture and his inability to contact Laura. 'And now,' he said, 'she's engaged to be married. All I can do is wish her happiness.'

As Cliff drove away, Mrs Pembury saw Michael in the drive, so she left the house to speak to him.

'Hello, Michael.'

'Hello, Mrs Pembury.'

'Have you come to see Laura?'

'Yes. My gran said she was home, but I missed her.'

'By about a week, I'm afraid. She returned to France last Monday.'

The boy nodded. I came to tell her I'd got an apprenticeship at the Central Bakery.'

'Oh, that's nice. If you like, I'll tell her about it when I write to her.'

'Thank you.'

'It's no trouble.' There was something else on her mind that she had to ask him. 'Michael, did the man who's just gone say anything to you about Laura?'

'He just said she was in France.'

'Did he say anything else?'

'He said she was engaged to be married, and he hoped she would be happy.'

'Was that all?'

'Yes.'

'Are you sure?'

'Yes.' He was looking threatened. She tried a softer approach. 'Did he ask you for her address, Michael?'

'No.'

'So you didn't give it to him?'

'No, honest.'

'Good. You see, I want Laura to be happy too, and seeing him again would upset her. Do you understand?'

He nodded mutely. Whether that meant he did understand or that he was merely scared, she hoped he would remember the seriousness of what she'd told him. She'd always considered him to be rather a dull child.

She took her leave of him and went indoors to speak to Gloria. Richard and his wife Elsie were coming to dinner, and she wanted everything to be as it should.

10

'A perfectly awful thing happened today,' announced Mrs Pembury as the family gathered in the drawing room before dinner.

Harold Pembury winked at his son and asked, 'Are we to be shocked, scandalised or disapproving?'

'Oh, Harold, I wish you'd take things more seriously.'

'Go on, then, Alice. Tell us the worst.'

'Very well, then.' Satisfied that she had the family's attention, she related the story of Cliff's telephone call and his visit. 'I had no idea who he was at first, and you'll never guess.'

'Probably not,' prompted her husband.

'He turned out to be that wretched man Laura got herself involved with when she was stationed in Winchester.'

Elsie, usually so quiet and shy in Mrs Pembury's company, asked, 'The naval officer? Cliff? But he was killed, wasn't he?'

'Apparently not. He was shot down and taken prisoner. He said he was unable to write to Laura when he was in captivity, because he had no address for her.'

'Astonishing,' said Richard, 'but why did he wait until now to come looking for her?' He was a tall, spare young man with the same quiet demeanour as his father.

'Well,' she said in a tone laden with scepticism, 'he says he'd written to her via the Admiralty, but he'd received no reply, and when he heard that a fire had destroyed the Wrens' accommodation at *HMS Flowerdown*, he feared the worst. I must say he's a very plausible young man.'

'Or possibly an honest one,' suggested her husband.

'I doubt it. I don't know what they were thinking of when they gave him the King's commission. His father is a baker, you know.'

'Disgraceful.' Her irreverent husband shook his head in mock despair. 'Although it's not unprecedented. In nineteen-fifteen, they even promoted a grocer to second lieutenant. Of course, there was an urgent shortage of officers at the time, which may have explained such a rash decision.'

His wife glared at him. 'Harold, you are impossible.'

'I know.'

'Apparently, he's working as some kind of quack, a psycho-something-or-other, in Folkestone. Naturally, I told him I'd no intention of telling Laura about his visit, and I told him why.'

'Poor devil.'

Mrs Pembury favoured her son with the kind of glare she usually reserved for left-wing politicians and disrespectful workmen. 'There's nothing unfortunate about him, Richard,' she said.

'So you told him about Laura's engagement.'

'Of course I did. He needed to be told that his quest was pointless.'

'I imagine,' said Richard, that was the last thing the poor chap needed.'

His mother ignored him. 'And it didn't end there,' she said. 'I saw him outside, talking to Michael from along the road.'

'Laura's little friend,' explained Richard for his wife's benefit. 'She took him under her wing after his father was killed.'

'How kind.'

'Well, I satisfied myself that Michael hadn't given him Laura's address. You know how he insists on writing to her.'

'It's that milk of human kindness, mother. If you'll allow me to mix metaphors, it reaps its own reward.'

'I don't know what you're talking about, Richard. Anyway, I let Michael know in no uncertain terms how important it was that Laura didn't get to know the man was still alive.'

'Two young men,' mused Harold, 'sent on their way in the same hour, each with a flea in his ear.'

'And you did this, I imagine, because you were afraid Cliff might rock the boat, the plighted troth and all that.'

A Chance Sighting

'Exactly, Richard. Now that Laura has found a suitable man, I don't want anything or anyone to stand in the way of their marriage.'

'It's the end of the line, Reg, a brick wall, a closed door.'
'It certainly sounds final, judging by that cocktail of metaphors.'
'The old bat waited until the end to tell me that Laura was engaged.'
'Pretty cruel, I'd say.'
'What I can't understand,' said Cliff, transferring the phone to his other hand, 'is how Laura came to have a mother like that.'
'It's a mystery, but rogue parents abound, nevertheless.'
'I wonder what her father's like. She has to take after someone.'
'Yes, but it's an academic question now, isn't it, Cliff? What are you going to do tonight?'
'I haven't given it any thought.'
'Why don't we go down to the harbour, find a disreputable pub, and irrigate the problem.'
'That's the best idea I've heard all day.'

Michael lay in bed recalling the events of the afternoon. It was a shame he'd missed Auntie Laura, but he'd enjoyed talking to Cliff. He was nice. It was exciting, too, to learn after so long that he hadn't been killed. It was just a pity he couldn't marry Auntie Laura now.

Michael had always been wary of Mrs Pembury. She was scary, like the headmistress at his old infants' school, and she'd gone all out to scare him about Cliff. Part of him wanted to write to Auntie Laura and tell her about Cliff. He knew she wouldn't be upset. She would be happy because he was alive. The problem was Mrs Pembury and what she might do.

He fretted about it until tiredness overtook him at around four o'clock.

After three hours' sleep, he went to school feeling dreadful.

At breakfast the next day, Richard was buttering a piece of toast.

'You know,' he said, 'I long for the day when bakers will be allowed to bake something more palatable than the National Loaf.'

'And their sons will no longer be exalted to commissioned rank.' Elsie ran a hand through her auburn hair in a fair imitation of Mrs Pembury.

'I know. She's the most awful snob, and when I think of poor old Cliff—'

'And the little boy. That was awful.'

'He's not so little now. He's about fourteen, but it can't have been pleasant for him.'

Elsie put two more pieces of toast in the rack and sat down. A question had occurred to her, and she had to put it to Richard.

'Do you remember last week, when we came home from your parents'?'

'Yes?'

'You said you had reservations about Gerry. What did you mean exactly?'

'Basically, I'm not keen on him.'

Elsie took a spoonful of marmalade and transferred it to her plate. 'I know he was rude to you about being a meteorologist, but was that all?'

'No, I disliked him generally, and Laura confided that they'd already had a bust-up on the train. It was something to do with Laura's secret war work. That's why Dad took over the conversation when he did, to prevent it from blowing up again. He also had to forestall Mother.'

'How awful, but how good of your dad to leap to her rescue like that.'

'She'll always be his little girl, and he enjoys teasing Mother as well. Haven't you noticed?'

'I have, really. More toast?'

'Yes, please.'

She passed the toast rack to him. 'He was very rude.'

'Who, Dad?'

'No, I meant Gerry. You know, I'd rather have a meteorologist I love than a Hurricane pilot I don't.'

'He was a Typhoon pilot, darling.'
'Well, I was close.'
'You're like Laura, except she does it deliberately. Anyway, what are you saying? That you don't love Gerry? I must say, that's a relief.'
'No, silly. I'm saying that Laura doesn't.'
'How do you know?'
'Call it a woman's intuition, but we notice things.'
'What things?'
'More coffee?'
'Yes, please, but do tell me about those things.'
'You wouldn't understand, being a man, but we see things as well as hearing them, and they all tell the same story.' She poured him a cup of coffee. 'Laura loved Cliff. As far as I'm aware, she still does, except she thinks he's dead. If she goes ahead and marries Gerry, it'll be a recipe for disaster, and that's why someone needs to say something.'

11

Laura was in her office when the national phone rang. She answered it, wondering who might be telephoning her from outside the Council.

'Laura Pembury.'

'*Mademoiselle Pembury, il y a un appel pour vous de M. Pembury en Angleterre.*'

'*Merci. Je prendrai l' appel.*' She wondered what could have happened at home.

'Hello, Laura.'

'Dad, what's the matter?'

'Nothing at all. If it's not convenient to talk now, tell me when it is and I'll phone you again.'

'I can talk now. It's just that I wasn't expecting to hear from you so soon and I wondered if something had happened.'

'Your mother's going to skin me alive for telling you this, darling, but something *has* happened. I have news for you about Cliff. He's alive and well.'

'What?' Tears were already forming in her eyelids. 'He's...?'

'Yes, he's fine. Now, because of your engagement, your mother didn't want you to know this, but Richard and I had a chat this morning, and we both feel you have a right to know.' He told her about Cliff's visit and gave her an abbreviated version of his story. 'He's now living in Folkestone and working as a psychologist. No, I tell a lie. It says here that he's a psychotherapist.'

'He always said... he wanted... to... study psychology.' She began to sob uncontrollably.

'Darling, what's the matter?'

A Chance Sighting

'Nothing, Dad. I'm crying… with… happiness.'

'Well, if you can stem your tears long enough to take a note, I'll give you Cliff's telephone numbers. There's a business number and a private one.'

'Right,' she gulped. 'I'm ready.'

He read the numbers and she wrote them down.

'Now, are you all right?'

'I've never been better, Dad.'

'Good, because I have to go now.'

'Thank you, Dad. Thank you, thank you, *thank you!* Goodbye.'

'Goodbye, darling.'

When she'd put the phone down, she went to the ladies' room to wash. Her reflection in the mirror was horrendous, and she waited as long as she could before re-applying her make-up.

As she restored her looks, she recalled an evening in Winchester, and her birthday present of stockings and make-up from Cliff. The memory had her almost in tears again but it was sweeter than ever.

The rest of the day tested her concentration as never before. She had to finish a written translation by lunchtime, and then she had to attend the conference, translating instantaneously from French and then German.

The end of the day finally came, and Laura returned to her flat, where she had to endure the wait until she could make her call to Cliff. Strasbourg was two hours ahead of Greenwich Mean Time, and nine o'clock local time was about the earliest she could reasonably expect to find him free to talk.

At eight-fifty, she could wait no longer. With a trembling hand, she picked up the receiver and asked the French operator to connect her with Cliff's home number.

The process took what seemed like a long time but it was probably only a couple of minutes before she heard the ringing tone. It rang three times and then she heard his voice for the first time since 1944.

'Hello.'

'Cliff?'

'Yes.'

'It's Laura.'

'What? Good heavens! I mean how did you find me? This is amazing!'

'My dad found your number. He told me this morning that you were alive. I couldn't believe it.'

'I couldn't tell you I'd been taken prisoner.'

'I know.'

'Until four days ago I thought you'd been killed in the crash at *Flowerdown*.'

'I know. I wasn't there. I'd already gone to Greenwich.'

'This is incredible. After what your mother said—'

'She doesn't know. My dad and my brother decided to tell me.'

'Oh, good. Oh, bugger....'

'What?'

'You must think I'm no end of a lout. With all the excitement, I haven't congratulated you on your engagement.'

'Oh, that. That's a long story, Cliff. Let's not worry about it.' She thought she'd better check. 'Are you involved with anyone?'

'No.'

'Good for you. Cliff, we've got to keep in touch.'

'Yes, but this call must be costing you a fortune.'

'It is. Let's exchange addresses. You first. My pencil's poised.'

Cliff gave her his address and then wrote hers down.

'What are you doing there, Laura?'

'I'm an interpreter at the Council of Europe.'

'I knew it would be something posh. Good for you.'

She laughed. 'Same old Cliff.'

'Some things never change.'

'It's wonderful to talk to you but I must go.'

'Of course. I'll write to you.'

'You'd better. Let's not say "Goodbye".'

'Okay. Cheerio.'

'Cheerio, Cliff. Take care.'

'You too.'

Reluctantly but happily, she replaced the receiver. On the table beside her chair stood the photograph of Agatha with Cliff and his crew. They were smiling, and so was she.

A Chance Sighting

Cliff was glowing. Within two days, his fortunes had changed from tense expectation to crushing disappointment, and now he was elated. For someone recently engaged, Laura didn't sound particularly excited about it, unlike her mother. 'Let's not worry about it,' she said, and if she wasn't worried, he certainly wasn't.

12

It was unfortunate that Gerry should come to Laura's office the next day, when she was still coming back to earth after her father's telephone call and her conversation with Cliff. Her feelings were in turmoil, and she knew she couldn't cope with him until she'd had a little more time to herself.

'I'm sorry, Gerry,' she said. 'I really don't feel up to doing anything this evening.'

'You seemed all right yesterday.'

It was tedious, yet typical of him to argue. 'Yes, well, these things can happen overnight.'

'What's the matter with you, anyway?'

She thought quickly. 'Women's things,' she told him.

'Oh.' Clearly, he was on unfamiliar ground. 'How serious is that?'

'Look, Gerry,' she said, 'in the absence of a note from Matron, can't you simply accept that I'm not feeling up to an evening out?'

'We needn't go anywhere. I could bring a bottle of wine to your flat and we could have a quiet evening in.'

She sighed heavily. 'You're like a limpet with a one-track mind, Gerry. Save your wine. I'm not playing in or out tonight, full stop.'

He left, disgruntled, but reappeared the next day, when she agreed to see him at her flat that evening. He turned up with a bottle of Burgundy. 'Come in,' she said.

'Have you a corkscrew handy?'

'We're not going to need that, Gerry.'

'Why not?' He sat familiarly on the sofa. She took the armchair opposite.

'I have something to tell you.'

A Chance Sighting

'Oh? Has this, by any chance, something to do with yesterday's extraordinary performance?' His eye fell on her ringless left hand, and he demanded, 'Why aren't you wearing your ring?'

'Listen, Gerry. I'll come straight to the point. I'm not going to marry you.'

'Don't be ridiculous, Laura. Of course you are. We're engaged.'

'No, we're not.' She leaned over and placed the box containing the ring on the occasional table beside him.

'What the devil do you mean by that?'

'Just as I said. I can't marry you. I'm sorry, but that's the way it is.'

'I see. Don't you think I'm entitled to an explanation, however bizarre?'

'You'll probably think it's bizarre,' she admitted, arranging herself more comfortably to address the question. 'When you asked me to marry you, and I asked you to give me time to make my decision, I think I should have taken a little longer.'

'You're making no sense, Laura.' He put the bottle of wine on the table and said, 'Let's open this and pretend none of this silliness ever happened. Will you fetch two glasses?'

'No, I shan't. I'm telling you it's all over.'

'At least tell me what brought you to this extraordinary decision.'

'All right. Do you remember my telling you about a pilot I knew in the Fleet Air Arm?'

'Oh, the Shagbat pilot, but he's dead. I'm sure you told me that.'

'As it happens, he's not. I only found out about it on Thursday. He was taken prisoner, although I'd no way of knowing that at the time.'

He gave her a raised eyebrows look and said, 'So, now you're going to marry him instead, I suppose.'

'I don't know. I've only just learned that he's alive, so I've no idea how things are going to work out between us, if they ever do, but that's not the point.'

He looked mystified. 'What is the point, assuming there is one?'

'The point is, Gerry, that this latest development has convinced me that I'm wrong for you, just as I know you're the wrong man for me.'

Still perplexed, he shook his head at the apparent nonsense of it all. Finally, he said, 'Look, take twenty-four hours to think about it. I'll come back tomorrow evening, and we'll see if you've come to your senses.'

'No.' She was angry now. 'Can't you accept that I'm not going to marry you?'

'You still haven't given me a convincing reason for this absurd decision.'

Summoning what remained of her patience, she said, 'To put it simply, Gerry, I don't love you. I don't think I ever could, and that would be an impossible basis for a marriage. Even you must see that.'

'I just don't see how your feelings for me can have changed in such a short time, simply because this character has suddenly risen from the dead.'

'In that case, you'll just have to accept that they have.'

'I mean to say,' he protested in an incredulous tone, 'I've actually been ousted by a web-footed wave hopper.'

'If you're going to be insulting, you'd better leave now. In fact, I think you should.' She rose to her feet and handed him the boxed ring before going to the door. 'Go now. I'm sorry it didn't work out. I hope you find someone who can return your feelings.' She opened the door and stood aside for him to leave. 'Goodbye, Gerry.'

'I wonder how long it'll be before he finds out you're bloody frigid!'

'Goodbye.' She waited until he was over the threshold, and then closed the door firmly, turning the key.

She poured herself a gin and tonic with shaking hands and took it back to her armchair. She felt guilty about disappointing Gerry when it must have seemed to him that things were going so well, but he'd just tested her patience to the limit.

He was convinced, as well, that she was about to throw herself into Cliff's arms, and that was by no means certain. She was overjoyed that he was alive, and he seemed equally delighted that she had escaped the incident at *HMS Flowerdown*, but that didn't necessarily mean that they could continue as if their separation had never taken place. It would be naïve of either of them to think so.

A Chance Sighting

Six years had passed since Cliff's disappearance, and much could change in that time.

Cliff had already spent some time in fruitless conjecture. He'd always remembered Laura in the most affectionate way, but now she was engaged to someone whom Mrs Pembury regarded as 'a most suitable young man.' It was inevitable that she should become romantically involved with someone; in fact, on reflection, he was surprised to find her single after so long. It was nevertheless disappointing that she was spoken for. On the other hand, he'd been conscious of her delight at learning he was still alive, and maybe.... He had no wish to live in a fool's paradise, but those memories she had of him must count for something.

13

March

The post was delivered shortly before Cliff left for work. There was an official-looking letter and one that bore a French stamp. He opened it hurriedly.

Dear Cliff,
Thank you so much for your letter. Your characteristic turn of phrase, the expressions you use, and your way of seeing things took me straight back to 1944. So little, if anything, about you has changed, and it's too wonderful for words that you and I are in touch again.
I'm sorry I haven't replied sooner; the fact is, I've been through a harrowing time recently, and I had to wait until I felt more settled. The fact is I've broken off my engagement to Gerry.

At this point, Cliff's pulse went up a gear. He read on.

I could never feel for him what he so obviously felt for me, and marriage was therefore out of the question.
And so life goes on. I'm delighted to hear that your practice is growing. I remember your saying you wanted to change from English to psychology. How did you go about that? I taught French, German and Russian for a couple of years at a school in Kent, but I had to change to something different. I was simply unable to settle down in the job, but then the Council of Europe was formed, and I got in quickly. I enjoy the work and, on the whole, I enjoy living in Strasbourg, although it's a long way from home.
Do tell me more about your brother's wedding. You made only a

A Chance Sighting

passing reference to it. By the way, I was based in Scarborough towards the end of the war. What a coincidence! I also found a bakery on my travels. As far as I remember, it was called 'J. Stephens, Baker and Confectioner.' Could that have been your family home? I must have stared for ages, because a lady, possibly your mother, came out and asked me if she could help me. She was very nice and friendly. Believing you'd been killed, I didn't want to mention you for fear of upsetting her, so I made up a story about looking for a haberdashery. If only I'd known. The shop, by the way, was in Sandringham Street. Was I getting warm?

Please write soon, even though I've taken so long, and look after yourself.

Yours with love and best wishes,
Laura. X

He told Reg about the letter when they met for coffee later that morning.

'Things sound promising,' agreed Reg, 'but I should be inclined to apply the soft pedal if I were you, at least for the time being.'

'Would you?'

'Look, old chap, I want things to work out for you but, if you don't mind my saying so, you're too close to the situation to see it clearly. Take a step back and try to see it through her eyes.'

'What's on your mind, Reg?' Cliff refilled the cups and waited to be enlightened.

'To begin with, there's nothing in that letter to tell you that she's ready, at this stage, to take up where you both left off, if you'll excuse my clumsy grammar.'

'I'm no pedant, Reg, and I agree with you so far.'

'Good. Now, the poor woman's just been through the break-up of her engagement and, even allowing for the fact that her feelings for the man were less than wholehearted, a broken relationship inevitably leaves behind it a trail of emotional detritus. Memories, associations and so on have to be allowed to leave the system only when they're ready.'

'I see what you mean, Reg.' He was looking down at the coffee things and he remembered something. 'Just a minute,' he said, reaching into his desk drawer and taking out a bag of wholemeal biscuits. 'I'd forgotten about these,' he said.

'How long have they been there?'

'Only since this morning.'

'In that case, good for you, but we'd better not get carried away. There's two weeks' biscuit ration there.'

'So we have to make them last two weeks. Hitler really had something to answer for, didn't he?'

Reg smiled at a memory and said, 'That's the kind of remark that could have got you a month in the cooler at Marlag Nord.'

'At least. As it happened, they gave me a fortnight for making a feeble joke about the Master Race.'

'I remember.'

'Have a biscuit anyway.'

'Thank you. I don't mind if I do.' Reg took one and snapped it in half before taking a nibble with appropriate reverence for such a rare luxury.

'*Apropos* of the other thing, I'll heed your advice. At some stage, Laura will no doubt make a visit to her home, and then I'll know much more. It's always easier face to face.'

He sat down that evening to write to her. He'd left the wireless set tuned to the Third Network, which was broadcasting John Mortimer's play *What Shall We Tell Caroline?* He found it unintrusive; in fact, he preferred something playing in the background because it aided, rather than hindered, concentration.

Dear Laura,

Right, he'd made a start, but how was he going to address the subject of her broken engagement? He couldn't really say how sorry he was, because it was clearly untrue. After further deliberation, he picked up his pen again.

I can only imagine how difficult it must have been for you to break off your engagement, and I hope the occasion was relatively painless, at least for you.

A Chance Sighting

This was where he had to lighten the mood, but not too much.

You told me you'd gone from Flowerdown to Greenwich. Does that mean you eventually weakened and accepted a commission? It would certainly explain one mystery, that you did find my family's bakery when you were in Scarborough. The address you gave is spot on. My mother thought of you when she saw your uniform, but then she saw that you were an officer and not a PO Wren. I haven't spoken to her since your letter came, but she'll be surprised when I tell her the truth. 'Fortune brings in some boats that are not steer'd.'

You asked me about my brother Ted's wedding. What a lavish affair it was, despite rationing and the usual shortages. The two families pooled their coupons so that Ted and my dad could bake the cake, and the girls in Vera's office saved up the little paper discs out of their hole punches to use as confetti, but the pièce de résistance was the wedding gown, which would not have disgraced the daughter of a viscount. Actually, Vera's a lovely girl and she deserved the best. Ted looked smart as well, especially as my mother had made him go out and buy a new pair of black shoes. He'd gone shopping earlier with the best intentions, but he'd returned with brown ones. He can be a drip, as you can imagine from this story, but the final embarrassment wasn't his fault, and it occurred during the ceremony itself, when the couple knelt at the altar, and everyone could see, marked clearly on the arches of his shoes: $17^s/6^d$ incl. Purchase Tax!

Speaking of bakers, did young Michael write and tell you about his apprenticeship? I met him outside your parents' house as I was leaving. He was very disappointed to find you were no longer there, and we had quite a chat. He's a nice lad and he's very fond of you, as I've no doubt you know.

I think it's wonderful that you're working for the Council of Europe. I imagine we both heard more than enough during the war about hatred and revenge. Surely, nobler and finer motives beckon. All right, Mr Churchill put it more eloquently than that, as he always will, but I'm allowed to agree with him.

I'm thinking of buying a car. Petrol rationing is a nuisance, of course, but it can't last for ever. Do you remember the Austin Seven I had in Hampshire? It was still parked at Worthy Down when I returned from Germany, and I ran it for a while until, being an impecunious student, I had to sell it.

You asked me about how I switched courses. I actually met my tutor at Marlag Nord, the prison camp in Germany, and he taught me so well that King's College London knocked a year off my course. I stayed there and took a higher degree in psychotherapy, which is what I'm doing now.

Do write and tell me about your life over there. I feel guilty already, writing so much about myself.

Take care.

Love and bestest of wishes (there is such a word as 'bestest'. I just made it up),

Cliff. X

14

APRIL

Dear Laura,
I now have my new car, a Wolsley 10/40 saloon, economical and with very low mileage. It was registered in 1939 and subsequently laid up during and since the war. I'm so delighted with it I've enclosed a photo that I took as soon as I got it home.

Regarding your work, how marvellous it must be to have politicians hanging on your every word, even if it's because they don't understand German or French. As I see it, to make politicians listen is an important step, the next being to make them answer questions, preferably with some regard for the truth. That would be a great achievement. Go to it, Laura!

Thank you for asking after Ted and Vera. They're both well and enjoying life as far as circumstances allow. I should explain that Vera was delivered of a baby, one of the female persuasion, last week. She's rather small at 5lbs, 10oz., but she makes a great deal of noise, especially at night. 'Though she be but little, she is fierce!' I don't know if Shakespeare ever had to suffer a crying baby at night, but playwrights, unlike bakers, don't have to be up at four o' clock every morning. Her name, by the way, is Valerie, and I've yet to see her, but I suspect the christening will be organised soon, and I shall be summoned to the family bosom.

I forgot to say, in my last letter, that I told my mother that the Wren officer was you after all, and that you were reluctant to mention my name for fear of upsetting her. Well, several handkerchiefs later, she wrote to tell me what a charming young lady you were, but of course, I didn't need her to tell me that. It's a strange thing, because she's not normally given to tears. I wish she'd get her facts right, though. She's been telling people that I'm now a successful psychopath. English can be a tricky old bugger, can't it?

Ted has just received his Palestine 1945-48 General Service Medal. He was too young for the war but he was caught up in the unpleasantness after it, so I'm glad he's got the recognition he earned.

Please tell me more about Strasbourg. It sounds like a place with an identity problem, or maybe I'm wrong.

Until then, take care.
Yours with love and the bestest of best wishes,
Cliff. X

Cliff was surprised to receive a letter almost by return of mail.

Dear Cliff,
What a delightful car you've bought. I now have photographs of Agatha (with three shady-looking characters beside her) and your new Wolsley. Could they be the two loves of your life?

That's good news about Ted and Vera's baby. I mean the birth, not the crying. You know, I see you as the ideal uncle. In years to come you could be the ultimate confidant, soothing her worries and quoting Shakespeare to her, even though you're a psychopath.

In a sense, you're right about Strasbourg. It's very much a mixture of French and German influences. You can see it in the architecture in all kinds of ways, and then there's the language. The official language of Strasbourg is French, albeit with a strange accent, but the people of Alsace have spoken Alsatian for generations and, before you make a joke of it, I don't mean 'Woof-woof'. Alsatian is a German dialect language with a lot of French influence. Even so, the city knows where it belongs, and so do I, which brings me conveniently to something I've been meaning to put to you.

I intend to take some annual leave, probably next month. Naturally, I'll be staying with my parents, but wouldn't it be nice if you and I could spend some time together? Let me know what you think, and then we can perhaps take it from there.

Yours with love and very best wishes,
Laura XX

A Chance Sighting

Cliff had intended writing to Laura that evening but, as he opened his writing desk, he was reminded that he was down to his last sheet of notepaper. It seemed he would have to leave his reply until the next day, when he would try to get to the shops.

He opened a bottle of pale ale and poured it into a glass. Then, after pondering the situation for several minutes, he leafed through his diary for Laura's number before picking up the telephone and asking the overseas operator to connect him.

He waited, and eventually he heard the phone ringing at the other end.

'Allo.'

'Hello Laura, it's Cliff.'

'Cliff! I'm really glad you called. How are you?'

'In rude health, as ever. How about you?'

'Oh, I'm okay, thank you.'

He thought he detected a sombre note. 'Is something wrong?'

'No, nothing's wrong. I'm just feeling a bit isolated, that's all.'

'Perish the thought. You're not isolated with me on the end of the phone.'

'No, I'm not,' she said, her tone lightening. 'You're right, Cliff.'

'Has something happened? I mean something unpleasant?'

'Well, fairly unpleasant. I had a visit today from Gerry, my ex-*fiancée*. He's annoyingly persistent and he took some persuading that I'm not going to change my mind. I think he was brought up to believe that if he asked often enough, he would always get what he wanted.'

'And I'm five hundred miles away. I can't do a thing to help you.'

'Don't worry, Cliff. I've told him that if he bothers me again I'll call Security. That would do his career no good at all, and he knows it.'

'Good for you.'

'As I said, there's no need to worry. I don't want to waste this call either.'

'That doesn't matter. I just wanted to say that it would be wonderful to see you again, always provided I can recognise you after all this time.'

'Of course. I'll send you a photograph.' She laughed shortly. 'I can't have you going off with the wrong person.'

'I was joking. I'll recognise you easily enough.'

'I'll send one anyway. After six years, you might be confusing me with someone else.'

'How could I ever confuse you with anyone? Lucretia, you do me wrong.'

'Who the heck is Lucretia?' Her voice was shaking with suppressed laughter. 'You've never mentioned her to me before.'

'I'm sorry. It was a slip of the tongue. I should explain that Lucretia was my pet budgerigar.'

'I don't think I can compete with a budgerigar.'

'She's in no condition to compete with anyone, having met her tragic and untimely end fifteen years ago.'

'Oh? What happened?'

'She had an unfortunate encounter with a vacuum cleaner. My mother, you see, was cleaning her cage—'

'Please don't! I can't bear to hear it.'

'Calm yourself, Laura. Her passing was swift and clean.'

'Oh, Cliff.' She was laughing freely.

'What?'

'You've cheered me up, even though I don't believe a word of your story.'

'I'm deeply wounded.'

'No, you're not, and I'm going to ring off now. This call must have cost you a fortune already.'

'Nevertheless, it's money well spent.'

'Even so,' she told him firmly, 'I must bring this conversation gratefully and affectionately to its close. Goodnight, Cliff, and thank you again for the best restorative ever. I'll be in touch with details of my movements, and I'm looking forward to seeing you again.'

'Goodnight, Laura.'

'Goodnight, Cliff.'

The call would doubtless be expensive, but it had been worthwhile.

On a whim, he sent Laura a photograph of himself taken, initially for his mother's benefit, after his release from captivity and after his promotion to lieutenant-commander. It was fair exchange.

A Chance Sighting

At the end of the month, Cliff travelled up to Scarborough for Valerie's christening at the Wesleyan Methodist church, where the minister looked with a questioning frown at the date of Ted's and Vera's wedding. Ted assured him that Valerie was born two months prematurely, a harmless yet convincing fib, given her modest birthweight.

It was an occasion that Cliff's father referred to as a 'teetotal jamboree.' Back home, though, they had a party, and the alcohol flowed quite freely.

In a quiet moment, Ted thanked Cliff for preparing all concerned for the news of Valerie's expected arrival.

'It was the least one brother could do for another,' Cliff told him.

'But you did it so... well, so that they knew something was up, but they didn't know, if you see what I mean.'

'I know, Ted. I'm not just a hairy chest.' He couldn't help adding, 'I hope you'll do the same for me if I have a negligent discharge.'

'I will, Cliff, but I can't guarantee I'll do it as well as you did.'

Cliff resolved to be extra careful.

15

Laura was due to arrive at Croydon Airport on the 20th May, and would be on leave for two weeks. She invited Cliff to the Pembury home on Wednesday, the 24th, and he arrived promptly.

Gloria opened the door and smiled in recognition when she saw him.

'Gloria,' he said, 'how are you?'

'I'm well, thank you, sir, and yourself?'

'Fighting fit, Gloria.'

'I'm afraid Mrs Pembury's not at home this morning.'

'Actually, it's Laura I've come to see.'

'I'll tell Miss Laura you're here, sir.' She took his hat and coat and led him to the drawing room, as she had on his previous visit.

He waited nervously. Six years had passed since their last meeting and, even after two telephone calls and numerous letters, he was experiencing the kind of tension he'd not known for years.

There was the sound of footsteps on the stairs and, a moment later, Laura entered the room.

'Cliff!'

Cliff held out his arms, momentarily bereft of words, and held her in a hug that was the culmination of six years' frustrated longing. If such a thing had been possible, he would have preserved that moment for all time.

When they broke apart, her eyes were wet.

'I'm going to ruin my make-up if I'm not careful,' she said.

'You're a welcome sight, all the same,' he assured her. She was wearing a pale green dress buttoned down the front, with a V-neck and short sleeves. She was the most welcome sight.

'Are you ready for coffee, Miss Laura?' Gloria must have been waiting for an opportunity to interrupt the reunion discreetly.

'Would you like coffee, Cliff?' Laura was dabbing at the corners of her eyes with her handkerchief.

'Yes, please. Coffee would be very welcome.'

Laura nodded to Gloria, who said, 'Very good, Miss Laura.'

'I'm thirty years old,' she told Cliff, motioning him to take a seat, 'and I still feel like a child when she calls me "Miss Laura".'

'Has she been with you long?'

'Almost as long as I can remember.'

'I suppose it's only convention.' He'd really no idea, being unfamiliar with the world of domestic staff, but it made sense.

'It is,' she agreed, 'but it's a feudal concept. I'll never have servants.'

He nodded absently. 'It'll be a saving.' In truth, he was still convincing himself that the reunion wasn't taking place in his imagination. Letters and phone calls notwithstanding, it still seemed to be the stuff of fantasy.

She also waved the matter aside, saying, 'I still can't believe this is happening. Have you driven here?'

'Yes, Reg gave me his petrol coupons for the next two weeks.'

'How kind.'

'Not really. He's just thankful I'm not there to bore the pants off him about your leave and the arrangements I've been making.'

She looked at him in surprise and asked, 'Have you been making arrangements?'

'Of course I have. I'm rather hoping you'll join me in a trip to London on Friday evening.'

'Oh? What do you have in mind?'

'A surprise, something I was going to do for you in Winchester before fate intervened.'

'Now I'm intrigued....' She stopped and asked, 'Is something the matter?'

'No, nothing at all.'

'You're looking at me strangely.'

'I'm sorry. I didn't mean to be so obvious. It's just that you look even better now there's no blackout.'

She smiled. 'Thank you. I think there was a compliment in there somewhere.'

The door opened, and Gloria came into the room carrying the coffee things.

'Thank you, Gloria. Just leave everything on the coffee table, please.'

'Very good, Miss Laura.'

'There's no cream, Cliff. It's a sign of the times, I'm afraid.'

'Milk will be perfect, thank you.'

She handed him his coffee with a grimace. 'Isn't it awful? We've known each other since the war, and we're both being ultra-polite and on our best behaviour.'

'I always behave like this, Laura.'

'No, you don't. It's because we're in my parents' house. My mother has this effect on me even when she's not around.'

Cliff's eye was drawn to a silver-framed photograph on a side table, and he stood up to examine it more closely.

'Third Officer Pembury,' Laura told him, standing up to join him. 'It was taken when I passed out at Greenwich.'

'What made you change your mind? You used to be adamant about not going for a commission.'

'My divisional officer persuaded me. I was.... It was when I thought you'd been killed. They found me a new draft – an appointment, as it happened – but it called for a three-oh, so I took a period of leave and then went on to officer training. It was meant to be the clean break I needed.'

It was the first reference she'd made to her state of mind at the time of his disappearance, and he felt so sorry for he that he slipped an arm round her waist and gave it a reassuring squeeze. She responded by turning to bring her cheek into contact with his.

'I'm glad you're back, Cliff,' she murmured.

They stood like that for several seconds, until fate intervened once more, this time in the shape of Mrs Pembury, who had returned from her appointment and was now speaking to Gloria in the entrance hall.

A Chance Sighting

When she came into the drawing room, Cliff and Laura had returned to their seats. Cliff stood up immediately and offered his hand.

'Good morning, Mrs Pembury. How are you?'

'Well, thank you, Mr Stephens. Will you be staying for lunch?'

'That's kind of you, Mrs Pembury, but I've arranged to take Laura out for lunch.'

'I see. Well, do take a seat.' Her manner was as cool as when he'd last left her. She looked up as Gloria came in with a cup and saucer for her. 'Mr Stephens will not be staying for lunch, Gloria,' she said.

'Thank you, Mrs Pembury.'

'I thought I'd show Cliff the Pantiles, Mother,' said Laura as she poured her coffee.

'Yes, that will be a novelty for him.'

'I've heard of them, of course,' said Cliff.

'Really? That's good.' Clearly, something was occupying her mind. Eventually, she said, 'Mr Stephens, when Laura came home she showed us a photograph of you in uniform. You were some kind of commander, I believe?'

'Lieutenant-commander,' he prompted her.

'Yes, quite. I've been meaning to ask you why you were wearing medal ribbons on both sides of your tunic. Was there a special reason for it, or was it simply unfamiliarity with the way things are done?'

He could only smile at her waspishness. 'The Royal Humane Society Medal and its ribbon are always worn on the right,' he explained.

'I see. Why on earth did they give you that?'

'I expect they were feeling generous, Mrs Pembury.'

Laura, who had been looking most uncomfortable since her mother's return, made a timely interruption.

'If you'll excuse us, Mother,' she said, 'we should be going.'

'Very well. When will you be back?'

'Late afternoon.' She stood up and looked across at Cliff, who was already on his feet. 'We'll be off, then. Goodbye, Mother.'

'Goodbye, dear. Goodbye, Mr Stephens.'

'Goodbye, Mrs Pembury.'

As they walked to the car, Laura said, 'I must apologise for Mother.... It's difficult.'

'I know. She sees me as a threat, even now you're no longer engaged to the man she thought was so suitable.'

'Oh dear.' Still embarrassed, she said, 'Wait 'til you meet my dad. He's the antidote. You'll like him.'

'He certainly pulled our irons out of the fire,' he said, stopping to unlock the car.

'Oh, this is lovely.'

'It's an improvement on the Austin Seven I had when we met,' he agreed, opening the passenger door for her.

'Your Austin Seven was very welcome that night Doris and I missed the last bus to *Flowerdown*.'

'I hope you realise that history is about to repeat itself.'

'Oh?'

'I'm going to need you to navigate into Tunbridge Wells,' he said, 'although I have the perfect excuse for not knowing my way around.'

'No sooner said than done, Skipper. Steer three-seven-five magnetic.'

'What?'

'I heard it in a film my dad was watching.'

He changed down as they approached the end of the road. 'Which way?'

'Right here.'

He made the right turn. 'You can't steer three-seven-five,' he pointed out. 'There are only three-hundred-and-sixty degrees in a circle.'

'It may have been three-one-five.'

'It's an easy mistake to make, Laura.'

'The aeroplane ended up in the North Sea.'

'I'm not surprised.'

'Take the next left.'

She continued to navigate until they entered Tunbridge Wells.

'You can park down here,' she said. 'It's a lovely day and it's just a short walk.'

They left the car, and she took his arm as they crossed the road and headed for the Pantiles.

A Chance Sighting

'Did you ever see your observer again?'

'Marcus? I saw the bugger every day in Marlag Nord.'

'I didn't realise that. What about the other man? The rating?'

'Woody? Yes, I've seen him a couple of times since we were released. He's okay now, teaching music to kids. It's what he always wanted.'

She gave his arm a squeeze and said, 'I'm glad you kept in touch with him.'

'I had to. I was his Fezziwig.'

'Wasn't he a character in *A Christmas Carol*?'

'Yes, I'll tell you about it one day when I'm not feeling quite so modest.'

'Okay, here we are in the Pantiles.' She looked at him quizzically and asked, 'Don't you want to know why it's called the Pantiles?'

'Yes, I just thought I'd keep you in suspense.'

She smiled at him sweetly. 'The upper walkway, which you haven't yet seen, was paved with red clay tiles that were shaped in wooden pans prior to firing, hence "Pantiles". That was in the eighteenth century. By the next century, they'd been replaced with stone slabs.'

Cliff looked around at the colonnaded shop fronts. 'Absolutely charming,' he said.

'Let's find somewhere to eat.'

They strolled along the walkway, stopping occasionally when Cliff pointed out some feature that appealed to him, until they came to a restaurant that looked promising.

'I've been here before,' Laura told him, 'but it was before the war.'

'A half-term treat?' Cliff had heard about them.

'A treat, yes, but I'd left school by then. I was at university.' She indicated the door to the restaurant and asked, 'Shall we see if we can get a table?'

'Why not? You're on holiday, and it's a treat.'

'That's true. Come on.'

In the event, the restaurant was only half-full, so they secured a table by the window with no difficulty.

'Let's see what they've got,' said Laura, opening the menu. She frowned as she ran down the page, until something caught her eye, when her frown became a look of surprise. 'Here's something I haven't had for years,' she said.

'What's that?'

'Welsh rarebit. It'll be made with Government Cheddar, but I'm still game.'

'I've never had Welsh rarebit,' Cliff admitted, 'but, if you recommend it, I'll make it my next venture into the unknown.'

'Steady, Cliff.'

'It's all right, Laura. I can handle it.'

Without thinking, he reached across the table and took her hand. Then, as she met his gaze, he released it quickly. 'I'm sorry,' he said. 'I was checking that you really existed.'

'You mustn't apologise. I know exactly what you mean. When my dad told me you were alive I couldn't believe it at first, and then, when he persuaded me it was true, I burst into floods of tears. I'd been convinced for so long that you'd been killed.'

'It was a narrow escape,' he admitted, encouraged to some extent by her disclosure.

She looked at him in alarm. 'What happened?'

'An enemy fighter attacked us from astern, so I dived, hoping he'd follow too closely and take the early bath in the oggin, but he was too wily for that. Instead, he blew up Agatha's engine, perforated her hull and showered Woody's leg with shrapnel.'

'Oh, no.'

'He's okay now.' He spared her the unpleasant images of Woody, lifted injured into the armed trawler, and then on his return, emaciated and with mutilated hands.

Mercifully, the waitress came to the table to ask if they were ready to order.

'We'd both like the Welsh rarebit,' Cliff told her.

'The Welsh rarebit, and to drink, sir?'

Cliff looked across at Laura, who motioned him to choose. 'I shan't have much,' she said.

'In that case,' he told the waitress, 'a half-carafe of the house dry white, please.'

'Certainly, sir.'

A Chance Sighting

Laura leaned forward to say, 'Tell me how you learned about the crash at *Flowerdown*.'

'I heard about it first from a subby who came to Marlag Nord. He'd only heard about it, but he reckoned there were lots of casualties, and I decided that must have been the reason you never replied to my letter. I thought you'd been killed.'

It was her turn to take his hand and squeeze it. 'Poor Cliff,' she said. 'Where did you send the letter?'

'Ah well, that was the problem, you see. I couldn't write to you at *Flowerdown*, obviously, and I didn't have your home address, so I sent it to you care of The Admiralty. I marked it "Please Forward", and I underlined "Please" three times. I couldn't plead harder than that.' Six years on, his expression mirrored the hopelessness of his cause. 'But it never reached you.'

'How did you address it?'

'As I recall, "PO Wren Tel. Laura Pembury, care of Postal Section, The Admiralty".'

'And you didn't have my official number. In any case, I wasn't a P O Wren for much longer.'

'Fate was always one step ahead of me.'

She nodded sympathetically. 'But then you learned that there were no casualties.'

'That's right. A man came to me for help. It turned out that he'd spent some time at *Flowerdown* on rest and recuperation.'

'Yes, they used it because of the facilities. I think they'd been on the Arctic convoys.'

'He told me that. He was there at the time of the crash, and he told me how the padre had rounded them all up and given thanks that everyone had been spared.' He opened his hands in a weary gesture. 'If I'd known that in nineteen-forty-five,' he said, 'I'd have come looking for you sooner.' He straightened up to let the waitress place the carafe of wine on the table.

'Shall I pour it, sir?'

'No, thank you. I'll do it.'

'But fate has its own timetable,' said Laura when the waitress was gone.

'So it's not true that "Our remedies oft in ourselves do lie, which we ascribe to Heaven."'

'I'm all agog, Cliff. Do break the suspense.'

'*All's Well That Ends Well.*'

'Let's hope so.' Her response sounded cryptic, but Cliff still had an agenda to pursue.

'Are you free on Friday evening?'

'I can be. What do you have in mind?'

'I have two tickets for Christopher Fry's *Venus Observed* at St James' Theatre.'

'How could I refuse?'

16

At Lewisham, they joined the London to Hastings road, which would take them to Bilshurst. Laura was quiet at first, allowing Cliff to concentrate on the traffic. That morning's announcement that petrol rationing was over had brought motor cars on to the roads in surprising numbers, possibly for no better purpose than to celebrate the fact.

After a while, she said, 'I'm still pinching myself. I actually met Sir Laurence Olivier.'

'I told you there'd be a surprise.'

'But to go to his dressing room....' Words evidently failed her. 'I didn't believe you at first when you told me to call him "Larry".'

He noticed that traffic was bunched up ahead, and slowed down accordingly. Also, rain was beginning to fall. 'He doesn't answer to his title,' he reminded her.

'Such modesty.'

'And he's not superhuman, as you'd know if you ever saw him try to land an aircraft.'

'But he's world-famous.'

'That's true.'

'Why did he call you "The Angel of Mercy"?'

'Did he?'

'Yes, when we arrived at his dressing room.'

He picked up speed as the traffic thinned out. 'It was just a silly nickname they gave me.'

'But why?'

'They didn't need a reason. The wardroom was full of overgrown schoolboys.'

'You're being modest, Cliff.'

'I'll tell you about it some time when I'm not being quite so modest.'

'That's the second time you've said that. You're holding out on me.'

'The traffic's easing now,' he observed.

'And you're changing the subject. I'll go on nagging until you tell me.'

'All right.' He sighed theatrically. 'But it's not much of a story.'

'I'll let you know.'

He took a deep breath, preparing himself, and began. 'We were scrambled to search for the pilot of a Mustang, an American fighter. The conditions weren't too promising; the wind had increased since take-off, and the sea state was pretty unwelcoming, so we had to find him and pick him up before he drowned.'

'But how did you fly in bad weather?'

'The Walrus could fly in conditions that kept most aircraft on the deck,' he told her. 'It had that in common with the Swordfish.'

'I remember hearing about that.'

He nodded. 'Anyway, he was the luckiest bloke alive because, against all the odds, Marcus spotted him in the water.'

'In a heavy sea as well.'

'Yes.'

A sudden squall obliterated the windscreen until the wiper restored visibility.

'It wasn't the easiest pick-up we'd ever made. For one thing, we nearly lost Woody over the side, and Marcus was thrown against the hatch by a spiteful wave, and knocked unconscious, but we had a job to do. Between us, Woody and I got the pilot on board, we patched Marcus up, and he gave me a course for home before passing out again.'

'Poor man.'

'Marcus? He'd do anything to gain attention.'

'Don't be rotten. I'd slap your wrist if you weren't driving.'

He smiled at the thought. 'We're only just reunited and you want to hit me.'

'Yes, but I'd rather hear the rest of the story.'

'Okay. We brought the pilot back to Worthy Down. An ambulance took him and Marcus to hospital to be checked over, and we thought that was the end of it, but worse was to follow. We learned that the pilot had been a reporter in civilian life, and he'd given the story of his rescue to his old newspaper.'

'Which one?' Laura was evidently hooked on the story.

'It was one of those state-wide newspapers, not a national one, like *The Washington Post* or *The New York Times*.'

'All right. Go on.'

'You keep interrupting me. Anyway, he wrote his story, describing Agatha making her descent "like an angel of mercy". That's how the name stuck.'

'But it's nothing to be ashamed of.'

'Maybe not, but the story's not over yet. The Royal Humane Society wanted to know the ins and outs of the operation, and that's how Marcus, Woody and I came to receive their award.' He shrugged. 'At least they honoured all three of us, which was only right because it really was a team effort.'

'Quite right.'

He nodded his agreement. 'Then the US Air Force conferred another medal on us. It was very embarrassing.'

Laura was silent for a moment, and then she said, 'You were all heroes: you, Marcus, Woody and Agatha.'

'Yes, Agatha should have had a medal. Instead, all she got was a burial at sea.'

'But you'll always remember her.'

'Always. In fact, if you come down to the office, I'll show you an oil painting of her.'

'I may take you up on that.'

They drove on in silence, Cliff because he'd said more than he'd intended, and Laura possibly because it had given her cause for thought.

Eventually, she said, 'Take the next turning left. It's signed to Pembury but it'll take us to Bilshurst.'

'Presumably your name comes from the village.'

'Originally, but we weren't related to the lord of the manor or anyone important.'

He indicated left and took the turning. 'I know.'

'How do you know?'

'If you'd been so well-connected, you wouldn't have been quite so excited about meeting Larry Olivier. It stands to reason.'

'No, it doesn't. Aristocrats exist by accident of birth, whereas Larry is what he is by sheer ability.'

'You're a true egalitarian.'

'I should say so. Aren't you?'

'I try to be, but my superiors keep putting me in my place.'

'You're evidently keeping the wrong company, Cliff.'

He drew up beside Laura's garden wall. 'Thank you for coming, Laura.'

'Thank you for a wonderful evening. The play was excellent and I now have a name to drop.' She held up a finger, as if remembering something. 'I really enjoyed your company as well.'

'I always enjoy yours.' He slipped his arm round her shoulders.

'You know, Cliff, it's our fourth date since nineteen-forty-four.'

'Is that all?' He lowered his head to touch her parted lips with his. Then, encouraged by her passive compliance, he kissed her deeply for the first time since Winchester.

Eventually, and with a tangible effort, she said, 'I must go. Thanks again, Cliff.'

'Until tomorrow, then.'

'Yes, I'm looking forward to it.' She slipped out and closed the car door behind her.

She let herself in quietly. Her mother would be in bed, and Gloria was off-duty. Her father was in the drawing room listening to Mozart. At least, it sounded like Mozart. He looked up when she entered the room.

'Hello, darling. Help yourself to a drink.'

She poured herself a cognac and sat down with it, content to listen to the music.

When it ended, her father switched off the wireless set and said, 'Tell me about your evening, Laura.'

A Chance Sighting

'It was wonderful, Dad. We saw an excellent play and I met Sir Laurence Olivier in his dressing room.

'Really?'

'Yes, we're on "Larry and Laura" terms now.'

He laughed good-naturedly.

'And I discovered that I'd been spending the evening with "The Angel of Mercy".' She went on to tell him Cliff's story, and he listened appreciatively, reacting occasionally with a look that showed he was impressed.

'He's a remarkable young man,' he observed finally.

'Yes, he is, and I want to invite him here for dinner before I return to Strasbourg.'

'Of course.'

'There's just one snag.'

He nodded minutely. 'Leave everything to me, Laura.'

The screeching noise began as Cliff entered Cheriton High Street and it wasn't long before water vapour was billowing from beneath the bonnet. He pulled in beside a telephone kiosk and called the RAC.

'My engine is screeching and the radiator's boiled,' he told the telephonist.

'Where are you, sir?'

'Cheriton High Street, Folkestone.' He gave the operator a few landmarks and prepared himself for a long wait.

The road scout surprised him by turning up after only twenty minutes. He parked his motorcycle combination in front of Cliff's car and stopped the engine.

'What's the trouble, sir?'

'The engine's making a horrible noise and the radiator's boiled,' he told him.

The RAC man lifted the bonnet and said, 'Just turn the engine over, sir.'

'The radiator's boiled,' he reminded him.

'Just a few turns, sir. It won't take any harm.'

Cliff started the engine, and the screeching began immediately. He switched off the ignition.

'It's the water pump, sir. The bearing's gone.'

It made no sense to Cliff. 'I know the car's eleven years old,' he said, 'but it's been laid up most of that time.'

'That's just it, sir. All that time without oil, and then everything starts up and the oil flies round in all directions, trying to reach everything that needs it.' He tutted sadly. 'It's a lot to ask of the lubrication system. Only to be expected, really.'

'What can you do?'

'How far have you to go, sir?'

'Not far. I live in Folkestone. Only about two or three miles.'

'I can fill up the cooling system so that you can get home, sir. You need a new water pump, and that's a garage job.'

'That'll be a great help. Thank you.'

He parked outside his flat fifteen minutes later, relieved to be home but less than enchanted with the so-called joys of motoring. He would have to phone Laura in the morning to tell her he was unable to call for her.

17

'Hello. Is that Mr Pembury?'

'Yes. Who's calling?'

'Good morning, Mr Pembury. It's Cliff Stephens.'

'Good morning, Mr Stephens. You'll want to speak to Laura, I imagine, but I'm afraid she's not here. She popped out earlier to the shops. I don't know when she'll be back.'

'That's a shame, but it gives me an opportunity to thank you for putting Laura and me back in touch. I appreciate that more than I can tell you.'

'Think nothing of it, old chap. I was only doing what I could for my daughter.'

'You certainly did that, sir. By the way, would you be kind enough to give Laura a message, please, when she returns?'

'Of course I will.'

'That's kind of you. You see, Laura and I were going to a dance this evening, in Folkestone, but the water pump on my car's leaking and the garage can do nothing about it until Monday, so I'm afraid I'm unable to come over and pick her up.'

'I see.' He paused for a few seconds and then said, 'I'll give her your message, but don't write the whole thing off because of that. She's quite capable of catching the train, you know.'

'Don't you think she'll mind?'

'Not in the least, old chap. If you like, I'll ask her to give you a ring when she comes in.'

'Thank you, Mr Pembury. I'm very grateful.'

'It's no trouble at all.'

'Goodbye, sir.'

'Goodbye, Mr Stephens.'

Mr Pembury replaced the receiver and poured himself another cup of coffee just as Mrs Pembury entered the room.

'Good morning, Alice. Shall I pour you some coffee?'

'Yes please, Harold.' She took her seat at the table.

'You really should eat breakfast, you know. One of these days you'll walk out of the door and faint over the nearest flower bed.'

'I doubt it.'

'You've been warned. Anyway, I've been meaning to speak to you about a different matter.'

She looked at the clock and frowned. 'Aren't you going into the office today?'

'No.'

'Why ever not?'

He shrugged. 'Richard is more than capable of dealing with anything that crops up and, as I said, I have something to discuss with you.'

'Well, what is it?'

'It concerns Laura and Mr Stephens.'

'Oh.' Her mouth closed firmly, accentuating the lines of disapproval that emanated from her compressed lips.

'They were at the theatre last evening.'

'So I understand.'

'Mr Stephens introduced Laura to Sir Laurence Olivier. It was an instant success, apparently. Laura tells me she and Sir Laurence are now on first-name terms.'

'What?' Her mouth fell open.

'"Larry and Laura", I believe she said. 'Of course, Olivier and Mr Stephens became close friends during the war, when they served on the same air station.' It was a mild exaggeration, but Mr Pembury knew better than anyone the hollow route to his wife's approval.

'Good grief.'

'I learned something else about Mr Stephens.'

'Oh?' It seemed that the great thespian had opened her mind to new possibilities.

'Laura had to wring the information from him and even then she was obliged to read between the lines to appreciate his account fully. He is a particularly modest young man, a quality you may well have overlooked.'

'Well? Go on.'

'Very well. He and his crew were awarded the Royal Humane Society Medal for a particularly courageous rescue carried out in hostile weather conditions. They could easily have forfeited their lives, but they carried out the operation to save the life of an airman who was in danger of drowning.'

'Good grief. But I had no way of knowing that.'

'No, but you know it now.'

Her expression had relaxed, and she spoke without sourness. 'I suppose so.'

'You object to him because his father is a baker.'

'Well, I....'

'Whereas I am a grocer. No more and no less than that. I sell groceries, beers, wines and spirits.'

'We've been through that so many times, Harold. All right, but where is this leading?'

He finished his coffee and reached for the pot again. 'Laura is clearly fond of him.'

'Apparently.'

He finished pouring coffee, replaced the pot and looked directly at his wife to say, 'I should like her to invite him here to dinner, when I shall expect him to be treated with the respect to which he is entitled, and the warmth and hospitality due to a guest and close friend of our daughter.'

'Very well, Harold. What you've told me puts a different complexion on the matter.' She added, 'I wish you'd told me those things earlier.'

He made no reply. Some of his wife's foibles still defeated him.

Laura phoned shortly after ten.

'Hello, Cliff.'

'Hello, Laura. You got my message, then.'

'Yes, I'm sorry to hear about your car, and you haven't had it two minutes, have you?'

'Oh well, the RAC man says it's only to be expected when a car's been laid up for a long time. Bits that haven't been lubricated become dry, and apparently the oil can't be expected to do everything at once.'

'No one can, Cliff.'

'It's a tall order after several years,' he agreed.

'Even so, it's a nuisance for you.'

'It's an almighty nuisance, but when I spoke to your father, he said you might come by train.'

'Of course I will. I haven't danced with you for.... Oh, dear. "Six years" has become rather a *cliché*, hasn't it? Anyway, I wouldn't miss it for anything.'

That was encouraging. 'Tell me when your train's due to arrive and I'll meet you at the station. It's the least I can do.'

'Ten-past four.'

'I'll be there.'

'Good, but there's something else I have to tell you. My mother – all of us, in fact – would like you to come to dinner next Wednesday if you can make it.'

'I'd love to, but—'

'Don't worry; she'll be on her best behaviour. It was her suggestion, by the way.'

'But how did that happen? I was Public Enemy Number One last week.'

'Let's just say that my dad is a diplomat.'

'He sounds more like a magician. No, sorry, that was uncalled for. I'd love to come. Thank you.'

'Good. I'll see you at ten-past four. 'Bye.'

18

Laura stepped off the train and allowed Cliff to relieve her of her case.

'My frock and shoes,' she explained. 'I didn't want to travel in them.'

'You'd have caused a sensation.'

'I'd have looked downright silly,' she said, accepting a kiss on the cheek.

'This way.' He offered her his arm and they left the station. 'It's very annoying about my car,' he said. 'I wanted to transport you from door to door. Instead, we have to hoof it.'

'I'm not fragile, Cliff. I walk occasionally, you know.'

'It's just as well.' He led her across the road and they continued on their way along Cheriton Road and Cheriton Gardens to the bottom of Manor Road. 'Our consulting rooms are along here,' he said.

'Oh, shall we have a look, seeing as we're here?'

'By all means. Not that there's much to see.'

'You mentioned a painting of Agatha.'

'Yes, I did. It's not much further.'

They reached the building, and Laura stopped to admire the brass plate. 'Oh, my word,' she said. ' "C. W. Stephens, MSc. (Lond.)" How very impressive.'

'Not really.'

'I'm allowed to be impressed.'

'All right.' He unlocked the door and let her in. 'A solicitor and an accountant have the ground floor,' he explained. 'We're on the first.'

They took the stairs and came to an oak panelled door, which Cliff unlocked and opened.

Laura looked around her, clearly searching for something.

'Are you looking for a couch?'

'Yes.'

'I don't use one. It's not like *The Seventh Veil*.' It had become a routine disclaimer.

'Oh dear.' She looked further and suddenly gave an exclamation of delight when she saw the painting. 'There's Agatha! How wonderful. What's happening? Is she landing?'

'No, taking off. Putting down was a much wetter business altogether.'

Laura's face had taken on an enchanted look. She said, 'She's beautiful.'

'I suppose she had a kind of homely appeal,' he agreed.

'No, I mean she's beautiful because she saved so many lives.'

'Okay, I'll grant you that. Now, we should get back to the flat for you to change, and then we have to eat before we go to the Leas Cliff Hall.'

The dance was excellent, although Cliff had reservations about some of the music.

'It's become something terribly sophisticated and grown-up,' he complained.

'Really, Cliff,' said Laura. 'Music was too grown-up for you in nineteen-forty-four. The nightingale stopped singing in Berkeley Square some time ago, you know.' She was wearing a flared dress in apple green that more than made up for the music.

On the whole, they enjoyed the evening, although Cliff had to admit to himself that he enjoyed Laura's company more than the dance itself.

The last waltz was 'Now is the Hour', a number made popular two years earlier by Bing Crosby. Laura danced with her cheek pressed against Cliff's, saying at the end of the number, 'I hate that word "Goodbye". It's so horribly final.'

'Okay, let's not use it.' He wasn't keen either.

They joined in the applause for the band and then headed for

A Chance Sighting

the exit. Cliff had ordered taxis there and back, and they were soon at the flat, where Laura used the spare bedroom to change back into her travelling clothes. The taxi stood outside, ticking over.

'I really don't want to go,' she said, 'but I must if I'm going to catch the ten-twenty train.'

'I'll come with you.'

'You don't have to. I'm a big girl now.'

'No, I insist.' He reached for his hat and coat.

In the dark privacy of the taxi, they sat close and, as they pulled up outside the station, Laura kissed him and said, 'No, I'll be all right now. I'll see you on Wednesday. Thank you for a lovely evening.' Before he could object, she had picked up her case and disappeared into the station.

The driver turned in his seat to ask, 'Back to your place, sir?'

'Yes, please.'

'I don't like the look of that sky, sir. I reckon we could be in for a right old downpour.'

'You could be right.'

Cliff was unlocking the door when the rain came, sudden and fierce. He hurried indoors, thankful that by that time Laura would be on the train. He hung up his hat and coat and poured himself a gin and tonic. Suddenly, the room felt unnaturally cold for late May, so he switched on the electric fire.

He'd recently treated himself to a gramophone and several of the new long-playing records, and he searched through the shelf for one to put on. He pulled out one of Ambrose and his orchestra because it suited his celebratory mood. He lowered the needle and sat down to enjoy the music.

After a while, his attention wandered, and he found himself going over the events of the evening and the past week, most of which had been unbelievable.

The music, the gin and the warmth of the fire created a cocktail of comfort, and it wasn't long before he had dozed off.

The doorbell was an intrusion, and he forced himself into wakefulness, wondering who on earth could be calling at.... He looked at his watch. It was almost a quarter to eleven.

He opened the door to find Laura, soaked and distraught, on the doorstep.

'Cliff,' she panted, 'may I use your phone?'

'Of course. Come on in. Let me take that wet coat and hat.'

She peeled off her coat, but she was clearly soaked to the skin.

'There are no trains,' she told him. 'They've found an unexploded bomb up the line near Ashford, and they've stopped all the trains.'

'Stay here,' he said. 'I don't know what you're going to tell your parents, but you're welcome to my spare room. You can have a bath as well. It'll warm you up.' He shook her coat over the doormat. 'You know where the phone is, don't you?'

'Yes, and thank you. I'll take you up on your offer.'

He took bath and hand towels from the linen cupboard, along with sheets and pillow cases for the spare bed. Dropping them temporarily on the bed, he found pyjamas and the old blue rayon dressing gown from his time at Worthy Down, and left them on the cork-topped linen box in the bathroom. He had to admit failure where slippers were concerned; she would have disappeared inside his size tens.

He was running a bath when she came to find him.

'I've told my dad I'm staying with a friend,' she said.

'Well, it's true enough.'

'A *female* friend. My mother would have asked questions, but he's just satisfied that I'm safe.'

'Safe as houses,' he agreed. 'Okay.' He turned off the hot tap. 'There are towels, pyjamas and a dressing gown on that box.' He stepped outside, leaving the bathroom for her, and said, 'Chuck your wet clothes out here and I'll hang them up to dry.' He remembered something else. 'Oh, and I've found you a spare toothbrush. It's on the basin shelf. When you're dry, come and join me in the sitting room.' He left her adjusting the temperature of the bath water, and set about making up the bed in the spare room. He'd found two pillow cases that didn't match the sheets, but he didn't think she would care too much about that.

When he'd finished, he found her wet clothes outside the bathroom, and he hung them carefully with her coat and hat on the clothes horse in front of the electric fire. Her brassiere and stockings he suspended from the mantelpiece, secured by the clock and two candlesticks.

After a while, Laura came into the sitting room, drying her hair and trying not to walk on the pyjama trousers, which were far too long for her.

'That towel's wet, he told her. I'll get you another one.' He searched the linen cupboard again and found another hand towel while she took her seat in the armchair.

'Are you ready for this?' He took the towel between his hands and set about drying her hair.

'My father used to dry my hair when I was little,' she told him. 'He used to sit me on his knee and recite nursery rhymes while he did it.'

Cliff took up the cue. 'Rub-a-dub dub, three men in a tub. Who do you think they were?'

She joined in. 'A butcher, a baker, a candlestick maker. They all jumped out of a rotten potater.'

It was his turn. 'Little Miss Muffit sat on her tuffet, eating her curds and whey. There came a great spider that sat down beside her, and she said, "Buzz off, you're R A".'

She laughed. 'I never had the Ration Allowance. I was always vittled on board.'

'Spoken like a true seafarer.'

'You sailors always made fun of us when we used navalese.'

'Who are you calling a sailor? I was one of "the Navy's cavalry".'

'So you were,' she agreed. 'Did you know that song was written originally for a film about the US Navy Air Force?'

'And we pinched it from them. It served them right for not inviting us to the Boston Tea Party, or whatever they got up to.'

'Were you absent from school the day they did history?'

'No, I just wasn't listening.' He ran his fingers through her hair and said, 'I think you're dry now.'

'Thank you. Have you seen my handbag?'

'Here it is.' He picked it up and handed it to her.

'Thank you.' She took out her hairbrush. 'And thank you again for drying my hair.'

'I look after my visitors.'

'You certainly do.'

'Would you like a drink?'

'Actually,' she said, looking a trifle embarrassed, 'have you any cocoa?'

'I may have. The previous tenant moved out in a hurry for some reason, and left lots of stuff behind.' He went into the kitchen and explored the food cupboard, emerging eventually with a tin of Fry's cocoa powder. 'I've found it,' he called, pouring milk into a saucepan and lighting the gas.

'I'm sorry to put you to this trouble.'

He looked over his shoulder and saw her in the kitchen doorway. 'It's no trouble. I'm learning a new skill.' He spooned cocoa powder into a coronation mug, also a relic of the previous tenancy. When the milk came up to temperature, he poured it on to the cocoa. 'There,' he said, stirring it industriously.

'Oh, thank you, Cliff.' She reached out to take the mug, but he lifted it so that it was beyond her reach.

'I'll carry it,' he said, 'and you can concentrate on keeping your pyjama bottoms off the deck.'

'You think of everything, Cliff.'

As they returned to the sitting room, she looked at the items dangling from the mantelpiece and put a hand to her mouth, leaving one trouser leg to concertina on to the carpet.

'What's the matter?'

'I've just realised, I left my underwear in that pile of clothes.'

'It's all right,' he assured her, 'I kept my eyes tightly closed all the time I was handling them. Those things are a mystery to me anyway.'

'I believe you.' She sank back into her armchair and tried her cocoa, which was hot but evidently drinkable. 'This is lovely,' she said. 'They used to give us cocoa regularly on the night watches at *HMS Flowerdown*.'

'You Wrens really knew how to live the high life.' He resumed his seat on the sofa.

She ignored the remark, clearly having something else on her mind, because she asked 'Do you remember telling me about your brother's wedding?'

'Yes.'

'You mentioned a fabulous wedding gown, and I couldn't help wondering how they managed that, when clothing had only recently come off the ration.'

'Ah, I supplied the silk. I left the clever stuff to the dressmaker. She was a local by-word in *couture*.

'Silk?' It was as if he'd mentioned spun gold.

'Yes, I'd been keeping it for such an occasion.'

'But how did you come by it?'

'It was one of the spoils of war. It happened towards the end of 'forty-two. Agatha rescued the crew of a Junkers 88, complete with their parachutes, which they'd been using as shelter from the rain and spray.' He smiled at the memory. 'I'll never forget Woody shouting, "The dinghy's gone down, sir, and we've won three silk parachutes." Trust Woody to think of that before sinking their *Gummi-Boot*.' He broke off from his narrative to say, 'It's a lovely name for a dinghy, isn't it? The Germans have such a way with words. Anyway, we each took a parachute. They were a lucky find at a time when manufacturers had changed over to synthetic fabrics.'

'What a lucky girl, too, to have a silk gown for her wedding.' She mused about that and said, 'It's a good story. All this and having my hair dried plus cocoa and a bedtime story. I feel quite spoilt.'

'I'm full of bedtime stories.'

She surprised him by joining him on the sofa and asking, 'Will you tell me another?'

'About what?'

'About the letter you wrote to me from Germany.'

'All right.' He put his arm round her shoulders, and she snuggled up to him. 'I can still remember that letter word for word; it was so important at the time.'

'What did it say?'

'It said, "Dear Laura, as you can see, I've been taken prisoner. I hope you weren't too worried when you heard I was missing. I don't like the idea of your being at all anxious, but I suppose you must have been. I hope my colleagues have kept you informed. Chin up! This war can't last for ever, and we'll see each other again." He was reciting with his eyes closed. He could see the huts, the barbed wire, his fellow prisoners and the guards very clearly. Most of all, though, he recalled his helpless frustration at being parted from her.

"I treasure those few evenings we spent together, as I'm sure you do. In the short time we've had, something very special has developed between us, and I long for the day when we can be together again."

'I said something about the letter form being so tiny, and having to write in pencil because we weren't allowed ink. It was very primitive. I asked you to write soon, and I promised I would.' Self-consciously, he said, 'I know it wasn't Shakespeare but it came straight from the heart.'

He heard a sniff and looked down. 'Please don't cry,' he told her. 'Everything's all right now.'

'I know. It's just thinking about how you were feeling, and I know how I felt when I thought you were dead.'

'It's all in the past,' he said, giving her the handkerchief from his breast pocket.

'Yes.' She blew her nose and smiled again. 'Thank goodness.'

She felt soft and snuggly in his pyjamas and dressing gown, and he held her close, discreetly inhaling the scent of soap and relishing the moment, mindful as he did so that those loose-fitting garments presented the only barrier between him and her naked body.

She looked up at him fondly, and he bent to kiss her, but then conscience intervened and he held back.

'What's the matter, Cliff?'

'I'd be taking advantage.'

'No, you wouldn't. Kiss me.'

'I mustn't.'

'Kiss me. Please.' Her lips were parted innocently, but they were no less persuasive.

He kissed her, scarcely maintaining his resolve until she asked, 'Have you got one of those things people use?'

He nodded.

She seemed to consider the option, and then said, 'I love you, Cliff.' It was an admission of the most ingenuous kind, but for him it was the final inducement.

A Chance Sighting

'I love you too.' He kissed her again, gently loosening her sash and pyjamas so that her exquisite breasts lay partially exposed, and he kissed each in turn.

Her breath quickened. She said, 'Take me to bed.'

'Are you sure?'

'I've waited six years, Cliff. We were going on leave together, remember?'

He kissed her again before rising to his feet. She followed him to the bedroom, still clutching her pyjama bottoms to keep them above her ankles.

He undressed hurriedly, but she was in bed before him, waiting. He kicked away the last of his clothes and slipped in beside her.

'I love you,' he said again, enjoying the satin feel of her naked body, and scarcely able to believe that she had uttered those same words only a few minutes earlier.

'I know. Isn't it wonderful?'

He kissed her lips, her chin, her neck and her breasts, where he lingered for a while before traversing the flat plain of her midriff with a series of soft kisses.

She moaned lightly and then shuddered when his hand explored further.

After a while, he leaned away from her to reach into a bedside drawer.

'What are you doing? Don't go away.'

'I'm not going anywhere.'

'Come back to me, Cliff.'

He returned, taking her in his arms again. Her eyes registered momentary surprise, and then she gave a tiny gasp of welcome.

He was awake before her. The sun slanted into the room through the aperture created by the hastily-drawn curtains, highlighting her half-uncovered body beside him. On a whim, he raised himself on one elbow to kiss her, and she stirred slowly. Eventually, she opened her eyes and focused on him.

'It's that man again,' she said sleepily.

'That's a wireless show.'

'That as well? What's your name and what are you doing in bed with me?'

'My name is Clifford William Stephens and it's my bed. You're my visitor and you're very welcome.'

She closed her eyes, pretending to digest the information. 'I remember you now,' she said, 'but I didn't know you were called William until just now.'

'As you can see, I have nothing to hide.'

She lifted the sheet to peer underneath it and nodded her agreement. 'Yes, the secret's out now.' She lay back, closing her eyes blissfully and said, 'I'm sure not every girl's first time could be as wonderful as mine.'

'I've no idea. Yours was the only debut I've ever attended.'

She closed her eyes dreamily. 'It was lovely.'

'Yes, it was.'

She snuggled against him more closely and said with a hint of wonder, 'I was a virgin until just a few hours ago.'

'Do you mean,' he asked, giving her a strange look, 'that you'd *never* eaten meat or fish?'

'That's *vegan*, you fool.'

'Really? And I suspected Mary Shelley wasn't all she claimed to be. I wronged the poor woman.'

'I think she'd have understood.' She stroked his arm soothingly.

'Do you? I hope so.'

'Anyway, how did you know Mary Shelley was a vegan?'

'I read about it in a book called *Well-Known Names and Little-Known Facts*.'

'It doesn't sound very absorbing.'

'It was too boring for words. I was glad when I finished it.' On reflection, he said, 'I could tell you a better story about names.'

'Oh, good. That's how it all began, as I recall, with a bedtime story.'

He drew her close and began. 'A man came to me for help. He'd been a leading seaman in the war, but I told him we were to meet as equals and on Christian-name terms if we were to make any progress. He agreed, and we got on famously. I called him "Norman" and he called me "Cliff", even though he still thought of me as an officer and himself as a rating. Later, however, when he was describing his experiences to me, he faltered. The pain of recollection was making it difficult for him to organise his thoughts.'

'It would. It's only natural.'

'That's true, darling, but bear with me.'

'Okay.' She settled into her pillow to listen.

'I asked him if he'd like a cup of tea, and just guess what he said.'

She waxed thoughtful. After a moment, she said, 'No, I give in.'

'He said, "Not 'alf, sir".'

Smiling at the picture he'd painted, she said, 'It was that commanding presence of yours.'

'No, it was early training. It dies hard, they say.'

'I know.' She raised the covers. 'Back in two shakes.'

He lay there in thought. One question remained and it had to be asked.

When Laura returned and resumed her place beside him, he said conversationally, 'I love you.'

'I love you too.'

They kissed at length, as if putting the seal on their relationship. When they eventually broke apart, he said, 'As we're agreed on that, do you fancy signing on for the duration?'

She smiled at him and said confidently, 'Not 'alf, sir.'

The End

Lightning Source UK Ltd.
Milton Keynes UK
UKHW020808211219
355800UK00002B/78/P